LOST AT SEA

Lost At Sea

Copyright © 2023 Bronwyn Harrison

All rights reserved.

This book or any portion thereof may not be reproduced or used in any manner whatsoever without the express written permission of the publisher except for the use of brief quotations in a book review.

Paperback ISBN: 978-1-7399188-9-7

Illustrations by: Rebecca Newbold

Edited and formatted by Curious Cat Books, UK

Fonts free for commercial use: Papyrus Serif, Trajan Pro, Times New Roman

A copy of this title is available through the British Library.

First Edition.

Also available as an e-book.

LOST AT SEA

By Bronwyn Harrison
Edited by E. Rachael Hardcastle
Illustrated by Rebecca Newbold

My debut novel is dedicated to Samuel, Noah, Florence and Elliott.

Acknowledgements

My debut novel has taken a number of years in its construction and I have many people to thank including my family and friends who have given me so much support and encouragement. In particular my husband Ian who has been patience personified as I disappeared for hours working on my computer. The support from Rebecca and Leonie in their help with ideas for the book cover, for which I am so grateful—the final design by Rebecca. I also need to thank my cousin, Pauline and friend, Joey for their 'honesty' in proofreading!I wish to thank Rachael Hardcastle, my publisher from Curious Cat Books, for her wonderful work but more than that, giving me the confidence and sense of belief that I needed. Above all, for sheer inspiration from Samuel.

Lost At Sea

PROLOGUE

A solitary candle stood guard to battle against the all-encompassing darkness. Outside, the wind howled and cried, like a drunken man's fist flaying and shaking with rage, battering in frustration on closed shutters.

In the centre of the room in a large four-poster bed, Thomas Castle slept fitfully. His skin, yellow and paper-thin, made pallid by white linen sheets, shone with beads of sweat that dribbled lazily down his face. Dry spittle encrusted his breathing—shallow and rasping—as each inhale brought a shudder through his thin body; yet, despite the pain, barely a flicker appeared on his face. His breathing became increasingly weak and irregular, gasping as a drowning man would fight to cling to life.

Thomas had been a larger-than-life figure of a man. As he gasped and hung on to life, his youngest son, William sobbed unashamedly at this pathetic, gaunt man whom he had loved and adored, and who now lay dying. Grace, William's wife, stood behind him with her hands placed lightly on his shoulders, unable to give her husband any words of comfort.

In the shadows on the opposite side of the bedroom, Thomas Castle's eldest son, George stood quietly, his mind working frantically but his face showing no emotion. Wishing to hide his true feelings, George leaned back into the shadows and grimaced at his younger brother's outpouring.

Their father, who had a reputation for honest trading in his working life, was a fool. It seemed the youngest son would add yet another weakness—that of a simpering fool. It took all of his self-control not to spit out his true feelings, but time would serve him well. Teeth clenched and head lowered, he glanced upwards at his sister-in-law, Grace. He blamed her influence for the suffocating morality of Castles' Merchant Traders.

Things were going to change. As the eldest son, George would inherit the business and would bring a ruthless edge into their trading. He had different ideas on trading in the new century.

A knock on the bedroom door woke him from his daydream. Grace moved silently to open it and let in the local parson, who was a friend of the family. Very Reverend Ralph Greening was a large man dressed in black, except for his white collar. He walked with a slightly ingratiating stoop.

He whispered quietly to Grace, who nodded, and then the Reverend moved towards William, placed a gentle hand on his shoulder, and bending down whispered words of comfort. Grace pointed at George; Reverend Greening walked around the bed towards him. George stood up, nodded curtly, and stepped back.

Moving silently to the head of the bed, the Reverend placed his hands on Thomas's head, then knelt stiffly at the bedside to pray over losing a good man. The candle flickered in relief.

Thomas Castle took one last breath, shuddered, and died.

Grace whispered to her husband and then offered George her deepest sympathy. The Reverend Greening stood, his knees having had the best of their life.

"If I can help with funeral arrangements, anything,

please let me know. Thomas was a good friend to the church," said the Reverend.

Grace nodded. "Thank you, but..."

George, with fists clenched to his side and barely able to control his anger, stormed to the door, stopped, and turned.

"I need to remind you, I am now the head of this family. Father is dead, and it is my responsibility to look to the future of the business. I will speak to the family solicitor and have the will read with all speed. Grace, I will leave the funeral arrangements to you. I suspect my brother will be indisposed. Good day."

Grace's eyed blazed at the perceived disrespect, took a deep slow breath, and with appraising eyes and tight lips whispered, "Thank you, George. Your father deserves to be treated with every respect. You will help me, I hope, Reverend Greening?"

"Willingly, my dear. Willingly," replied Reverend Greening.

Grace continued, "Forgive me, gentlemen. I must see to my child. He needs his supper. I will see you first thing tomorrow morning."

Heart pounding and head thumping, George walked out of the bedroom and down the stairs without a backward glance. He paused at the hat stand to collect his hat and gloves, picked up his stick and then opened the front door, stepping into the street.

Shaking with anger, George was relieved the ordeal was over (for that was how he saw it). An ordeal with fools. A cold arctic blast hit him, bringing him back to the here and now. It momentarily took his breath away. His eyes were stinging and his breath appeared as mist.

He instinctively hunched his shoulders, pushed his hat down hard on his head, and thrust his gloved hands in his pockets to face the weather head-on. He knew he had to confront the hostility heading his way from the Castle family. Unless, that is, he could somehow circumvent it.

His favourite Inn, "The Rat and Barrel" tempted him, but it was midnight, and he needed his wits about him for the morrow. He stopped and turned to return to his own rooms, which were above Castles' Merchant Traders Warehouse. The name would have to change, he mused. His rooms were comfortable enough and private. He groped in his coat pocket for his key to the only door to his sanctuary. Away from the raised eyebrows and disapproving looks, he cared not one jot.

He had a parlour and a small kitchen. Not that he did any cooking. Smiling, he walked into his bedroom and from a cupboard by his bed produced a small bottle of golden nectar with a glass. He peered in to look for mouse droppings. Despite his best efforts, mice were ever a problem as his bedroom was above the warehouse. He spent as little time as he could in his room—cleaning was women's work. He decided it was safe and poured himself a small measure of brandy.

Lifting the glass in salute, he said, "Here's to me," and emptied the glass.

He undressed. Leaving his black leather boots by the door, he folded his clothes neatly, before placing them on a chair and then getting into bed.

George slept fitfully that night, spending most of the time staring at the ceiling. He made plans, although they could not be finalised. His brother and sister-in-law would be horrified by what he was contemplating. Grace was the shrewd one of their partnerships, which said little, but he would have to be alert. She was as wick as a barrel of monkeys. George must not underestimate them, and he had to play a careful hand. Perhaps he would pay them a visit in the morning and pretend to be the distraught brother? They would smell a rat. No, he needed to get his business settled quickly first. He had to get control of his father's company.

Up bright and early the following morning, George polished his boots to a high shine. After a wash in what was bitterly cold water, he dressed in his best dark blue velvet jacket, white linen shirt, blue cravat, and grey trousers. A large highly polished silver mirror with an ornate surround was his pride and joy in the bedroom, rescued from his father's warehouse. He was not the most fashionable man but strikingly handsome, with short, light brown curly hair and a neatly trimmed moustache. It gave him a rather rakish look. This, together with his brown-green eyes, made him popular with the ladies.

On the top of a chest of drawers were a clothes brush, a comb, and a variety of pleasant pomades. He combed his thick, brown curly hair, selected his favourite scent, and brushed his coat and hat within an inch of their lives. He had to portray himself as an astute trader. Carefully placing his pocket watch and chain into his waistcoat pocket, and picking up his silver topped and tipped walking cane, he left.

George headed away from the Bristol docks toward the city centre. Aware of his clean boots and immaculate dress, he kept away from the slop and detritus in the middle of the narrow streets. The first thing he must buy himself, he thought, was a horse. To be separated from the riff-raff and the muck. He was looking for Jeremiah Sykes and Company Family Solicitors. He had seen Jeremiah Sykes Senior some years ago when he visited the family solicitor with his father. Having had to stop for directions from some wastrel, he eventually found himself outside the door to the solicitors' rooms.

To the left of a dark green door was an impressive plaque that announced, 'Jeremiah Sykes and Sons, Solicitors'. George saw the name and casually walked up the three steps to the door, rapping three times with his cane. Composing himself for the conversation that must inevitably take place, George was determined to maintain a cool exterior.

Eventually, the door opened. A tall man with thick, dark wavy hair appeared with a formal air and asked, "Can I be of help, sir?"

George cleared his throat. "The name's George Castle. I would like to speak to Mr Jeremiah Sykes." George then pointed his stick at the plaque.

"Oh, you mean my father? I am his son, Joseph. Father is busy presently, but please come in. Could I tell him the nature of your visit? It may help."

"Of course," said George. "I am the eldest son of Thomas Castle of Castles' Merchant Traders. Father has sadly passed away. You will understand we have business matters to address."

Joseph Sykes nodded and smiled. "Please wait here. I will be but a moment." A short while later, he returned. "Follow me and my father will see you now."

George followed him up a set of stairs onto a large landing with paintings of prestigious clients on the walls. He stopped to observe the names of those surrounding him and the expense of employing such an eminent solicitor. Father must have been unstable or astute.

Joseph opened a door at the far end of the landing. He beckoned to George and nodded to his father.

"George Castle for you."

Jeremiah Sykes glanced up from a pile of papers, leaned back in his chair, and looked long and hard at George.

"Thank you, Son. You have work to do, I believe? Good, good."

The door closed, leaving George standing in front of Jeremiah Sykes like a pupil before a schoolmaster.

"Please, sit."

George sat on the comfortable leather chair placed in front of the desk.

"Now, I understand you are here about your father's business?"

"That's correct, sir," replied George, who cursed his instinctive use of 'sir'.

"Eager. Don't you think? I can call you George? Good, good. Your father only died last night. Still warm, I bet."

Jeremiah Sykes, hands clasped gently on the desk in front of him, stared at George. He struggled to control his panic. How did the solicitor know his father had died last night?

He took a deep breath. "Yes, but you will understand better than I the need to keep continuity—the good name of Thomas Castle. Merchant Trading is a tough business. I, *we*, cannot allow the business to display any weakness or fault. I am sure you will understand why..."

"You need to have your father's will read at the earliest opportunity. Yes, yes. I respected your father, Mr Castle. He was a good man, an astute man, and a shrewd judge of character. After all, he chose *me* as his solicitor." Jeremiah laughed at his quick wit, which broke the tension a little.

George continued. "Father would have done likewise, I think. Acting decisively, I mean."

Jeremiah nodded. "When would you like the will to be read? Next week, perhaps?"

George pursed his lips as if in thought whilst his mind raced over how to deal with this clever man. He decided upon caution.

"As soon as you are able, Mr Sykes, sir. As soon as you are able. I have things I must get on with."

"Fine, let us say in fourteen days, at ten o'clock, at your home. Let me know the funeral arrangements. I would like to pay my respects."

At that, he picked up his pen and continued to write. The meeting was over. George got up from his chair, nodded, and left.

***

As he left the solicitor's, George smiled. One down and one to go, he thought, and walked with his normal swagger towards Black's Coffee House, his favourite. Jeremiah Sykes watched him from an upstairs window.

Lost At Sea

It was a relief the coffee house was nearby. Though it was popular with many traders, he needed to meet one man—a slave trader by the name of Vincent Marchant.

He crossed the road and walked towards the coffee house. George stepped spiritedly up the steps to a black door with a smart, polished brass doorknob. He pushed it open and stepped inside. The smell was breath taking. However many times he visited Black's Coffee House, the aroma of tobacco, soft brown sugar, and coffee never failed to take his breath away. He closed his eyes before breathing in the heady mix. George removed his hat and carefully placed his expensive soft leather gloves in his hat. Whilst doing so, he glanced around the room.

There was a gentle hum of sound like a busy, contented beehive. Now and then raucous laughter would erupt and fill the room. The conversation lulled as people looked around to find the source of the noise before continuing, and the hubbub would rise again.

George saw the familiar face of Vincent Marchant. He put his cane under his arm, casually glancing at his reflection on a long mirror by the entrance, placed to allow those leaving to look presentable. George sauntered towards the rear of the room for that was where the prime seats were (away from the noise and stench of the street, as well as the draught from ill-fitting windows). They supplied the best cuts of meat or pieces of cheese and the freshest bread to these tables.

Vincent Marchant was at the rear where he could see the comings and goings and particularly, who sat with whom. Shrewdly, those wishing to speak to him had to do so publicly; Vincent was not one to hide his presence, nor indeed his influence. He saw George enter but made no indication. He was too clever to give a sign or advantage to any future customers, whether a buyer or seller. George walked towards him whilst Vincent continued to eat his dinner of ham, cheese, and warm baked bread. In front of him was coffee, a small glass of rum, and a bowl of brown sugar.

There could not have been two more different men. Vincent was an experienced, hard-working and a self-made man; short and round with little hair, and a few somewhat stained teeth. George, on the other hand, was well-groomed with a full set of his own white teeth. Vincent's scruffy appearance did not fool George, for he hoped to emulate him as a successful trader (but without the foul breath and crude manners).

"I am glad to see you here, Vincent. We will soon have a common interest and I hope we may do business. My father has passed away and as the eldest son, I will be the head of our family business."

Vincent held a fork to his mouth with a piece of ham poised. "I've heard, George, my condolences. Join me."

Vincent pointed to the chair next to him continued to eat, concentrating all his attention on his food. George took a piece of bread from the plate and cut a small slice of cheese.

George continued, "Slave trading, that's where the money is."

Vincent coughed and spluttered. Red-faced, he continued to gasp, trying to catch his breath, before grabbing his glass of rum and slurping a mouthful. George watched, unsure of what this outburst meant.

Wiping his mouth of spittle, rum, and food, Vincent smiled. "Shock is what it is! Shock! A Castle, a slave trader? Well, I never!"

He shook his head in amazement and took a second drink of rum before clearing his throat once again.

George nodded sagely. "It is the 18th century, and we must move with the times; progress or perish, progress or perish. Slave trading is where the money is, so that's where I wish to be. But I will need some advice from a man of your stature, Mr Marchant."

Vincent Marchant waved his hand modestly. "You have a plan, Mr Castle?"

"Call me George, please. I need to convert one of my existing ships or purchase a new one. When I say new, I mean a slaver."

Vincent nodded. "Seem to know what you're talking about, George. I need to think about it. To buy a slaver or convert one. Let me order some more food."

He waved frantically at one of the young serving lads who hurried over to the table. "Yes, Mr Marchant, sir."

"More food, lad, more food. Only the best for my guest, mind. More rum as well."

George watched the scurry of activity that followed as the coffee house owner brought food to the table.

"Hope everything is to your satisfaction, sir?"

"It is indeed. George, may I acquaint you with Mr Wilfred Black, proprietor of this coffee shop? Excellent it is, too. Mr Castle is a friend of mine, so Wilfred, mind you look after him well."

When faced with his best customer, Wilfred Black could only nod with agreement.

After a pleasant meal, George was ready to take his leave. Vincent placed a hand on his sleeve.

"I am sure I can be of help. We need to keep this matter private, you understand? Business dealings such as this are… how shall I put it… sensitive? They certainly are for you, George." He smiled at that and continued. "I will send a messenger who will only speak to you. Understand?"

Unsure of whether he understood as it all seemed a little secretive for something so simple, George had enough sense to nod his head and purse his lips.

George, face relaxed, casually gathered his hat, gloves and cane, bowed nonchalantly to Vincent, and strolled from the coffee house. George considered the secrecy as proposed by Vinny Marchant and a seed of doubt entered his mind. Could Vincent be trusted? As if on cue, Vincent opened his jacket pocket removing a small notebook and pencil, and wrote furiously whilst things were fresh in his mind.

George walked slowly along the quayside deep in thought and decided to visit his brother and wife. He knew he had to tread carefully if he was going to have his way with the family business and be above suspicion, at least for the moment. He knocked on the front door, which was opened by Grace who looked tired and stressed.

"How are you, my dear? You look exhausted. Could I speak to William?"

Grace opened the door and stood back, unsure as to the reason for the pleasantries from her brother-in-law.

She walked down the hallway and to a door on the right, knocked lightly, and opened the door to the office where the family business was run.

"William, George is here."

William Castle was at his desk checking the ledger of costs for refitting the recently acquired Swift, which was currently anchored in the Bristol dock. William stood and walked around his desk to meet his brother. George smiled gently.

"William, how are you? I am sorry I was so ill-mannered last night, but like you I was, am, upset at the loss of our father. Please say you will forgive me."

William gave his brother the benefit of the doubt and reached out to shake George's hand.

"We have a lot of things to resolve, George and better we do things together, don't you agree?"

George nodded. "Well said, William. Well said indeed. If I may say, Grace looks exhausted. She has a lot to deal with I suspect and with a child as well. What can I do to help?"

William sighed, and his head dropped momentarily. "The funeral arrangements have to be made and then we will need to have the will read. "

"Ah," replied George smiling, "some good fortune there. I met father's solicitor, Jeremiah Sykes. I have told him of our father's death. He sends his condolences and will be available to read the will after the funeral and a proper period of respect, of course. I believe our father would not want us to let Castles' Merchant Traders, which he built from nothing, to languish because of our indecision."

William nodded, offering his brother a seat. They

then planned the funeral. William was glad George was there to share the burden and perhaps this was the new beginning they both needed. George was the more outgoing of the two. A charmer. If he was honest, he hoped George would share in the running of the family business.

***

The funeral went well, or as well as funerals could go. William and George sat together in the office awaiting Jeremiah Sykes for the reading of their father's will.

George as charming, and as ever made his brother laugh at the many scrapes they used to get into as young boys. There was a gentle tap on the door and Grace peered round, delighted to see the grey of William's face had lifted, if only momentarily.

Not wanting to break the moment, she hesitated before catching the eye of her husband.

"Mr Sykes is crossing the square. I will bring him through."

William nodded and turned to George, who smiled.

"Everything will be fine, William. This is a new beginning. You'll see, you'll see."

Grace opened the door and there stood Jeremiah Sykes, complete with horn-rimmed glasses and a top hat. Every inch a solicitor of experience. He knew he would need every crumb of that today, for George had not fooled him for the length of an ant's blink. Smiling, he removed his hat which he gave to Grace, and then placed his large brown leather briefcase on the desk. George, who had been sitting behind the desk calmly, stood and offered Mr Sykes a seat next to William.

The solicitor was business-like and spoke quietly, yet firmly. "I have a lot of papers as you can see. It would be helpful, Mr Castle, if we could exchange seats, just for now. Thank you."

George had carefully planned this meeting, or so he thought. He had deliberately placed himself in the main chair so he could be seen as the dominant partner. Jeremiah Sykes swiftly turned the tables and George did not know whether this was intentional or a coincidence. Grace stood and watched Mr Sykes, intrigued, and thought this was going to be an interesting meeting. George tried to gather his composure and turned to Grace.

"Thank you, Grace. Perhaps you could organise some refreshments?"

Mr Sykes shook his head. His dark brown eyes were as unfathomable as a bottomless pit, and overshadowed by brown shaggy eyebrows seeming to have a mind of their own. He looked up.

"Not for me, Grace, and dare I suggest not for you. You need to be present for the reading. Please take a seat."

This was certainly not what George had expected, and he was about to object. William held his breath as to the outcome of the will and what it would mean for his family, in particular, the future of his son. So, the moment was lost on him.

"Now then gentlemen and Grace."

The solicitor nodded and smiled at Grace. He was enjoying himself. Mr Sykes, now seated, opened his brown leather, well-worn satchel and removed papers which were carefully tied in bright blue ribbon. He placed his satchel to one side, undid the ribbon, and sifted the papers, placing them precisely in front of him. Then thoughtful for a moment, he changed the order and position of his papers.

William sat deep in his own thoughts. George watched intently, mesmerised by the papers on the desk as if he were watching a dealer with cards at his club. Grace watched Mr Sykes's demeanour and importantly, as she had learnt, his eyes. That was always the tell-tale sign. Mr Sykes gave nothing away.

He picked up the first pile of papers and tapped them gently on the table. Instinctively, he glanced up and looked straight at Grace. Their eyes met momentarily, and he winked at her. Startled, she blinked. The moment had gone, and she wondered whether she had imagined, what could she call it… a conspiracy?

Mr Sykes cleared his throat. "Let us begin. I have here the last will and testament of Thomas Castle. This will was made by your father five years ago in September 1707 and written by me. Your mother witnessed his signature. He altered his will a year ago when he knew his health was failing. Thomas Castle, gentlemen and lady, was an accurate judge of character. You are most fortunate. Indeed, you are!" The solicitor nodded as if to himself and continued. "I will read the entire will. By that, I mean as initially written and then as amended."

He raised his eyes above his spectacles and stared at each of them.

"Yes!" The three spectators nodded in unison.

"The first will begins: To my sons. I have spent my

life wanting to leave both of my sons a legacy that you could build upon. Castles Merchant Traders has been a lifetime's work but as night follows day, I could not have done this without the love and support of your mother." Jeremiah Sykes paused and looked up to smile at them all. "Where was I? Yes." He continued, "My dearest wish is both my sons follow me in this glorious business and that is why I have encouraged you both to become part of, but it has to be your choice. Whilst you are brothers, you are different boys and are now young men. You, George, are flamboyant and charming. You, William, are quiet and industrious. We are in exciting times with great opportunities for expanding our trade and so I am leaving Castles Merchant Traders to you as equal partners. My wish is for you to continue the Castle tradition of honesty and fair play with other traders, for that has served me well."

William smiled and turned to Grace who sat impassively, her mind active as to the implications of what had been said. Could William really work with his brother? Could they trust George, who had a somewhat high-handed, arrogant, and a less than honest approach to people and business? George sneered and could barely contain himself.

Equal partners, honesty, and fairness! Not for him.

"However, as stated," the solicitor continued, "the will was changed some twelve months ago when your father recognised his health was failing and an increasing burden was on you, George and you, William. And, might I add, you, Grace."

George, now alert, turned quickly to look at his

sister-in-law who sat passively at the back. As if on cue, the fire in the grate that had been a slumbering bystander, spat and crackled into life.

"My health is now failing, and I have watched you, my sons. It was you, William who took the burden, with help from Grace. You, George were content to let your brother and his wife take the greatest share of the burden whilst you still shared the benefits. There would be a conflict if you had to work together. I see now it would be a mistake. I, therefore, leave Castles' Merchant Traders to William and Grace. For you, George I leave the sum of £5000. This should be sufficient for you to make your way in life."

The room was in absolute silence; a calm before the storm. George's eyes were glazed and smouldering, and then it happened. As a man possessed, he stood, picked up his chair, and hurled it across the room. His hands formed into fists and with white knuckles menacing, he bellowed, spittle flying from his mouth, anger in full force like waves crashing mercilessly against a helpless ship.

He stared at Jeremiah Sykes and then at William and snarled at Grace, that fount of goodness and kindness. Grace was a daughter of a parson who believed in education for girls. God preserve us. Then an aura of calmness washed over him. Jeremiah, William, and Grace sat wide-eyed at the transformation of the man. This now somewhat subdued man was more chilling, more frightening. Now in absolute control, he turned to William.

"You cheats! You! You! This is my inheritance, and I will have it."

Their solicitor watched unmoving. He had witnessed worse.

"Mr Castle, George, remember this is your father's will. These are his wishes. So do not be too hasty. If you would call on me, say tomorrow morning, I will have your money ready for you."

George stormed out of the house, barely remembering to collect his hat and cloak. Outside in the bitter winter afternoon, the cold slapped his face, bringing him back to his senses and the stark reality of what had just taken place; his plans had blown away into nothingness. He needed to think.

What to do? What to do?

The wind blew hard, yet George seemed oblivious. He needed to see Vincent, or perhaps not. Vincent was a shrewd man and could sniff out any weakness at one hundred paces. George had to learn quickly or else be undone. He needed to keep his counsel. He was a man on his own now and if he had to act alone, so be it. Heading toward his rooms, George pushed a hand into one of his coat pockets, took his scarf out, and wrapped it around his neck to face whatever was thrown at him head-on.

The following morning, George arrived at Jeremiah Sykes Solicitors. He knocked briskly on the door and Joseph Sykes opened it.

"Good morning, Mr Castle. Father is waiting. Thank you for being so prompt."

George nodded curtly and followed him up the stairs onto the landing and to the office door of Jeremiah Sykes. Joseph tapped the door lightly and opened it slowly.

"Mr Castle is here."

"Thank you, Joseph. Do come in, Mr Castle. Please sit down." Mr Sykes indicated the large leather chair in which he had sat a few days earlier. "Can I get you a drink? I have had an arduous morning already, George, so I am going to indulge myself in a large glass of French brandy. Only the finest, of course."

George nodded and sat down. Jeremiah Sykes strolled to a large cabinet next to his desk, opened it, and picked two fine-cut glasses. From behind other items, hidden away, was a bottle of dark liquid. Nodding to himself, he poured three fingers of very expensive French brandy and handed one of them to George, who was curious at what he thought was a change in the solicitor's attitude—respect, even.

Jeremiah watched quietly for a reaction, for that was what he had expected and prompted. He was curious what young George Castle was made of. The impression of the young man before him was not the greatest, but Jeremiah recognised George had an edge, had something about him. What that something was he intended to find out. After all, the sum of money left to his son by Thomas Castle was not paltry and the solicitor hoped George was not a fool who would waste the hard-earned bequest. Jeremiah also knew from long experience not to be judgemental too quickly, for people are not always what they first appear. George Castle may become a wealthy man and scorn a solicitor that mistreated him.

"You may well be wondering, Mr Castle why I appear to be treating you with such kinship."

George pursed his lips but did not drop his guard for

one moment. The solicitor was a clever, nay shrewd man, and George was a quick learner.

"Something like that."

"I thought so, indeed I thought so. Straight to the point, Mr Castle. I am a man of few words. You understand I see many clients. Joshua brought me your father's file, so I could refresh my memory. It is not the greatest these days. Your father was a man of exceptional talent and, moreover, the shrewdest man I have ever had the pleasure of meeting." Jeremiah shook his head in wonder and continued. "His philosophy of business was of fair trading, but you already know that. He had unwavering faith that this was the road to good trading. I suspect from our previous conversation you disagree."

Jeremiah stopped and waited for a response from George Castle, but none was forthcoming. George remained passive. Jeremiah leaned back in his chair. He was enjoying the challenge of this young man.

Nodding, he continued, "Your father and I often discussed the future of his business, and at the beginning when you and your brother were young boys, Thomas would talk whimsically of a future company with his two sons at the helm. He knew, however, that any company had to have one leader—a manager with ultimate authority. In the beginning, George, that was you."

The solicitor saw the slightest flicker of emotion and he knew competition between the two brothers was George's weakness.

"However, as time passed, your interest seemed to wain somewhat, whilst your brother, William showed a passion and understanding of fair trading, which was what your father believed in."

Yet again a flicker momentarily passed over George's eyes like a cloud flitting across the sky. Just as quickly, it disappeared.

"Your father recognised the difference in his sons; you, the eldest, handsome and charming but easily distracted and a little cavalier in his manner. His youngest, quiet, steadfast, and dare I suggest more honourable."

"Boring, he is boring," George interrupted with eyes flashing. He could not help himself. "William has no ambition, no desire for great wealth. I have. William is mediocre and so Castles' will be mediocre. I have the ambition to make Castles' great."

George was angry and quickly realised he had been shouting and glanced at the solicitor whose face was a picture of calmness and serenity.

He nodded. "Please, Mr Castle. I understand. I am here to help."

"Ha!" replied George. "Weasel words, Mr Sykes."

"Where was I?" continued Mr Sykes, pondering a moment. "Ah, yes! Your father understood his sons. He knew the direction you may well take the company in. Listening to you the day you came to see me, you had plans of your own, slave trading perhaps. I am right, am I not?"

George, embarrassed, flushed like a small child who had been caught stealing. Is there anything that this man did not know?

"Your father had originally left his company to you, believing William would find work easily as an accountant, or a clerk. We even discussed a solicitor's apprenticeship with me. Your father then decided you and William should be partners before finally recognising the son best placed to continue his beloved company with the ethics he aspired to, was in fact his youngest son. He believed your cavalier manner and charm would make or break you—wealth and riches or poverty and depravation. He thought you were capable of great things but he could not, would not risk his beloved trading company, so he left you a sum of money, and not a small some either."

George was silent and for a second Jeremiah Sykes thought he had not heard. He coughed lightly. George turned slowly gathering his thoughts.

"I wanted to be a trader," he said quietly, "not sitting at a desk making tiresome entries into a ledger, adding up figures and costs and profits and loss and… I wanted to be out with father buying and selling and travelling to faraway places, exciting places."

"George, your father knew you better than you realise. Think about how you would like to use the money he has left for you. Think carefully and come and see me tomorrow. You may wish to put some of your inheritance into a savings fund with one of the more reliable companies. I have a client, a good friend, who is an investment banker and closely involved with the South Sea Company that pays reasonable returns for shares in the company, which may be of some use."

George arose from his chair, nodded, and left.

Several days later, George stood outside the Old Bristol Gentlemen's Club. He had an appointment there with an investment banker, Jonathan Jerome, arranged by Jeremiah Sykes. Even the steps leading to the front door eschewed class. The railings were immaculate in black, without a chip or mark. The steps were spotless, and the open dark blue door had a brass doorknob in the shape of a lion's head, gleaming.

George dressed in a recently purchased well-fitted green velvet jacket, with matching cravat, grey fitted trousers, and highly polished plain black shoes, minus the current fashionable buckle which he detested. After all, he was not vain. He wore a smart grey hat with a dark grey band around the base. He had retrieved a pair of grey leather gloves from his own limited supply. In his right hand, he held his black walking cane with a decorative silver handle and tip at its base. He looked and felt the part of an elegant gentleman.

Light-footed, he walked up the steps past the main door and into a hallway with a coat stand and table, upon which were hats and matching gloves. Also, discreetly on the side was a silver plate with calling cards. He had barely set foot in the hallway when, from a glass-panelled door at the far end of the hall, a smartly dressed, clearly vigilant doorman in a black and dark blue waistcoat appeared.

"Can I be of help, sir?" asked the doorman.

George quietly said, "I am here to see Mr Jonathan Jerome."

Puzzled, the doorman replied, "Ah, you mean Mr Bernard. Please, sir, this way. He is waiting for you. It happens all the time—gentlemen being confused, that is. I reckon he does it deliberately. Jonathan B Jerome. Bernard, sir. B for Bernard."

George laughed and relaxed a little. "And what is

your name?"

"David Charles, sir. Has a nice ring to it they say, better than Davy Charles. Can I take your hat and gloves and your cane, Mr Castle? They will be quite safe."

George handed his hat and gloves to David. "I'll keep the cane if you don't mind. They are replaceable, the cane is *not*," he said.

David nodded and put the gloves and the hat on the table. "Safer than the bank here, sir," chirped David.

He followed the doorman. It took all his efforts not to stare at the opulence of the lounge. The walls were covered in blue with gold velvet curtains decorating the windows. It was breath taking, there was no other description George could envisage. There were blue leather chairs, and a light grey-blue and gold-coloured carpet. The lounge was empty but for a table by the bar on the left-hand side of the room, where a gentleman sat smoking a large cigar and reading a newspaper.

"Mr Bernard is behind the newspaper, Mr Castle. He always has his head in the financial papers. Very successful if I might say."

"Has he paid you to say that?" responded George.

David shook his head and laughed. "No, sir, but he looks after my savings, small that they are. I own shares. Me an investor, who would have thought? Doing fine as well, sir. Don't ask me with who, confidential and all that." He tapped his nose and winked. David walked towards the table and coughed lightly. "Mr Castle is here, sir. Can I get you both something to drink?"

A voice from behind the paper muttered, "Mister

Castle will have the same as me, you young scoundrel. I will have a refill. We need our wits about us."

"Coffee it is, then." David disappeared behind the bar and then returned to his post—a seat by the glass panelled door.

The paper rustled as he folded it neatly revealing a slim, elegant young man, clean shaven and with bright green eyes which had a sparkle that seemed all-knowing, as well as neat, copper-coloured straight hair. Whilst casually dressed, he was a man of unmistakable quality.

"Mr Castle, please take a seat. You will have gathered from David I am Jonathan B Jerome, but please call me Jonathan. Forgive me for ordering coffee."

George replied, "Thank you and please call me George."

The coffee appeared as if from thin air, carried by a server with the same coloured black jacket and trousers as worn by David. However, the waistcoat was a darker shade of blue. The server placed the coffee jug on the table, along with brown sugar.

"Do the honours, James," said Jonathan.

"As you wish, sir."

They paused for the server to leave.

"George, Jeremiah Sykes has asked me to provide you with financial advice on an investment. On shares and savings and such like."

George nodded. "I have a sum of money—an inheritance from my father. My younger brother has inherited the business."

"So, we could say you are momentarily unemployed,

with I believe a sum of £5000, and you will need an income; perhaps a saving fund providing you with one?"

"Correct. I will need some of my inheritance for somewhere to live as well as monies for day-to-day living. It is worth mentioning I feel badly let down by my father. I am the elder brother, after all. I have a point to prove."

Mr Jerome smiled. "Your father's company was a merchant trader, I understand. Profitable but risky. Ships sink, traders cheat, and goods get spoiled. You might find that we can do better, so do not be too downhearted."

On the floor at the side of his chair was a battered brown leather case, with a long shoulder strap and two buckles which he undid with care as if fearful the briefcase would simply drop to pieces. Mr Jerome placed it on the table in front of him and, opening it gently—with love, even—withdrew a small notebook. He closed the leather case and placed it back on the floor.

Smiling at George, Jonathan removed a small silver pencil from his inside jacket pocket, opened the notebook, and wrote the date neatly on top of a new page: '25th January 1712. George Castle Esquire'.

On the next line, he wrote 'Accommodation' followed by 'Club Membership'.

He continued, "You will have to stay where you are for now. You need to be a member of a gentleman's club for respectability, contacts, and trade. There are no better clubs than this one. There are, however, formalities for membership at the Old Bristol

Gentleman's Club and that will take some time. Now, to your inheritance. £5000 is a goodly sum. I recommend you invest in the South Sea Company which is a new British company, established by an Act of Parliament to trade with Spanish America, including slaves. Crucially, the South Sea Company gives a good and guaranteed interest rate. Now, whilst it is intended to boost trade in the South Seas, it is in the Government's interest for the South Sea Company to flourish. Being an early investor whilst the share price is low and with a good interest rate, it is an excellent investment. I possess shares in the South Sea Company, and I suggest you do likewise and as much as you can afford. Castles' Merchant Traders, however, are opposed to slave trading, I believe. Is that your position, George?"

George shook his head. "Anything but! Had I been running my father's trading company I would have looked towards slave trading as my primary source of trade. In fact, I have spoken to Vincent Marchant about the possibility of converting one of our ships to a slaver." Jonathan Jerome winced. He poured coffee into their empty cups and continued. "My advice is to keep well away from Mr. Marchant. He is a rogue."

George nodded. "An investment in the South Sea Company is a good risk?"

"I cannot say there will be no risk. No investment is without risk. Obviously, you need to consider the credibility of the company. Credibility, George. Credibility. The company has it in bucket loads."

Jonathan was animated, eyes twinkling like stars in the night sky. Certainly, Jonathan seemed very confident. George considered, well informed.

"Might I ask you, Jonathan, where this information has come from? Is the source reliable?"

"Good question. Much of the information is open to the public but some parts of the agreement are still confidential. I will also add my source is impeccable. As I have said, I have investments in the South Sea Company of my own that is how confident I am. Also, I need to keep many a confidence, George, including yours. I need you to trust me. What is said in here, stays in here. I need your word on that."

Though he would not divulge the source of his information, it was an 'impeccable' one, and the confidence flooded out of Jonathan like a fast-flowing river about to burst its banks. George looked enthralled as he tried to absorb the information and keep an inner calm.

George was not wealthy by Johnathan's standards, and he understood he had to know his own limits and realistically how much he could afford to lose.

"How much do you think I should invest? You need to understand my inheritance is all the money I possess."

Jonathan nodded, leaned back in his chair, and closed his eyes. He muttered to himself as if thinking through the question before considering an answer.

"If we invest say half of your inheritance in South Sea Company shares, which will take twelve months to earn any profit. To spread the investment and reduce the risk, we can place a lump sum in a bank whilst we look for other investments. There will be less profit in that but greater security leaving you a reasonable sum to use right now. As image is everything, I would suggest you accept—if I can manage it at a good rent for you—rooms here at the club, as they are quite prestigious. And buy new clothes. You must look the part."

From the inside pocket of his dark red well-tailored jacket, Jonathan produced a card which he straightened neatly before placing it on the table.

Tapping the card with an elegant forefinger, he said, "My tailor. Tell him I sent you. There's another thought." George frowned. "There's more?"

Jonathan laughed, tapping the card again. "Calling cards. You need your own."

He turned the card over and wrote neatly in the limited space available some details of yet another acquaintance, and then signed it.

"I understand, George. You do not know me, and I am asking you to trust me. Speak to Mr Sykes, please. I hope by being cautious with your investment, it will give you the reassurance you need. In time we will hopefully be able to be more adventurous if you would like me to handle your finances. Believe me, this is the time to do so with English trade expanding. Who says wars are bad? Wars are excellent for trade. After all, armies need to be fed, they need to be watered, and they need a uniform and cannons. And firearms. I am here most days but do not linger too long."

George nodded and smiled. "I will consider this. It has been a difficult time for me, and I have a lot to think about. But I will not delay. Two days, at the same time and place?"

Jonathan nodded and George stood, picked up his

cane, and walked to the door, where David was waiting with his coat and gloves.

He glanced at the large mirror on the wall to see whether the reflection gave any sign of the sweat dribbling down his back and the anxiety he felt. His gut reaction was to do the business there and then, but something stopped him and a voice in his head advised caution. Without so much as a flicker of an eyelid, he acknowledged the warning and remained silent.

"Everything all right, sir?"

"Yes Davy, everything is all right."

CHAPTER ONE

10th July 1720

The young boy sat looking out of the garret window. He leaned against the wall with his knees bent, peering above rooftops to the Bristol docks and beyond. From here, he could see ships of all shapes, types, and sizes, and from there, he could imagine life at sea. Sam's favourite post was the crow's nest whence he would envisage looking, eagle-eyed, for land and pirates. Clutching his cuff in his right hand, he wiped the condensation and mist from his breath on the window. He looked at his sodden sleeve and grimaced. His mother would not be best pleased.

Sam was excited. The 10th of July 1720 was a very special day, for now, he was ten years old. That was important enough, but even more so was his father had promised him on his tenth birthday, he would become a member of the family business. His desire to sail the seven seas and perhaps become a captain of his own ship was one step nearer.

He leaned against the wall and stretched his legs out on the window ledge. He was stiff. This may be his favourite perch, but it was cramped as well as damp.

Then he saw a tall, slim upright figure, wearing a three-cornered black hat walking on the main street from the dock. It was his father. Samuel stared hard. Was he hiding something in his coat? A parcel perhaps? His father looked up and waved. Samuel, not wasting a moment, jumped off the window ledge, crossed the room, and opened the door to the stairs. Within a single breath, he hurtled down the stairs two at a time but lost his footing in his desire for more speed.

Stumbling, he was grateful for his mother's arms at the bottom. She heard the commotion and realised her husband was on his way home with a birthday surprise.

"Careful, Samuel. You will not pass your tenth birthday if this is how you carry on."

"Father's home, Mother. It looks like he has a parcel underneath his jacket. Could it possibly be for me?"

Grace shrugged her shoulders, and a nonchalant look spread across an already passive face. She was determined not to spoil her husband's surprise for Samuel.

The door opened, and there stood William Castle, face beaming. "I am ready for my lunch. It has been a very long morning."

Ignoring Samuel, he walked towards the kitchen where the cook, Mrs Harper, was laying the table for the midday meal. With her was her daughter, Alice who was standing by the cooker in deep concentration. Alice wore a brown linen smock reaching just above her ankles and was protected by a multi-coloured apron on account of the spillages from the various mixtures she attracted.

"Ah, Mrs Harper, what is Alice watching?" enquired Mr Castle.

"Sorry, sir, can't be telling you; it's for Master Samuel's birthday. It's all about the timing, sir. One minute late, that's all it takes."

Alice glanced at Mr Castle, then at Sam, and blushed. William smiled his broadest at Samuel, then at

Mrs Harper and Alice.

"Will Sam have time to open his present before the mystery appears from the oven?"

"Yes, sir. Ten minutes."

William Castle sat at one end of the table inviting everyone to join him. "You as well, Alice. As you know Samuel is ten years old today, and so he formally joins the family business. He needs to know the importance of facts and figures, prices, commodities, profits, and losses. Samuel must learn how to buy and sell, to learn to trade is not about glamorous faraway places. It is about honesty and fair play. About looking men in the eye and judging whether they are paying their dues or robbing you blind. Your grandfather, Thomas was the best man I knew at judging characters; you must learn about that, Samuel. But let us forget the serious part for a moment and enjoy your tenth birthday. Happy birthday, Son."

Like a magician, he put a hand inside his coat—a coat with innumerable pockets from which over the years he had pulled trinkets and presents to the delight of his wife and son. William produced a long parcel wrapped in brown paper and tied with red ribbon as befitting a tenth birthday. This he handed to Samuel. Samuel slowly untied the red ribbon and removed the brown paper, revealing a long item wrapped in oil canvas.

Holding his breath, the now ten-year-old boy removed the oil canvas cover and there it was, in all its glory. Sam stared in disbelief at the beautiful, shining telescope. They had engraved it with the words 'July 10th, 1720, the 10th birthday of Samuel Castle.'

Lost At Sea

Speechless, Samuel caressed it gently and with some encouragement put it to his left eye to look through the kitchen window. Taken aback at the closeness and enormous size of the window, he staggered backwards to be rescued yet again by his mother.

"Perhaps not a good idea; you will need to take the telescope outside and look at long distances," laughed William, "though not just at this moment. After our luncheon."

Dorothy Harper coughed politely. "Sir, Madam, Samuel. Alice has a present. Go on, Alice show him."

Shyly, Alice put her hand into her apron pocket and produced a small item wrapped in colourful, if unusual, tissue paper. It fitted snugly into her palm.

The cook nodded at her daughter. "Carry on, Alice,"

"When Father went across the sea, he always brought a present back—something he made or carved, for me. I have two of these, Master Castle. I would like you to have one."

Sam took the small parcel from the palm of Alice's hand. Alice blushed from the top of her head to the tip of her toes and scrutinised her very interesting hands, embarrassed. Samuel tenderly unwrapped the present and saw the most exquisite ivory ship. "Father told me it was carved from a whale's tooth. It took a bite out of the ship but broke its tooth, then swallowed the ship whole. Father was lucky he fell overboard and clung to it for days and days until his rescue. The tooth is lucky, and it will keep you safe if ever you are at sea."

Samuel, wide-eyed, was speechless at the whole spectacle of a whale swallowing a ship like the Swift.

Dorothy smiled fondly at her little Alice, who would

sit enamoured and spellbound at her father's feet as he told her stories of mermaids and whales and man-eating monsters. So lifelike and full of fantasy were his stories, her mother had to tell her husband, 'Not to fill little Alice's head with nonsense.'

Samuel thanked Alice and smiled at her for her thoughtfulness and generosity.

"Alice, this is the most wonderful present. I will keep it close to me always, I promise."

"With all this excitement we forgot about the oven!" cried Mrs Harper. "Quickly, Alice, we need to get the birthday surprise out."

Helped by her mother, Alice carried steak and ale pie from the oven and placed it on the table.

"My favourite," sighed Sam.

"Five plates, Mrs Harper. You and Alice must join us!" said William.

The luncheon was most enjoyable but there was much work to be done for William. He had to return to the Swift, which was being loaded to depart for Portugal. It was due to set sail in the morning. Sam was to accompany him, complete with the telescope.

At two o'clock in the afternoon, father and son left their home to return to the Swift to complete the manifest and to give Captain Joseph Featherstone an amount of cash. Grace was careful indeed in the amount she supplied and insisted the captain signed for the money and provided receipts. She was wise enough, however, to know receipts could be forged. Previous captains thought with a woman in charge, it would be easy to pull the wool over her eyes, but Grace was astute as well as intelligent and had been in the trade long enough to see through that, and to make her presence felt.

She glanced upwards through the window, and in the distance saw her husband and her beloved son, each wearing a three-cornered hat, brown jacket black trousers, and boots. William was tall and slim and her son was gangly, hopping from one leg to another like an over-excited baby sparrow. Fortunately for Samuel, the telescope was safe in his father's inner coat pocket again. A sensible precaution, she thought.

It had given Grace a great deal of pleasure to see her son take a step, even such a small one, into the family business. Samuel had moved from under his mother's wing to now being under his father's. Wherever practicable, Samuel would accompany his father to some meetings and visits he had to undertake. Always with his beloved telescope either in his hand or in his father's pocket, as Sam and his telescope would become inseparable.

The office as they liked to call it, was at the front of the house in a room with the largest window, which provided Grace with a deal of natural light. This is where she spent most of her time making entries into the company ledger which contained prices, profits, losses, wages, and other essentials. At the rear of the ledger were notes on all their customers, good or bad. More useful were notes on those who cheated or fiddled. Those who watered down the liquor, placed the floor sweepings in the tea and chalk in the flour, or who under weighed and swapped casks. The fly-by nights, the rogues and wastrels.

She sat at the desk, instinctively passing her right

hand over her hair to ensure it was tied neatly and firmly, and then glanced at her hands. She rubbed the callous on her right forefinger through years of writing, then gently smoothed her white cotton smock as she switched her mind from her husband and son to the work in hand. The daily completion of the company ledger—their Bible—without which they could not function or perhaps more accurately *she* could not function.

They built the reputation of Castle and Sons Merchant Traders upon hard-nosed but honest trading. They had learnt not to trust those who were supposedly honourable men, the customs and excise men, constables and justices, even parsons. God forbid.

On the walls around the room were large maps of the world. They differed in that some contained details of hazards such as Cape Horn, Cape of Good Hope, and the Saragossa Sea. The largest map was of the routes of their own ships and the ledger contained details of each journey, such as stop-off points, any unscheduled breaks in the journey, and the date of return. Much was guesswork as communication was poor and news often weeks behind, but Grace understood she needed to have as much information as she could. Yet another lesson learnt was she had to show those with whom she worked and traded that she knew what she was doing —wherever possible, remain one step ahead. It had been her suggestion they should formalise Samuel's position in the company.

She had taught him well. Mrs Harper had been willing to look after Samuel from birth along with Alice, to allow Grace to do her work. She had thought long and hard but decided against it. Instead, she purchased a small cot which she placed next to her in the sunlight. In times of deep concentration, she would speak her thoughts out loud to him and she found doing so helped to clarify her mind. It helped even though it seemed rather strange to share her thoughts with a baby, particularly on the occasions her husband entered the room and stood behind her whilst she was having a detailed conversation with Samuel, aged twelve months, on the amount of tax to be paid on three kegs of rum.

Grace had been most fortunate in her life not only with her husband and child but also with her parents. Grace's father had been a Rector and married a teacher. Her father Rector Harold Finch was well-read and enjoyed good debates. His wife, Jane was forward-looking and inspirational, telling Grace with application and fortitude she could achieve great things. Grace was a quick learner and even at an early age started helping her mother in the classroom. Initially, simple things: carrying books, writing words on the chalkboard, counting pencils and reading extracts from selected books.

Grace used this experience with Samuel. Teaching him his numbers, she used bags of flour or sugar, or sacks of coffee as counting bags. With letters, she wrote the words on sacks, bags or crates. His first written word was in fact 'cocoa'. The dilemma was often those writing the words on bags could not spell themselves, and so Grace had to keep a close watch. To be fair, Samuel was a clever little boy and sponge-like, quickly absorbing any information he was presented with. Grace recognised the environment her boy was in on a day-to-day basis was a good one. It was inventive and never boring. Sam learnt geography from the routes of their ships, history from wars, and even those in which England was not involved but which affected their trade.

In time, he sat beside his mother and copied her entries into the ledger on a chalkboard. Later, he could make the entries himself in neat handwriting, supervised by Grace. She taught him everything she knew in the practical sense of how to run a successful merchant trader. What he had to learn himself was the human element, not least that people are not always what they appear. Yes, she could teach him to examine the quality of the goods they received, to count the sacks, to check the money they were paid. Alone, he had to learn about the pitfalls of a business such as theirs and how to make judgements, who to trust, and who to turn to in a crisis. There would be some hard lessons and some disappointments too, but he had to make his own mistakes.

Her chick was about to take his first flight from the nest. She hoped the landing would not be too bumpy. The time was right for William to take Sam from home to experience day-to-day trading. The face-to-face haggling, the bluster, the promises, and whether they could be kept.

Lifting her hand to replace yet another escaped lock of hair, she then picked up her pen and dipped it in ink to make her painstakingly slow but accurate entries. There was literally no space in the many columns for error. The opening of their front door and Sam's laughter broke her concentration. William put his head around.

"Hello there. How are things with you?" he whispered.

"There seems little point in whispering, William. Has Sam been noisy all this afternoon?"

William grimaced. "Unfortunately, yes. The Swift has set sail and I have the papers here." He tapped his jacket pocket protectively.

CHAPTER TWO

16th July 1720

The room was in darkness and George sat on a well-worn brown leather chair, stretching his long limbs by placing his feet on a red, leather-clad buffet. He had promised himself a matching brown leather buffet, but that was for another day.

It was midnight and George relaxed after a hard day; he smiled at that thought, for he did not do hard work unless you included gambling and womanising. He laughed out loud but there was no one at hand to share his laughter.

On the right-hand side of the chair, there was a small table with a bottle of brandy. He loved his brandy, and this was the time he enjoyed it most. It was the finest money could buy (or customs men could buy to be more accurate) but it was not for sharing. Next to the bottle was a beautifully carved glass with a large measure. In his left hand was a thick cigar with ash ready to fall like a small drop of water hanging precariously from a petal, getting larger and larger until it burst. The ash landed on a well-placed plate. He had burnt a hole in a very expensive Turkish carpet when he was worse for wear one evening. Next to the brandy was a solitary candle, still and upright like a soldier on guard.

He picked up the glass and held it close to the candlelight to marvel at the colour of the swirling liquid. As if in unison with the candle, the glass and brandy performed the most wondrous magic, changing the room to a dancing collection of shadows. It was mesmerising.

George dozed gently; the brandy and the warm summer night were a toxic mix. He was in danger of dropping his glass when a sudden movement gave him a jolt. He glanced up at the picture above the unlit fireplace—a picture he had purchased after the reading of his father's will, when his brother inherited the family business. George's hatred was such that he could not say the words, 'Castles Merchant Traders' out loud. He bought the painting of some unknown cutter at full sail across the sea, as a reminder of what he believed should have been his inheritance and a focus for his sheer loathing.

Staring at the picture with sails billowing and waves crashing across the deck, the ship seemed to come alive. George could hear the voices of the men shouting, the wind howling like a pack of wolves spitting and snarling, lightning flashing, thunder rolling, and waves crashing onto the deck with such ferocity and anger the ship seemed to shudder with fear and anguish, before crashing from the top of the wave into a hellhole.

Totally wide-eyed in terror, George sat motionless, sweat pouring from his brow. His hair raised at the back of his neck. He was living in the moment. The ship was the reminder, the driving force of a burning hatred he had for his father and his brother. Until exhausted, breathless, and in sheer panic, he broke the spell by throwing his glass into the hearth.

Bronwyn Harrison

***

It was the 17th of July, a week after Samuel's birthday. Samuel was sitting in his favourite perch—nonchalant and relaxed with his back against the wall, knees under his chin, and his telescope placed on the ledge ready for instant use. In his mind's eye, he was back in the crow's nest atop a ship's mast keeping watch, looking for land or an enemy fleet, or even Alice's whale. He laughed out loud at Alice's tall story before pondering the possibility of the story being true. After all, Alice's father was a well-respected captain, so who was he to mock?

It was late afternoon, and the weather was not the best for his telescope. Outside, the rain was drizzling and whilst he was sheltered inside, he was learning quickly that he had to keep his telescope both dry and clean at both ends. He could not see through the misted window, with or without it!

Sam held his sleeve cuff with his right hand, painstakingly wiping the window. He peered through the clean glass to look for something exciting upon which he could point his telescope. It was then he noticed on the opposite side of the road a boy, perhaps a little younger than himself. He watched the boy as he paced up and down, hesitating, before looking across the road in his general direction towards the front door rather than at the attic. Intrigued, Sam placed his telescope on the window ledge, before jumping down. Against his right eye and with his left hand holding the telescope steady, Samuel took a step back to focus on the boy, as well as staying out of sight.

Lost At Sea

He scanned the opposite side of the street until—after a moment's panic that the boy had disappeared—he pinpointed him once more standing and staring across the street towards their house and warehouse. Holding the telescope steady, Samuel watched him. He could see he was scrawny. The boy had a cap on his head which he straightened before placing it purposefully back. He then pulled his jacket down and straight as if trying to make himself more presentable. Sam also noticed he kept looking inside his jacket, then patting it firmly before glancing up at the window. Sam could not avoid his glance and so remained still. He could hardly do anything else.

The boy marched across the street and a short while later, Sam could hear knocking on their door. He closed the telescope with care and placed it back in its oilskin cover. His routine ended abruptly, however, as Sam ran across the room and down the stairs to see his mother appear from the office.

"There's someone at the door."

"I heard," replied Grace.

"It's a young boy," continued Sam. "I saw him through my telescope!"

"Spying now?" Grace shook her head with mock indignation.

"I wasn't spying, Mother. I just saw him there and wondered what he was up to."

Grace smiled. "We will soon find out."

She walked to the door and opened it. Puzzled at first, she looked right and left before glancing down. In front of her was a small, thin boy who seemed in need of a good feed. The boy grabbed his cap with both hands having momentarily forgotten his manners. He cursed inwardly, not daring to repeat it to a lady.

"Hello, missus," he said in a loud voice, puffing himself to all of three foot high. "I'm wanting Master William Castle if you please. I have a message." He tapped his jacket pocket knowingly. "Important it is, and urgent."

His words drifted away like a leaf in the breeze.

"I am Mrs Castle. You can leave a message with me. I will see my husband gets it promptly." Grace held a hand out and waited.

The boy took a deep breath whilst he considered. The silence hung like snowflakes soundlessly falling to the ground.

"Can't do that. I have to hand it personally to him and wait for a reply. My orders." Confidence getting the better of him, he continued, "If I return tonight then I will get a shilling. Sorry, missus, I need to see Master Castle."

Grace studied the lad. "Hmm, I see. You had better come in. Samuel!"

Must be serious, thought Sam, as Mother's using my Sunday name. "Yes, Mother?"

"Tell your father he has a visitor. I will take him to the kitchen."

Grace ushered the boy into the kitchen where Mrs Harper was hard at work with Alice alongside her, peeling potatoes and carrots for their supper.

"Mrs Harper, we have a visitor. I think whilst he is waiting for Mr Castle, he might as well have something to eat."

Grace looked at Mrs Harper, nodding towards the

boy. She frowned, because Mrs Castle was always very careful about strangers in the house.

"I think, Mrs Harper, he could do with something to eat."

"Ah." She smiled. "I think you're right, Mrs Castle. Let me see what we have."

"But I need to return with an answer straight away," pressed the boy.

The temptation of a hungry boy being offered food was written all over his face, as clear as their trade routes mapped on the office wall.

"I understand, but Mr Castle will need to consider his answer before writing his reply. In the meantime, Mrs Harper, I am sure you can quickly rustle up something for him to eat."

Playing the game now, Dorothy Harper pondered long and hard. "Does the lad have a name?"

"I don't think so," replied Grace.

Both women looked at this small boy and waited.

"It's Noah, missus."

Grace nodded at Mrs Harper.

"Right, Noah, come with me. Wash your hands over at bowl yonder, then sit down at the table."

Hesitant and a little frightened, he stood looking down at his feet, wringing his cap as if he was about to throttle it.

Grace came to his rescue. "Noah, please, I'll tell you what I will do. I will see Mr Castle and ask him to come in. Meanwhile, do what Mrs Harper says. You can eat while you are waiting. I will tell Mr Castle about the shilling. Sam, come with me."

Grace disappeared, followed by Sam, who was

bewildered.

"I don't understand, Mother. We know nothing about him. Is he who he says he is?"

Grace patiently placed both hands on her son's shoulders. "Sam, whatever his name is, he is scrawny." She continued, "I wonder when he last had a meal. This morning, like you? Unlikely! Surely you do not begrudge him something to eat?"

Chastened by his mother's tone, Sam nodded. "I am sorry. I didn't think."

"I know. Now go back in there and do not stare at him. Treat him kindly."

Grace left her son and tapped lightly on the office door, before opening it.

"William, you have a small visitor."

Without looking up, William replied. "Not another rat, Grace. God forbid, not another rat."

Grace laughed an infectious laugh that always had the effect of taking William's mind away from what he had in hand.

"No. This one has two legs. A young boy called Noah has a message for you and you alone, and, if he can take the reply by tonight, he gets a shilling."

"Must be serious then, a shilling."

"He looks half starved," continued Grace, "and so Mrs Harper is in charge."

William put his pen down on the desk and followed Grace from the office and to the kitchen. She opened the door and there sat Noah with a bowl full of mutton stew and a slice of bread. Mrs Harper talked animatedly, whilst Sam sat quietly watching. The boy looked up and dropped his spoon looking guiltily down at his food.

Smiling, William said, "What do you think of Mrs Harper's stew? Is it any good?" He winked at the boy who, with a mouth full, nodded and grinned. "Mrs Castle tells me you have a very important letter. If you let me have it, I can prepare my response. I understand there is a shilling at stake."

Noah wiped his hands on his jacket before carefully removing a sealed letter. The boy stood and handed it with great decorum to William.

"Do you know who it is from, Noah? It is Noah?" continued William.

"Mr George, sir," replied Noah.

William frowned, lips tight as he concentrated on the unfamiliar name. "Mr George? The name is not familiar."

"Mr Castle. Mr George Castle."

William and Grace stood motionless like a rock against the barrage of the sea. A wave of emotion crashed over them both. The boy rescued them as he took their reaction, or their lack of it, to be they did not know Mr George.

He added, "Your brother, sir. I run messages for the Bristol Gentlemen's Club. He asked me to bring the message and return... promptly. Yes, that was the word, *promptly*."

Grace recovered the quickest. They had seen little of William's brother since the reading of the will some eight years ago. The odd glance here and there, and the occasional snippet of information. He was doing well. The letter was intriguing.

"Thank you, Noah. For a moment you had us at a

loss. He needs a reply promptly?"

She smiled at the boy and then turned to look at Samuel who was staring hard at his parents and about to speak. Grace silenced him with a gentle shake of the head and a finger to her lips.

"Look after Noah for us."

The Office door was closed behind William and Grace as they left. The revelation shook William. He stared at the letter, before Grace ushered him to the desk and his chair, and then sat beside him. William was pale-faced, and his hands shook.

"I wonder what he wants, after all this time."

Grace gently put her arms around her husband. "Let's open it and see. Do you want me to light a candle?"

He shook his head. He opened the top drawer of the desk and picked up a letter opener. Gently, he slid the end of the small knife-like object into the envelope, leaving the red wax undamaged. Inside was a single sheet of paper. It may have been several years since he had read his brother's writing, but William recognised it immediately.

The Old Bristol Gentleman's Club
July 20th, 1720

William,

I hope this finds you and your family well; your son must be ten years old or so by now. I am sure this letter will have come as a surprise to you for we have not spoken since the date our father's will was read. My associates tell me Castles' Merchant Traders is doing well. You may know through the trade I have done well for myself and am a rich man, although not rich in the way you are with your family. I think it is time for us to let bygones be gone.

I have a proposition for you. The source of my good fortune has been the sum of money our father left to me and, with wisdom and sound investment, I have made a great deal of money and would like to share my fortune with you. They have offered me a wonderful opportunity for a small investment you may well be interested in, and the potential returns are excellent.

I cannot say more; secrecy is the basis of sound investment, and we need to act speedily before the cat is out of the bag. I hope you will meet me at the Old Bristol Gentleman's Club where I will introduce you to my partner. It will impress you; I am sure.

Lunchtime is the best time. The next two or three days should suffice.

Give the boy your response today. I cannot stress the urgency.

George

William leaned back in his chair and read the letter slowly. Grace watched his eyes, which initially brought a smile to his face, followed by a pursing of his lips and then a puzzled frown. She had learned patience and waited silently as William read and then reread the letter. He placed it in front of him and without a word, slid it toward Grace. She glanced at her husband, picked up the letter, and read. As letters normally start with pleasantries, she quickly read past them to the main part of the letter. An investment! She considered it long and hard.

William had been shocked at his brother's anger after they read the will. Whilst he understood George's frustration, it was not of their making. It was his father's decision after all.

William glanced sideways at Grace. "I don't know what to make of that after all this time!"

Grace nodded in agreement. "I know, but he has partly answered the first question. Eight years! Why now? He writes he wishes to put things behind him." Skimming the letter, Grace continued. "Ah, here it is. 'Let bygones be gone' and then of course he offers you an opportunity to share his good fortune with an investment. The question is, do you believe him or is it about getting your money?"

"Our money," William quickly corrected, "but what do we do?"

Grace then said what was on William's mind. "Do you wish to see your brother and put the past behind you, or not? If you do, then meet him. The investment is a separate matter and I think you need to remember that. I will leave you to your response, William." She put her arms around her husband and whispered. "Follow your instinct, William."

William patted her hand and nodded.

Grace slid from his shoulders. She gently kissed his cheek, turned, and walked out of the office. As she entered the kitchen, a sight of gentility and kindness stopped her in her stride. Mrs Harper was sitting next to Noah, encouraging him to have some of her stewed apple with cinnamon and cream.

"Come on, lad you need fattening up. Am I right, young Sam or not?"

Sam was sitting on the opposite side of the kitchen table and solemnly declared, "Definitely scrawny, Mrs Harper, but perhaps he doesn't like your stewed apples either."

Playing the game wonderfully, she took a deep breath to take her to her full height, even though she was sitting. She looked at Sam and wagged a finger which was covered in cream.

"Now you listen here, my lad, there's nothing wrong with my stewed apples."

Noah, wide-eyed, and pale-faced, turned his head, first to Sam and then to Mrs Harper.

"Prefer your stewed plums, Mrs Harper, if you don't mind my saying," continued Sam.

Noah shook his head and said, "I've got to eat what I'm given when I'm given it and if I'm given it."

Sam stood up and walked around the table placing his hand on Noah's shoulder. "Noah, we're only playing. We meant no harm."

Noah smiled shyly.

Samuel stopped and hesitated, and before he could say another word, saw his mother standing in the doorway.

"I see you are entertaining Noah." Looking at him, she smiled. "I hope Mrs Harper and Sam are treating you well. If not, they will have me to answer to! Mrs Harper, have you got something he can take with him? Are there others at home Noah: mother, father, brothers, and sisters?"

At that, tears welled and were in danger of overflowing like a blocked river about to burst its banks. He stared down at his food and cried. Closing his eyes tightly, he took a deep breath. He sensed these were decent people who were concerned about him, really and truly.

"Our dad's at sea. Unsure whether he's alive or dead. I live with Ma, my little sister, Florence, and my older brother, Billy. Ma takes in washing for Mr Jonathan, and my brother and I do errands, take messages and such, like Mr Castle's."

Sam was silent for a moment as he absorbed what was being said by a boy of his age, born to different circumstances.

Grace nodded. "Find Noah something to take home if you please, Mrs Harper."

Mrs Harper said, "Right you are."

Grace followed her to the larder. "Something for all the family."

Mrs Harper was a kindly soul but nobody's fool. She'd had a tough life and her beginning was like that of young Noah. She too had seen hardship. Experience had taught her poverty brought both the best and the worse out of people.

"Don't mind my saying, ma'am, but are you sure about this? Giving food away. There'll be beggars at the door."

Grace nodded. "They wouldn't dare if they knew you would be the one opening it."

Mrs Harper laughed out loud with an infectious laugh that brought a smile to Grace's face. "Quite right, ma'am. I'd box their ears."

Grace continued, "I understand what you are saying, and I am grateful, but I sense the lad is genuine. "

Leaving Mrs Harper to her own devices, Grace tapped on the office door. On entering, William was still at the desk, head bowed, mouthing the words. Lips pursed, brow sweating, and pausing here and there, he considered alternative wording. Writing a letter was, she believed, to be an art form, and she recognised the subtleties and interpretation or even misinformation that was sometimes required. William liked to be straightforward in his dealing and enjoyed the face-to-face haggling with other merchants. He was a shrewd trader, but his skill was in watching for sweaty palms, the blinking of eyes, and the nervous licking of lips.

Grace closed the door. "How is it going, William?"

"Nearly there. I will have to rewrite it. See what you think."

He handed the sheet of paper over and looked at his ink-stained forefinger in disdain. Grace quickly scanned the letter and raised a smile at his clumsy way with words, but she understood the tone and thought he had done well for a man who was unfamiliar (or rather inexperienced) in letter writing.

"Would it help if I rewrite the letter? I am a little quicker and neater. The boy needs to be off with your reply."

William sighed, nodded, and stood to allow Grace to take the letter and walk to her own desk.

He moved towards a cabinet that was placed at the furthest corner from the window. The cabinet was made of yew. Good quality too. William had an eye and had done well with this purchase. He enjoyed good quality whether it was furniture or brandy, and his trader's instinct came easy to him whatever he was buying. He smiled because he had haggled well when he bought it. The cabinet had two glass doors that were locked. It was no good placing temptation there for those traders who visited him, and he was of the opinion even the most honest man had his price. Not necessarily money, either. He removed a key from an inside pocket, opened the cabinet, and reached behind the liquors. There, he placed his hand on a small bottle of his favourite brandy. French brandy to be accurate. He sighed in admiration of the pleasure to come from this golden liquid.

William removed a glass and with the bottle made his way to his preferred chair. He sat in his rather worn-out green leather chair, with its battered arms which he stroked affectionately and intimately as he would a dog, then poured himself a generous measure and placed the bottle on the floor at the side. He sagged back, stretched out his legs, and before taking a sip of the brandy, closed his eyes and placed his hands and the glass on his stomach.

Grace slid William's draft letter to one side. She took a clean sheet of quality paper normally saved for their good clients, picked up her quill with her left hand, and dipped it in the inkpot.

She realised she had to take care with William's letter. George had to believe he was the writer. George, it seemed to her, believed she had too much influence over her husband. This was far from the case but the skill of writing an excellent letter was to understand the mind set of both the receiver and the writer. What was left out was as important as what was put in.

Dear George,

Your letter finds us well, and it is indeed a pleasant surprise to hear you have done well for yourself.
  I am a most fortunate man with a good wife, and you are correct in your assumption our son has just reached his tenth birthday. My greatest desire is he will follow me into Castles' Merchant Traders and continue our good name.
  I have heard of your success in investments and such and agree that time has moved on and we should let bygones be gone. It will be good to see you again after so many years. The investment opportunity you propose seems interesting and I will gladly listen to your proposals.
  This is a busy time for me and if speed is of the essence, it would be helpful if we could hold the meeting here. I could see you tomorrow, say twelve noon.
  The boy you have sent is most pleasing and is worthy of a suitable reward.

William

Nodding with satisfaction, Grace placed her pen down to one side, picked up her blotter, and carefully dabbed the letter. She could see the brandy glass precariously placed on his stomach as it moved up and down in time with his deep breathing. He had fallen asleep. She got up from her chair and walked to his side. Removing the glass before it would spill, she gently shook his shoulder.

"William, I have finished. Come and read it. See what you think."

William blinked before staring at Grace in confusion.

"Your letter, William, come and read it," she repeated.

She handed him his glass and pointed to the table. Beaming at his wife whom he loved more than words could say, he got out of his chair and sat down at the desk to read the letter.

"It's an excellent letter, William. You have it right. Pleasant but not too eager, I think."

"It reads much better now, Grace dear, thank you."

William signed the letter and placed it in an envelope. Grace had simply written, 'To be delivered by hand to George Castle Esquire.' The letter was sealed, and Grace then went to the kitchen where she handed it to Noah. He was waiting with a canvas sack full of food.

"I'll be off, missus. Sorry, Mrs Castle. Thanks for everything."

Noah smiled at Mrs Harper and nodded toward Sam.

***

It had been a warm July day and after a languorous day of idleness George made his way to the Old Bristol Gentlemen's Club, anticipating the letter of response from his brother.

George was at his regular table and was in animated

conversation with his business associate about the South Sea Company's latest share offer. Since his first investment after the death of his father, the value of shares in general and the South Sea Company in particular had soared in value to dizzy heights and made George a lot of money. His advisor, Jonathan Bernard Jerome, however, was now advising caution. Their joint investments had done well, including the shared purchase of a trading ship, the Pegasus.

The King himself had become an investor and was now registered formally as the Governor of the South Sea Company, which had simply increased confidence.

"The share price of the South Sea Company is absolute madness and cannot continue. There will be tears, believe me. The markets will collapse, and the bubble will burst. For goodness' sake man, sell them now. Do not be too greedy. You will make a handsome profit if you sell now."

George laughed. "The markets are booming and we have to take advantage, to hang onto our shares. Keep our nerve. Who is to say the share prices will not continue to rise?"

Jonathan and George discussed the major investors in the South Sea Company. Many were men of probity and credibility and included members of the Cabinet. Even royalty. He smiled at his friend and shook his head in mock seriousness. George's energy and grin were infectious and sometimes he needed to rein in the enthusiasm of his friend.

"The share price may indeed rise further but it may well go down. None of those we have mentioned are in finance, or in banking, are they? We have done well so far, but we understand financially and economically this cannot go on. The risks are simply too great. There are only so many fools and only so much money. We know, do we not, through our contacts that the South Sea Company has used questionable means to prop up the value of its shares? Remember, not that long ago in June I think, the company was lending people money to buy its own shares. A strange going on. Not only that there are other new companies making extravagant claims, other ventures and frenzied speculation. I was told yesterday one company is advertising itself as a company 'for carrying out an undertaking of great advantage but nobody to know what it is.'"

Jonathan was becoming frustrated by George's inability to grasp the finer points of financial management and the serious game he was playing. George was in danger of getting his fingers burnt and Jonathan had to ensure George did not bring financial ruin upon him as well.

Jonathan continued, "How long can the company keep propping up the share prices or finding yet more ways of buying and selling their inflated shares? They simply cannot. Therefore, the company will collapse and those that are overstretched, will face bankruptcy because the shares will be worthless."

"What does your friend, John say, in the company I mean?"

Jonathan hissed. "Keep your voice down. If we are to keep our heads and our investment, we need to be circumspect. Men are greedy and corrupt in Government and out of it. Remember that. I tell you, George it will end in tears. Calm. Temperate."

Lost At Sea

It was a worrying sign. South Sea Company stocks and shares were, in his view, getting messy, and so any new shares had to be handled with care. Jonathan had sold a lot of his stake holding at a good profit, leaving but a few—should his judgement prove incorrect—and the share price continued to rocket. Even though the share price had continued to rise, Jonathan believed he had acted sensibly.

He was unsure, however, whether George had avoided temptation. Jonathan was also uncertain whether it was greed or arrogance on George's part. Either way, he walked a fine line between hell and high water. The shares were now heading ever upwards to a ridiculous price. A fortune won or lost.

Experience taught George Jonathan was an astute investor if a little cautious. George would hold his nerve a little longer. He leaned back in his chair and took a drink of red wine from the glass in front of him.

He closed his eyes when he heard a voice.

"Excuse me, Mr Castle, sir. There's a young lad at the door. Says he has an important letter for you."

"What was that Davy boy?"

"A boy at the door, who calls himself Noah."

Alert, George jumped from his chair. "Why didn't you say, man?"

George's interest in the boy aroused Jonathan and he languidly leaned over to refill his glass. Back in his chair, he nonchalantly moved to a more favourable position. Feigning attention to his wine and holding the glass to the light, swirling the contents expertly, sipping and pursing his lips with approval, he turned towards the door to watch the meeting.

George took the boy to one side away from interested ears.

"Have you got a letter?"

Noah nodded and surreptitiously produced a letter from his pocket. The boy understood this was a private matter and played the game well. He maintained a sombre face.

Noah continued, "I came as soon as I could, sir. I waited as you told me for his reply. You promised me a shilling."

Beaming, George placed his hand in a pocket and produced a shilling, tossing it in the air for Noah to catch. A shilling! He was rich!

"Wait there. I might need you again."

Noah gained the impression there may well be a reply but maintained his silence. George turned and walked back to the table where Jonathan was showing not the slightest interest (but had missed nothing).

"Did you receive your letter?"

George tapped his breast pocket knowingly with a grin from ear to ear.

"From my brother. I have invited him to join us in an investment. Maybe to get rid of some of the bad debts you keep talking about." George laughed at his own joke.

This investment was news to Jonathan. "Aren't you going to open it?"

George nodded and took the letter out of his pocket. He opened it and placed it on the table to read quietly. He watched, intrigued and saw the colour drain from his partner's face.

"What is it, George?"

Lost At Sea

"Fool."

"What?"

"My brother. He's a fool! Read it."

Jonathan took the letter and read it, re-read it, and read it again, shaking his head.

"Sorry... I... don't understand."

George snapped angrily. "That, there."

He pointed to the letter and the sentence which read: 'My greatest desire is that he will follow me into Castles' Merchant Traders.'

"Sorry, George, I still don't get it."

He watched as George's face became bright red, his eyes bulged, and he licked his lips before gasping for breath. Thinking he was about to collapse, Jonathan handed him a glass of wine.

"For goodness' sake man, what is it?" Yet a ten-year-old boy, who has done nothing—nothing, I tell you—comes before me."

Jonathan watched in astonishment as bile and hatred oozed from every pore like worms in a corpse.

"I thought you wanted to put your disagreement with your brother behind you?"

Exhausted, George slumped in his chair.

"I presume we will not be meeting your brother," continued Jonathan.

"I wouldn't miss it for the world. But I tell you, his son will not inherit what is really mine. I will have my inheritance by hook or by crook. I will bankrupt him and if what you are saying about the South Sea Company shares is true, they may be the means."

As astute as ever, Jonathan had already made his usual character checks on any trader or investor, and

William Castle's name in the quarters that mattered, were held in the highest regard for honesty and integrity. He always felt there was something George was not telling him and now he had his answer. Jonathan B Jerome wanted no part of whatever George was planning for his brother.

George dispatched Noah with his reply he would be there at twelve sharp on the morrow. He gave him sixpence, promising another if he got there by midnight. The immediate response had come as a surprise to William and Grace, not least that Noah, a boy of a similar age as their own son, was wandering around Bristol streets near midnight. Noah cared not one jot, for he had earned himself yet another shilling for doing very little. Grown-ups were a mystery to him, but a shrewd lad recognised his employer was an angry man, bitter, from the tone of voice he used. He liked William and Grace Castle, but he would have to keep things close to his chest and his mouth shut. Surprising what you can hear when people think you are not listening, or even better, stupid.

CHAPTER THREE

July 21st

George was on time and crossed the street to the front door of the Castles' home.

Samuel opened the office door. "He's here."

Information passed on, Samuel ran back up the stairs to return to his telescope and his imaginary crow's nest. He was pleased he had a proper target for his telescope, not that he needed one to see a man approaching in broad daylight.

Smiling, Grace welcomed George. She opened the door to her brother-in-law.

George smiled back. "Grace, you seem to have blossomed. I hope my brother is treating you well, otherwise I may have to steal you from him." He continued, "I'm afraid my acquaintance could not make it."

Ignoring the flattery, she turned and walked to the study.

"I see. Never mind. This way, please."

William was standing in front of his desk." George, you are looking well. Please sit down."

William had set two chairs. A bottle of port with two glasses had been placed on the desk, too. William poured and sat down. Grace left the men, not wanting to compromise her husband; they had agreed no decision would be taken unless both concurred. She recognised she was most fortunate in her husband for he treated her as an equal in unequal times—something she suspected George would not understand or ever contemplate. Grace was William's ace up his sleeve, and he would produce her when the time was right.

George was curious how Castles' Merchant Traders was progressing, and William chatted amiably about the expansion of the business. George nodded.

"And your progress, George? Look at you." William shook his head in awe and smiled fondly. "Every inch a successful man."

"I've done well for myself, with Jonathan's help. In fact, we have joint ownership of a trading ship, the Pegasus, which trades between Bristol and Lisbon. We are hoping to add a second ship. Jonathan has some wonderful contacts including within the South Sea Company, believe it or not. You must have heard of them?"

"Who hasn't heard of the South Sea Company? But it's not my line of business."

"But it's mine. As we speak, William, an acquaintance is looking at investments with that company and other opportunities and we hope you will join us. This is a good time for it. The latest investment opportunity is Irish Peat Bog, I kid you not. You will not regret it, I promise you, and it will be good for us to be together again. Father would have approved." George played his ace. George amicably tapped his brother on the hand. "Now is a good time to invest, trust me."

William nodded. "How much have you got in mind, for my investment, that is?"

"It depends. Our investments are always cautious. Should the South Sea Company with Government backing fail, then our country would be bankrupt and that would never happen, of course. It could not; think of all our trade overseas, and of our manufacturing base. I can assure you, should you choose to invest in the South Sea Company in particular, and it would be quite safe."

William frowned and paused in deep thought. "Surely, no investment can ever be totally safe, George, even with your contacts?"

George leaned towards him acting as William's greatest friend and confidant. "William, there are contacts, and there are my contacts." Looking around as if they were being overheard George continued. "They are Cabinet-level contacts and advisors to the King, impeccable sources, I can assure you. You must know that the King is the governor of the Company. You tell me who would be better than that! If the South Sea Company fails, then our country's finances will also fail. Impossible."

William looked unconvinced. "But the King is German, and the Cabinet is full of crooks."

George maintained his grin. He had to be convincing.

He laughed. "We know in all trades, yours included, William, there are the rogues and cheats. Parliament is much the same; the difference is we know who the rogues and cheats are and use that to our advantage. So, do not be put off. I should not tell you this, but one of our contacts is, the Deputy Governor of the South Sea Company. There are other investments as well. This is the time of great opportunities."

William was wide-eyed and speechless.

"You have heard of him, then?" asked George.

William nodded, but he knew names and titles were easy enough to throw about, particularly if you have been sworn to secrecy and if correct, what does it say about the management of the company?

"How much do you advise I should invest?"

George had spent some time working out or trying to work out, William's wealth; how much he could realistically afford to invest, what would tempt him further, and what would financially ruin him? George would then step in and rescue Castles' Merchant Traders. George had to tempt William with an investment only a fool would turn down.

"Well, the shares are doing well, and you will be in partnership with me and Jonathan B Jerome." George needed some notion of William's wealth and so plucked a figure out of the air and continued. "Say £3,000 to start with. You can always increase the investment." George had thrown the name of Jonathan into the plot for he was well known and regarded. George knew his friend would be angry at this presumption, but he cared not one jot.

William pondered. "That's a lot of money. Out of my league, I'm afraid."

"Come on, William, there is a guarantee for investors. What do you earn from your ship? What do you pay in insurance? Do not forget, my friend and I are investing much more than your £3,000. Would we do that if there was any risk?"

William shook his head. "George, I reinvested most of our spare capital in Castles' Merchant Traders in maintaining our ship the Swift."

Lost At Sea

George kept a straight face whilst his mind was alert, nodding in understanding. He had learnt William was looking for a shareholder in the purchase of another ship for longer hauls.

"I understand you need to keep your trading vessel sailing and in good repair and that costs money."

William nodded and sighed. George was getting out of his chair. Then stopped and sat down abruptly, placing his right hand against his chin as if in deep thought.

"I don't know why I did not think about this earlier. The South Sea Company has a monopoly of trade in the South Seas, and I also know they are looking for ships to trade. Now ship owners are contracted to the company and have the privilege of this monopoly. Let me arrange through my contacts a contract with the South Sea Company. Imagine having a ship from Castles' Merchant Traders trading in the South Seas, the Sugar Isles? Our father would be so proud! Think of that and of your son's future." George's voice trailed away quietly. "Maybe I could help? Possibly as a shareholder in a new ship, which we could then contract to the South Sea Company? Imagine what we could achieve!"

William stared at George, mouth wide open. All the answers to his prayers had been answered. It seemed too simple, too good to be true.

"Sounds interesting, George but surely a contract with the South Sea Company must have a price? I would need to know the exact cost, and I will not trade in slaves. Contracts mean solicitors. We will need extra Maritime insurance as well."

George knew he had his brother's interest now. "Not with the contacts I have in the Bristol Merchant Venturers, or Jonathan has. Nothing is impossible."

George cursed under his breath. Jonathan would be most indignant about his mentioning his name. Not once, but twice. In fact, it would most displease him about what he was proposing. George's business partner was of the view the contracts with the South Sea Company were dubious and possibly illegal. Jonathan was an honourable man for a financial adviser.

"It makes good sense for us to have a joint investment. You have the knowledge and experience in trading. What goods to buy, costs, and the markets and such like and I have the money to invest. I would be delighted to help the family business. Really, I would. A great legacy for Samuel, don't you think? Talk to Grace. Both of you should understand we need to keep tight-lipped about this, though. These contracts are not… how should I put it? Not public. I will leave you with your thoughts, William."

George left quickly, seeing the effect of his words on the expression on his brother's face.

The outer door shut with a bang. The door to William's study opened quietly and Grace peered round. William waved her in.

"How did it go, William?"

William shook his head, and shrugged his shoulders. "I am unsure."

Grace frowned. "You're unsure about what?"

He laughed. "About anything. I will be succinct, Grace. George offered me an investment opportunity with himself and his associate in the South Sea Company, with good returns for £3,000 invested. I told him I invested most of our spare capital in Castles' Merchant Traders and keeping the Swift in good repair. Then out of thin air, he plucks this grand idea for him to share in the purchase of a new ship, a larger ship, to be part of the monopoly trade with the Sugar Isles or the South Seas. It is as if he knew where our money was and what our plans were. I did tell him we would never trade in slaves."

William explained the issuing of contracts by the South Sea Company to take part in the monopoly trade the company had in the South Seas, and the importance of keeping the matter secret. William closed his eyes and shook his head as if irritated by bees swarming.

Grace sat quietly and thoughtfully. "We must be watchful, William. It all seems too contrived, don't you think?"

What is George up to? She thought.

William nodded. "Something isn't quite right."

***

July 22nd

Grace was sitting at her desk, working on the company ledger. William opened the door.

"Glad I found you, I am taking Samuel with me. I need to discuss our insurance with Joseph Blakeley. I have arranged a meeting at the Round Coffee House."

Grace smiled. "Good. This proposition by George has made me think about Samuel."

"What has this got to do with Samuel?" muttered William.

"We need to consider Samuel's future, William. We need to ensure not only his safety but his security. Now, that will be taken care of as long as one of us is alive and well to protect his interests."

"You are stating the obvious, Grace."

Hands on his hips, this irritated William. He had a lot of work to do, and he had not got the time to stand about regurgitating the obvious. Grace calmly continued. She did not want to patronise the man she loved, but sometimes her husband's lack of foresight was downright grating.

"Consider this, William. You and I are ill, very ill. Samuel is still a child and is incapable of running our company. What then? What if we die of disease or plague?"

William glowered. "What chance of that, Grace? What chance?"

"Remember your father, William."

As soon as she had said those words, she instantly regretted them. The sorrow in his eyes, the memory of his father and his painful death, was etched on his face.

"I am sorry, William, but we must consider this. What will happen to Samuel if something happens to both of us? We need a guardian to look after his welfare and protect his interest. Our solicitor, perhaps? We need to be sure, William."

William nodded. "It never occurred to me, Grace. You are right. I will need to talk to our solicitor. I may call on the way back. If I am delayed at all, I will send Samuel home."

Grace frowned and placed a wayward piece of hair behind her ear. William nodded as he recognised the sign when his wife had a notion.

"I smell a 'but William'!"

Grace laughed. "Our solicitor is Jeremiah Sykes and his son, Joseph? "

William nodded "and so..."

"And," continued Grace, "they are also the solicitors that represent your brother, George. I would not want our private matters compromised or misplaced."

William nodded. "I will give it some thought."

He liked Joseph Sykes and sensed he was building an excellent reputation for himself as an honest broker. It also appeared Jeremiah Sykes found that as the Official Solicitor to the Bristol Merchant Venturers, he had less and less time for what he considered to be the 'more mundane work' that he left to his son, Joseph.

Father and son walked into Bristol to the Round Coffee House where William had business to settle. Quickly resolved, he went to the City Office of Jeremiah Sykes and Son and was fortunate to find Joseph Sykes was available to see them. William expressed his concern. As he and his brother, George used the same family solicitors, could confidentiality still be maintained?

Joseph raised an eyebrow and looked at Samuel, who sat quietly next to his father, inspecting the small carved ship given to him by Alice.

William coughed and continued. "I understand this is sensitive for you, loyalty to your father and your family business, that is. But I need to know. Can I have absolute discretion with my family business?"

He nodded towards Samuel.

"Mr Castle, my father has showed to me he is too busy with Mercantile Law on behalf of Bristol Merchant Venturers to be, how I shall put it, involved with the 'day to day work of common folk'. His words, not mine. So, Mr Castle, if you are common folk then I am your man. I am also my own man, and you can trust me, truly you can. I have my own office in less grand surroundings than this, and, where I keep my private work private."

Joseph Sykes was too loyal a son to tell Mr Castle he despised his father and the way he worked. Joseph wished to help ordinary people, often with little money, to get justice.

William nodded. The predicament William and Grace had in protecting their son's interest was explained, particularly the concern shared by his wife about his brother. Joseph Sykes nodded and listened intently, making notes and punctuating the conversation with a question here and a suggestion there. The solicitor explained to William he would consider the legal position but suggested a viable solution could be to nominate a legal guardian for Samuel who would, in the event of their demise, act in Samuel's interest. Also, as their solicitor, he could oversee all legal matters until Samuel was of an age to look after his own interests.

"A final question, Mr Sykes. Would you consider being Samuel's guardian?"

Joseph Sykes frowned and said, "I would prefer those legal matters be separate from other issues. That way I can be truly independent, but I will think about it."

Pleased with himself, William returned home via the quayside. They made their way to the docks. Samuel chirped happily, telescope in hand, looking for a target on which he could focus. Arriving at the quayside, William saw the familiar black curly hair of the Harbour Master, Jeffrey Bryant who was over-seeing the loading of the Pegasus which was anchored broadside to the dock. The crew were busy checking sails and doing urgent repairs. Samuel was enthralled and had lots to see through his telescope.

"The Pegasus is a lovely ship, Jez."

At this familiarity, the Harbour Master turned and scowled before a broad grin crossed his face.

"William Castle? She is a grand ship, not big as ships go, but quick enough and good to handle, so I am told. A quick turnaround this time, to Portugal. I have sent a message to George and Jonny Jerome to come to the dockside so we can check the manifest before she sails in the morning. They shouldn't be that long if you hang on a while!"

"Jonny Jerome? He won't like that, prefers Jonathan," retorted William.

"I knew him when he was that high," laughed Jeremy, placing a hand waist high.

The Harbour Master talked amicably to William, who was losing all sense of time. A little while later his brother, George, and Jonathan arrived at the dockside. William talked to Jonathan about the investment proposal as suggested.

"The South Sea Company, Mr Jerome. George has invited me to join your..." William did not get another word out of his mouth before George grabbed him roughly and pushed him away. "For heaven's sake, William, keep your voice down."

Puzzled, William looked about him. "But George, there is no one else here but you and me and Mr Jerome."

"And Jeremy Bryant! Good God, William," exploded George.

Jeremy Bryant was busy with the ship's manifest.

"Did I hear mention of investment in the South Sea Company? Best avoid that like the plague," said a somewhat bemused Jonathan Jerome.

William decided he needed to talk about this investment further and told Samuel to return home and explain to his mother his father had been delayed.

"Mind you, Samuel, no dawdling."

Samuel grinned and strolled away, looking through his telescope as he did so. At this point, George said he felt quite unwell and needed to return to his room. Confused by his brother's outburst, sudden illness, and words of warning about the South Sea Company from Jonathan Jerome, William made his way home too.

How odd!

Grace was a little surprised at his late arrival.

Puzzled, William said. "I am sorry, Grace, but I met the Harbour Master on the quayside. George and Mr Jerome were due and so I waited to chat about their investment proposal. Mr Jerome told me to avoid investment in the South Sea Company like the plague and oddly he was totally unaware of any investment proposal. I sent Samuel ahead two hours ago to tell you I would be delayed."

Lost At Sea

Grace frowned. "But Samuel hasn't arrived home, William. Where on earth could he be?"

"I don't understand," continued William, "he should have arrived home long ago. I will walk back to the quayside. He has his telescope with him; you know what he is like. Probably, he has seen something interesting. Now, you are not to worry."

William strode purposefully back whence he had come from where he had last seen his son.

CHAPTER FOUR

The Pegasus—at sea, July 23rd

The ship was rolling in the heavy swell of the Atlantic Ocean, creaking and sighing like an old man climbing steep cold stairs. Waves crashed on the deck as the ship swayed. The Pegasus defied its name for she was hardly a sleek trading ship with poise and agility, cutting through with great speed. Quite the opposite. But to her credit, the Pegasus was agile, manoeuvrable even, and despite her shortcomings, she was well-loved by the crew.

The Pegasus was heading south from Bristol to Portugal. Aided by the river's pilots, tugs, and beacons, the ship had navigated the river Avon before sailing into the Atlantic Ocean with all its uncertainties and dangers. The irony was not lost on its captain. When not in his bunk asleep, Clive Fothergill spent most of his time on deck like a moth to a flame. He loved being at sea, standing—often alone—on deck, feeling the wind in his black curly hair and the spray peppering his face. He felt alive facing the elements which he both admired and feared, knowing they could crush the ship and dash their lives on rocks. The captain curled his lips like a snarling animal. He would have it no other way.

He gripped the deck rail and closed his eyes momentarily to calm his mind and bring him back to the task at hand.

Stroking the rail fondly he whispered, "Come on, old

girl; let's show the frogs a clean pair of hooves."

Experience had taught him the Pegasus had to take a wide berth of the French coastline because of brigands and pirates who waited for vulnerable ships. The Pegasus, like most small trading ships, had limited defences and so he hedged his bets by steering clear. This, however, meant a longer journey and facing the treachery of the Atlantic Ocean.

An experienced captain, Clive Fothergill preferred the odds against the sea as the survival of his ship depended on the skill of its commander and his crew. The crew of the Pegasus was both dependable and first-rate, which made his job as captain easier.

It was daylight, and visibility was good which made it an advantage to any ship. He stood upright—a tall slim man with a weather-beaten face, his clear blue eyes looking outward over the sea. He wiped his brow with his right hand, grimaced, and looked at the swollen joints of his fingers before stretching them slowly to stop them from stiffening.

The waves crashed onto the deck clearing away anything that was not tied down or secured. The saline water carrying the ship's filth in its wake covered the deck in detritus as well giving off an overpowering stench, before taking loose items overboard. It was not unknown for men to end up in the sea and with a small crew like his, it was a luxury the captain could not afford—a fact he would continually remind his men.

Captain Fothergill was content, however. The weather was nothing to trouble him and his best sailor was keeping watch in the crow's nest on the middle-mast. Instinctively, he glanced upwards and Johnny

Mason, true to form, was gazing seaward.

The captain stood watching the glow on the horizon like a large bloody orb. Strands of gold, orange and red flecked the sky. The sun, with a last sigh, disappeared. Clive Fothergill stood enthralled, never bored with the setting sun despite the number of times he had stood thus. Shaking his head with awe, he strolled to his customary position behind the wheel standing next to Caleb Joyce, who was holding it with tenderness and affection.

From the door leading below deck, a tall man appeared dressed unconventionally for a sea-going vessel. In his hands were two mugs.

"Your hot chocolate, Captain."

As ever, he was formal to his friend in front of his crew. He handed the hot drink to the captain.

"Thank you, Stephen. I see you have one. Milk must not be rancid, then."

Stephen James laughed out loud. "The cook reckons the milk will last two more days before it turns ugly. Needed drinking, and so I offered to help."

Clive Fothergill had a sweet tooth and a penchant for hot chocolate with soft brown sugar and fortified by a drop of rum. What the captain wanted the captain got, was Gus Brown's motto. How to keep 'the bloody milk from going off' was a dilemma for the cook. He did his best, always buying fresh milk whenever he could, and trying different containers in various parts of the ship. Below deck, above deck, fore, and aft, even over the side on a long piece of rope. But the sea salt always seeped in.

The last resting place for the milk churn was on the

foredeck by the bows where it was tied firmly and securely to combat the crashing waves. Fresh milk would last seven days on average and so for the first week, at least the captain was a contented man.

Clive Fothergill lifted the lid of his mug of hot chocolate and sniffed at it.

"I think the rum does the trick you see; an extra dollop and you can't taste the milk and somehow it stops it from curdling. Now there's a thought."

Stephen daydreamed over the complexities of alcohol and its action or reaction to sour milk. Captain Fothergill looked at Stephen James, who was the most intelligent and inquisitive man he had ever met and smiled inwardly at the familiar blank look on his friend's face. Stephen was thinking. Despite the tendency to daydream, sometimes at the most inopportune times, Clive was fortunate in his ship's doctor, and from an auspicious introduction on the deck of Pegasus some five years ago he had grown in admiration for him as a man, professional, and friend.

On that occasion, they were anchored at the Bristol docks after returning from Portugal. It had been his first trip as Captain, and it had been a very successful one. He had celebrated the conclusion of his first trip in his cabin when there was a hasty rat-tat-tat on his door. He opened the door sharply and glared at the sailor standing before him who dared to interrupt his first day of rest for many a week.

The pale-faced John Mason said, "You had better come quick, Captain, Seaman Joyce has had a nasty fall. Brown thinks he's dead."

Frowning, he did not trust his cook, Gus Brown's

ability to tell whether anyone was alive or dead. Even his cooking was debatable.

"God help us," he muttered to himself. "I will be on deck directly, Mason."

"Aye, aye, sir."

With that, Mason turned on his heels and shot up the steps.

On deck, the captain could see Caleb Joyce was flat on his back with Gus Brown, the cook and ship's medical man, who was leaning over the prostrate sailor. Joyce had fallen from the rigging, landing badly on the deck. The sailor was unconscious with blood seeping from a head wound.

Gus Brown stood hands on hips, a tear welling in his one eye, shaking his bald head in dismay. Clive Fothergill could see Joyce was in a bad way and cursed himself for his dilatoriness in the care of his crew. He had relaxed momentarily and thought they were doing their jobs safely, but a Captain's work was never done. He knew his medical man and cook was out of his depth who, for a seasoned hard-nosed sailor, was distressed at his own uselessness.

However, Caleb Joyce moaned, a fact that saved his life for, seeing he was alive, spurred the Captain into action. He demanded the crew find a doctor and quickly. Johnny Mason, a local man, asked the captain to leave it to him. He left the ship promptly disappearing up one alleyway which led from the dockside, returning hastily with a tall slim man wearing a rather worn, brown hat, with a leather satchel that was slung casually over his left shoulder.

"He's not a proper doctor, Captain but best I could

find. He is an apprentice."

Many things went through the captain's mind; the last thing he needed now was another incompetent medicine man but, before he could say a solitary word, the man before him, Stephen James, took charge.

Looking down at the badly injured sailor, he asked no one in particular, "This must be Caleb, and you," he said, turning to Gus Brown, "must be Gus? I might need your help."

Gus nodded.

After looking closely at the injured man's head wound, Stephen James stood momentarily deep in his own thoughts before turning to his newly appointed assistant and demanding the injured man be taken below before issuing instructions for clean water, bandages, and brandy.

"Quickly now, we have little time."

With his authority restored and now the new doctor's assistant, Seaman Gus Brown returned to his old belligerent ways, chivvying crew members to get a move on. He glanced upwards and saw the captain watching intently.

"If it pleases you, Captain."

"Carry on, Mr Brown. Well done. Keep me informed, doctor, if you please."

He nodded at the doctor and returned to his cabin to consider his thoughts.

The skill and dedication of the so-called apprentice doctor not only saved the sailor's life, but he also handled the crew with grace, courtesy and aplomb. Clive Fothergill was impressed and recognised the need for a medical man of some proficiency on board and asked Stephen James, who had returned the following morning to check the progress of his patient, if he would consider a position as the ship's doctor.

This was a simple enough decision for Stephen. He was the youngest of three sons to a well-regarded Bristol family. As the youngest, he had to fend for himself and took an opportunity as an apprentice to a local physician of some esteem, Doctor Alastair Simeon. Stephen, aged seventeen, was an intelligent and educated young man and he took to his work like a duck to water. However, the doctor's willingness to have the young Stephen as an apprentice had a price. First, his parents had to pay his board and lodgings for the first two years and second, the doctor had a liking, indeed zealousness, for alcohol (particularly whisky).

At the outset of his apprenticeship, Doctor Simeon's predilection for whisky was well disguised and Stephen learnt a great deal, not just about procedures and medication, but about new ideas and methods. Alastair Simeon, a clever and competent doctor, was a pioneer in the prevention and treatment of diseases amongst the poor in Bristol.

This was the challenge the young Stephen needed. Doctor Simeon enthralled him. At the beginning, Dr Simeon would take a nip of whisky to 'clear his head' or 'help him concentrate', prior to a difficult patient or procedure. A naïve young Stephen James accepted this explanation without question. Time, misplaced equipment and forgetting the names and conditions of his patients made him reconsider his opinion of the doctor and subsequently, he would check the patient's details and contents of the medical bag himself before accompanying Dr Simeon to the next patient. Gradually, Stephen took on more and more responsibility which he accepted with relish. That was until the occasion when he found Dr Simeon paralytic.

Despite everything, his five-year apprenticeship had been a wonderful experience, and the patients regarded him as a doctor in his own right, but he had to have the end of his apprenticeship formalised and legalised. He left Captain Fothergill with a promise to consider his proposition.

Meanwhile, the captain had to discuss the proposal of having a ship's doctor with the ship's owners George Castle and Jonathan B Jerome, arguing forcibly the benefits to the ship and indeed the crew of a fully qualified doctor on board. The owners agreed but only on the satisfaction of two conditions. They would not pay him on his initial trip until his contribution to the safe running of the ship was clear. And, the position of his apprenticeship had also to be finalised at the doctor's expense.

Clive Fothergill looked at his friend sipping his hot chocolate. It worked out well for them both. Doctor James was first rate as a doctor and the Pegasus and its crew were the healthiest, second to none.

As the waves reached every nook and cranny amongst the ropes neatly piled and secured, a figure huddled, knees under chest, with arms around them, head bent, and eyes closed tightly as if by doing so the cold, damp, and stench would go away. Mouths full of saltwater spat out, back aching, and head gashed and bruises, belied the lie. When would the misery end? What to do? Stay hidden and starve to death? Not much of a choice. A conundrum for a grown man, never mind a young boy.

Voices were loud and alert. "What have we here? Looks like we have a stowaway."

Captain Fothergill groaned. "If I had my way, I'd throw them all overboard."

The boy terrified froze as if a dagger made of ice had stabbed through his heart. Like a frightened rabbit, wide-eyed, he waited for a hand to grab his throat, but it never came.

He heard a voice in the distance. "Here you are, Captain."

It was Caleb Joyce who was lifting another boy from under a tarpaulin on the deck. He hoisted the lad aloft like a wriggling fish, slimy and slippery, arms waving like a windmill in a gale. The scrawny youth with fair skin and green eyes had long, curly ginger hair as unruly as the lad himself. He was fighting to release the grip of the sailor who held him by the scruff of the neck.

"Let go of me, you oaf," he squeaked.

Caleb Joyce stared quizzically. "What shall I do with him? Not only does he stink, he needs a good thrashing."

Captain Fothergill shook his head. "Bring him here."

Holding him at arm's length, the sailor held him for inspection.

"Name!" demanded the captain.

The boy had to think quickly, for he could not give his true name, William Thomas.

"Me sir? William, sir. Billy, Billy Wragg."

The captain frowned. "Wragging Billy? Now there's

a fine name."

The boy knew he had to brazen it out. "Yes. Now can this oaf let me go?"

"The oaf is happy to oblige, young sir." Joyce dropped him and the boy clattered to the deck with a thud.

Captain Fothergill looked at the boy. "Take the lad below and get him fed and cleaned up." He turned stern eyes on the stowaway. "And you, my lad, had better learn to behave or Seaman Joyce here will get his wish. Now think on."

He glanced threateningly at the sea. The boy sufficiently chastened, nodded, and followed the sailor down below.

Another boy under the ropes had laid still and lifeless throughout the scene that had played out only a short distance away from him. A flicker of recognition of what he did not know crawled slowly through his befuddled brain before it became becalmed once more. Barely conscious through fatigue, and loss of blood from a head wound, his head lolled from side to side with the movement of the ship. The ship shuddered as an enormous wave crashed onto the deck and the boy rattled about in his hideaway like a drunken man falling down steep steps, banging his head as he did so and knocking him once more into a semi-conscious stupor. The pain shot through his body like a cannonball, which had the effect of stirring what life there was left in him. He was dying, and he knew it.

Perhaps the captain will be generous once more? But two stowaways may test his patience. Even at such a tender age, the boy knew his life hung by a thread and so like a dazed, dying animal he struggled painfully to his feet. With his head throbbing and tears edging as if to overflow like a torrent, he struggled to climb atop a pile of ropes that had been his protection, his hideaway and shelter. Shaking like a new-born colt, long-legged, wet and weak, he stood, barely alive and pale-faced, like a ghost from the deep.

In a timid voice barely the strength of a gentle breeze, he whispered, "Sir, there's two of us."

Clive Fothergill continued to look out to sea, oblivious of the diminutive figure behind him.

"Excuse me, sir."

To be heard, the voice was a little stronger. The captain turned around and stared at the pathetic figure in front of him. The boy could barely stand; blood matted his light-coloured hair. He had a pale face with dark rings under his eyes and shivered uncontrollably. Having spent what seemed to him an eternity curled under the ropes, his legs could not hold him and he collapsed onto the deck. Caleb had returned on deck and was about to tell the captain young Billy was with the cook when his eyes fell on the bedraggled state of yet another boy.

Caleb Joyce snapped, "Not another."

"The child is barely alive, man. Take him below. Now, Mr Joyce," snarled Captain Fothergill.

Caleb Joyce had spoken out of place though only for a moment, and his captain would have none of it. The sailor nodded sheepishly and bent to pick up the bedraggled, sodden figure. Lifting the boy gently, he carried him below deck and to the kitchen.

"Gus, we have another one, but he is in a bad way."

Lost At Sea

Seaman Angus Brown stared at Caleb Joyce and ignored the familiar nickname used by the crew.

The cook glanced at the slight figure in the sailor's arms and grimaced. "The lad is in a bad way, bad way."

Angus Brown pointed to the doctor's room which was a converted storage cupboard opposite the ship's galley.

"Put him on the treatment table and fetch Doctor James. Be quick about it. Then bring clean water and rum."

The sailor, cook, and doctor's assistant followed in the wake of Seaman Joyce who placed the boy gently onto the treatment table. Angus Brown carefully examined the pathetic figure as best he could with one eye covered by a patch. He turned the boy to one side and cleared his mouth.

"Mustn't let him choke," he said to no one in particular.

"What's that?" muttered Seaman Joyce.

Doctor James wandered calmly into the small treatment room with his battered leather satchel. "What have we here, Augustus?"

Augustus was the formal name between the doctor and his assistant.

"He's in a bad way, Doctor."

Stephen James smiled at his assistant and nodded. "We had better get to it then."

The doctor leaned over the young boy who he assessed was nine or ten years of age, dehydrated, unconscious, with blood oozing from the back of his head, and blonde hair matted in blood.

"Augustus have you...?"

"Yes. Clean water, bandages and rum."

"We will have to act with all speed. Are you ready?"

The sailor nodded, recognising the serious state the young lad before them was in. Doctor James removed the boy's damp clothing before covering his modesty with a blanket. Stephen peered closely at the head wound, sniffed and pursed his lips. He stood and gazed into the distance, his eyes fixed nowhere in particular. Augustus was by now used to the peculiarities of the ship's doctor. He stood quietly, aware the doctor was concentrating hard on the task at hand.

"We need to clean this wound and stop the bleeding. He has lost a lot of blood and we do not have long. Get the rum in the bowl, clean my instruments, and tear me plenty of strips for bandages."

As his assistant moved quickly and efficiently to undertake these simple but important tasks, so the doctor turned the child gently to one side to examine the wound. As he did so, the blood oozed slowly from a nasty gash on the top of the head. The rudimentary instruments were already soaked in brine and they cleaned the wound with fresh water and rum.

"Needle and twine, Augustus."

Working quickly, the wound was stitched by Doctor James and then bound by Seaman Brown.

"Well done, Augustus. Well done indeed."

"Just doing me' job, Doc. What's his chances? Living, that is."

Stephen James pondered. "Let us agree on not good! We will have to keep a close eye on him and keep him from dehydrating. A damp cloth on his lips first, then drops of water. Slowly, slowly. Yes."

Lost At Sea

Gus Brown nodded. "Maybe this is a job for the lad, Billy Wragg?"

Stephen James frowned. "Is he dependable and can we trust him? This boy's life is at stake."

The doctor nodded towards the lifeless boy on the treatment table.

"As I see it, Doctor, this boy needs constant watching over and we cannot do it all. Better Young Billy than nothing."

Stephen James nodded in acknowledgement of the truth of his assistant's words.

"We will oversee the patient ourselves and see him through until tomorrow." This was an instruction from the doctor, not a request.

Despite his punishing schedule which had been set by himself so he did not dwell on past demeanours, the captain's mind would drift to the two boys and in particular the boy who was at death's door. In his thirty years at sea, starting as young as these two boys, he had never known two stowaways discovered on the same ship. Coincidence, perhaps? Caught in the moment, the captain left the deck and walked down the steps to find Stephen James leaning over the child—a tall man with copper-coloured hair, which seemed to have a mind of its own, blue eyes keen and lively, missing nothing. Whatever his lack of experience, thought the captain, the Doctor had a way with him and if he was honest; he admired him.

"How are things?" asked the captain.

"He is holding his own, just. I cleaned and bandaged his head. A nasty wound, Captain. Nasty," replied Stephen James. "As you can see, I have an assistant."

He nodded towards the boy, Billy Wragg.

Ignoring the boy, Clive Fothergill continued, "Bang his head, did he, Doctor?"

Stephen James stood leaning backwards to ease a painful back and shook his head. "Makes little sense, Captain. May I have a moment?"

The doctor placed his hand on his new assistant turning towards him. "Now if he falls to the front as so," he said and pointed to Billy's forehead, "then his injury must be to his nose or forehead."

The captain nodded.

"Now if he falls backwards, his injury will be at the back of his head so."

He pointed to the back of the boy's head. The doctor leaned over the injured boy and pointed to the bandage which was blood-stained.

"His injury is to the top of his head, so unless..."

"Someone dropped him on his head," chimed Billy Wragg.

"Quite so," continued the doctor, "quite so."

"This was an attack on the boy?"

"Captain, I believe so. This boy appears to have been attacked and somehow ended up on the Pegasus."

"And by the time we discovered him, we were at sea and the boy, had he not been found, would have died."

"Quite so," added Doctor James.

The captain pondered for a while. "Anything in his pockets, Stephen?"

The doctor shook his head. "His clothes are sodden and somewhat dishevelled. They are of good quality though except for his woollen jacket that is, which seems a little odd. He has a linen shirt, undergarments, trousers and the jacket, of course. The boy has also survived several days without food and water with a severe head wound. An undernourished child would not have survived. It appears he is well cared for."

Captain Fothergill replied, "Someone is going to miss him. A parent, perhaps."

The doctor nodded.

Clive Fothergill turned to the living stowaway. "Can you tell me anything? Now, no lies."

"You had better tell him, young Billy; he means it." Doctor James gently nodded towards the captain. "Tell him."

Billy knew he could not tell the whole truth, but it had to be near enough.

" Well, sir, I was on the docks to see if I could get anything, earn some money loading and unloading from the ships, run messages anything. It was getting dark and so I thought I'd head back home when I heard arguing. I hid amongst some large barrels. There was someone trying to be quiet, but they were not. I could hear someone moaning and then I heard a thud, and it all goes quiet. Then I heard muttering, then another thud. I daren't move in case they got me as well, but I fell asleep and woke up on the ship."

Young Billy Wragg thought he recognised his fellow stowaway but dare not admit to such for that might lead to the captain knowing who he was. That he would not, nay could not do. Billy was at the docks because he had hidden there after non-other than George Castle had accused him of theft—the shared owner of this very ship, the Pegasus. But he was not a thief.

"He was loaded along with the barrels," laughed the doctor.

"What about you then, Master Wragg? Where do you live; who are your parents?" added Clive Fothergill.

"He's tight-lipped, Captain, but he's a bright lad and I think he could be useful."

"Right, Doctor James he is your responsibility. On your head be it."

With that, the captain went to his cabin for his supper and rest.

***

At sunrise the following morning, Clive Fothergill was already on deck with his telescope in hand, scanning the sea. Caleb Joyce was at the wheel.

The cook had found young Billy somewhere to sleep in the galley. It was cramped but warm, and whilst he would not appreciate it in the summer, his bolthole would be warm in winter.

Stephen James sat by the bedside of the young nameless stowaway all night. The boy was dehydrated; his lips were parched and encrusted with who knows what. The doctor had to get water inside him somehow. So, after wiping the lad's mouth, he found a small spoon and stirred it in the brandy he'd used to clean the wound. Laboriously and gently, drop by drop, he dripped water on to his lips, then rubbed gently hoping this would help moisten badly cracked lips.

At dawn, he turned the unconscious boy on to his side and gently undid the cloth that bound his head. He sniffed the wound. He pursed his lips in deep concentration as a trickle of blood dribbled down the back of the boy's neck, joining the encrusted stains on the bed beneath him. With clean water, he tended the injury before taking the bottle of brandy kept for such a purpose, pouring a little into a small cup, and then carefully, he dripped it slowly on to the wound. This was (in his experience) one of the best ways of stopping infections. On a conscious man, it would have been excruciatingly painful. On the unconscious boy, barely a flicker.

The doctor bound the boy's head once again, and as he did, he considered the lad's circumstances. Hardly a stowaway—more a victim of attempted murder or a kidnapping gone wrong; either way, the boy may well be in danger if he returned home.

The name, Billy Wragg, did not quite ring true. He stood to his full height of six feet and placed a hand through his damp hair. As if by some intuition, the living stowaway appeared next to the doctor.

"How is he, Doc?"

Startled by the young boy's familiarity, Doctor James—normally temperate—stood to his full height and with the most withering look he could conjure, stared hard at the lad.

"If you are to live, nay, survive on board this ship then you must know your place and earn your keep. You do neither."

Chastised, Billy Wragg slunk away. He was confused. Bristol life differed from this. He had to earn enough to help his mother, brother, and sister as his father was away at sea. In fact, his father may well be dead. An intelligent lad, he realised life was different on board a ship like the Pegasus; he needed a friend.

Gus Brown was in the galley preparing the crew's meal to break their fast. The crew always seemed to be hungry, never satisfied, and were always moaning about their food.

"Gus, Mr Brown, sir, Doctor James reckons I have to know my place and earn my keep."

For all his smart answers and cocky attitude, Billy was a young lad. An innocent, even, compared with what this crew had seen and done. Gus lifted a hand and put one of his fingers under his eye patch and rubbed intensely.

"This eye. Bain of me life. Bain of me life!" He turned slowly and looked at the boy. "Words of wisdom, young Billy, me lad. The doctor's a clever man and you would do well to heed him. Our lives depend on this ship, on the captain, the doctor, the crew and each other. We all need to pull our weight. You understand?"

Billy stood for a moment and nodded as if to himself.

Later that afternoon, Doctor James and Augustus Brown stood at the side of the unconscious child. The doctor was worried.

"We have to get more water inside him, Augustus, or he will simply dry up like an old prune."

"But he'll choke!" replied a startled Augustus Brown.

The doctor nodded. "That's the problem. He may be unconscious for some time, but we must get water, clean water, inside him. Slowly, slowly."

Lost At Sea

Stephen James pondered staring down at the pale-faced boy. "How do we do it?"

Gus left and returned shortly with Billy Wragg.

"Go on, tell the Doctor."

"Doctor James, sir, I..."

Stephen James frowned, awaiting some clever retort.

The boy continued. "Gus, Mr Brown, has told me of the predict... uh... problem with him." Billy nodded at the unconscious boy. "I can sit and do what has to be done."

The doctor looked at Gus and stared hard. "This is serious. If we get it wrong, this boy will die. Can we trust him?"

Gus nodded and said, "I've told him if the lad dies through his incomp... these big words of yours, Doctor. If he gets it wrong, then he's fish bait."

True to his word, Billy sat by the unconscious boy, wetting a cloth and wringing it carefully so a single drop would fall onto the parched lips of the anonymous boy. Billy again thought he recognised him, but for the life of him could not remember how or where.

From time to time, Gus and Stephen would give the newly appointed assistant a rest and send him up on deck. There the crew would let him join in their attempts at fishing with long lines dangling overboard and tell him stories of mermaids and monsters of the deep.

The skill of Danny Johnson, the ship's carpenter, who would spend his quiet moments making small carvings for his children when he returned to Bristol, fascinated Billy. They were carvings of mermaids, ships, and such like from scraps of wood left over from the many repairs he had done. It was Danny who had built a makeshift cot for the young unconscious boy. It enabled the doctor and his assistants to better care for their patient.

The care and attention brought an improvement in the boy's condition. Doctor James asked Gus to provide some thin soup that could be dripped onto the boy's lips.

It was one morning at eleven o'clock as Stephen James took his turn with the unconscious boy to give young Billy a brief respite, when the boy sighed and opened his eyes before staring blankly at the ceiling, eyes glazed. The shock of seeing the boy awake made the doctor gasp for a moment. After all, he had been unconscious for several days and tested Stephen James's experience to the limit.

Speaking calmly and quietly, he said, "I am Doctor James and you, young man, have given us a real fright."

Closing his eyes and grimacing, his mouth moving fast as if in deep concentration, the boy stared at the doctor.

"I don't. I can't. Where am I?"

"You're on board the Pegasus out of Bristol. Can you tell me your name?"

The boy in deep concentration shook his head. "My name? My head hurts." He closed his eyes and drifted off to sleep.

Stephen James, exhilarated by the awakening of his anonymous patient, called for the cook who, sweating and with flour-coated hands, appeared. He told him and said he would tell the captain. The cook put the thought of the crew's supper out of his mind and sat next to the boy's cot.

On deck, Captain Fothergill was looking towards the horizon watching Lisbon—the prosperous and vibrant Portuguese Capital City—come into view through the haze. They had been fortunate and had made good time. The doctor strode towards his friend and peered through the summer haze. It fascinated him, the ability of a sailor to see the invisible, for all he could make out was, well, nothing.

"Good afternoon, Stephen. Lisbon ahead. We will dock soon and should be on our way back within fourteen days."

"Some more good news for you. The boy has regained consciousness if only briefly. He seems confused understandably, but he appeared to be surprised he was on board a ship."

The captain frowned. "Did he give any name?"

"Afraid not. If he keeps improving, we should learn more, but time is the best healer."

Clive Fothergill stopped for a moment and turned towards the doctor. "Well done, my friend, well done indeed."

"Thank you. Gus and young Billy need your thanks, too."

Captain Fothergill nodded and laughed. "Send them up, Stephen."

A short while later, the two doctor's assistants stood in front of their captain.

"The doctor has given me the good news that his patient has regained consciousness, albeit briefly, and he could not have done it without his two assistants.

Well done."

Billy beamed but before he could blink, Gus thanked the captain and said they were glad to help and were just doing their job. Billy nodded, and they turned to leave.

"Sailor Brown," said Captain Fothergill. "Better get on with supper and don't forget," he nodded toward the quickly appearing Lisbon port, "to replenish my milk and chocolate."

"Aye aye, Captain."

"You, Seaman Wragg, had better go below and help the doctor. Sharply now."

Shocked at the acknowledgement by the captain that he was a member of the crew, Billy shyly replied, "Aye aye, Captain."

With a grin as wide as the harbour entrance, Billy skedaddled down the steps to below deck.

CHAPTER FIVE

Bristol 24th July

Only seventy-two hours had passed since Samuel had vanished into thin air, and William and Grace had tried everything in that short time to find him. Samuel's disappearance made little sense—to simply disappear in such a short time was puzzling. As the hours passed with no news, the magnitude of the loss of their only son hit home.

On the one hand, William and Grace had to keep trading to ensure their company kept afloat; after all, it was Samuel's future. Whilst on the other, they had to find their beloved son. Grace insisted she would know through instinct if her son was dead. They agreed William would concentrate on the business, whilst Grace focussed on finding Samuel. Grace would, however, maintain the company ledger as this was critical to the company. William was not proficient at bookkeeping. Grace would need to work on the ledger at daybreak, to enable her to spend the rest of the day searching for their son.

They organised search parties with help from friends and the local constable. Posters had been hastily made and plastered all over Bristol. Still no news. They did not know what could have befallen their son or, truth be told, whether he was alive. In addition, a second boy named William Thomas had also disappeared that same afternoon.

Ironically, the last sighting of the second boy was by

George Castle. William, known as Billy (the elder brother of Noah), had taken a message from Jonathan B Jerome to George Castle asking him to meet him at the Pegasus. The ship was anchored at the Bristol docks. A somewhat drunken George had accused young Billy of theft and the boy was last seen running toward the docks.

Grace was unsure whether the disappearance of both boys was simply a coincidence or somehow linked. She decided young Noah Thomas, the brother of Billy, would be most helpful in the search for both boys and so with agreement from Noah's mother and Jonathan, Noah delivered messages and handed out leaflets with details of their disappearance and descriptions.

William's brother, George had been the perfect example of diligence and fortitude, providing support and even advice to his brother and distraught wife through the strenuous days. He used his many Bristol contacts, along with rewards to help track down his nephew, but he would not countenance any involvement with young William Thomas who had, in his mind, made him look foolish. George had the backing of Bristol financiers, whilst William looked to merchants and traders for help.

"Nothing makes sense," Grace opined. "If someone had hurt Samuel, we would have found him by now. It's as if he has disappeared from the face of the earth in a puff of smoke."

"I would have to agree with Grace there," said George, firmly. "It pains me to say it. If he was alive, we would have found him. If he has met some ill fortune then surely, we would have found his body.

Sorry, but it needs to be said. The longer this goes on the bleaker it looks."

George shook his head and did not try to wipe a tear from his eye.

William glanced at Grace. The toll of the last few days and sleepless nights were already etched starkly on her face.

"Is there anything else we can do?" His voice trailed away.

"I suppose we could try further afield. London, perhaps? I have contacts there," added George.

Grace shook her head. "Whatever has happened to Samuel has taken place here in Bristol. All Samuel is interested in is the sea, ships, and his telescope."

Grace had stubbornly refused to talk about her son in the past tense. The brothers stared at her. William adored his wife whilst George did not believe in such matters as love. Women were a convenience, and a pleasure, and Grace was thought of by him in such a way often.

Straight-faced, George nodded and smiled at Grace. "You are right, my dear. We must think positively and believe they will return Samuel to us safe and well."

One hour before sunrise, Grace slipped quietly out of her bed, trying hard not to awaken her snoring husband—a hard task at the best of times, but more so when in such a fitful sleep.

She shivered. It may have been mid-summer, but there was a chill on the early morning sunrise. Dressing quickly, finishing with a warm blue shawl, Grace tiptoed softly down the stairs and entered the kitchen which was always the warmest room in the house, on account of Mrs Harper's determination to bake bread at first light. Grace quickly warmed the rest of the milk to make herself a drink, into which she stirred a spoonful of honey. She sniffed at the warm, healthy drink and smiled.

Grace put on her shoes which were warming by Mrs Harper's oven and walked into the office, closing the door quietly. She lit a candle, which she placed on the desk before sitting down. Grace opened her ledger at the last entry.

This had been her morning ritual from the day her son disappeared. A religious woman of strong faith, Grace believed the key to Samuel's disappearance was not in London, Liverpool, or any other far-flung place. But, here in Bristol. She had been grateful for the help of her brother-in-law who had been the epitome of support and kindness. There was, however always a 'but' in her mind with George, dismissing the thought as she had every morning from that fateful day. In her mind, she had to keep concentrating on the task at hand: finding Samuel.

Immersing herself in her work and her daily routine helped Grace to keep her sanity. After three or more hours at her bookkeeping, she would then be ready to walk to the dockside and ask questions, hoping one of the handmade notices would come up trumps.

Many people insisted it was a fool's errand—sheer madness for her to walk the Bristol dockside and streets for Samuel. She would have none of it. There was an inner sense Samuel was alive and that sense, call it what you will, was still intact. It also seemed odd two young boys had disappeared on the same day which could hardly, or so Grace believed, be a coincidence.

Deep in concentration, she placed an unruly wisp of hair back in its correct place behind her ear. After a little while, a smiling William Castle opened the door dressed in his best brown trousers, linen shirt, and jacket for a meeting with David Harrison, a merchant trader with whom he did regular business. William tried his best to present to Grace as much normality as he could, but her determination was taking its toll.

"What do you think, Grace, will I pass muster?"

Grace looked up and pretended to ponder, sucking in her cheeks, raising her eyebrows and shaking her head.

"Just by the skin of your teeth."

William bowed. "Where are you going this morning, Grace?"

"I thought I would try the Harbour Master."

"Harbour Master? Good idea. Jeremy Bryant is a good man. Now, why didn't we think of him before? Well done. Well done indeed."

"What's he like? As a person, that is. It might help me when I speak to him."

"Honest as the day is long, full of his own importance though and may try, you're a female…"

"To treat me with disrespect or try to seduce me?"

William nodded. "Both, but just earn his respect."

He bent over to kiss his wife. He did not doubt Grace and knew not to patronise her.

Completing her morning work, she walked into the kitchen and smiled at Mrs Harper and Alice as she saw two freshly baked loaves of bread on top of the oven.

"Morning, Mrs Castle. Breakfast!" She nodded at

the bread. "And would you like eggs with that?"

"Eggs would be delightful, Mrs Harper, thank you."

Grace ate her breakfast as she thought about the Harbour Master and what her approach should be. William was an excellent judge of character, and his observations would give her an edge, at least at the first meeting. Upon finishing her breakfast, she returned to the office. She placed her papers, leaflets, and small journal in which she had catalogued minutely every detail of every conversation she'd had and visit she'd made, into a beautiful deep red satchel in the softest Italian leather—a gift from William. She put on her best coat, mauve-coloured felt hat (which she knew brought out the best of her colouring) and matching gloves before setting forth to find the Harbour Master.

Grace was annoyed with herself for not thinking of speaking to the Harbour Master before. In fact, he ought to have been her first port of call. Although it was a long walk from her home, the Harbour Master's house was simple enough to find. It was stone built and with her eagle eye for detail, she could see it was of recent construction, with clean lines and with no sign of wear. Perhaps a sign of the recent modernisation of the ever-growing Bristol dock.

It was twelve noon by the time she arrived, and an indignant housekeeper made Grace wait. She had a wizened face and an expression as sour as a cup of a month-old milk. Not that Grace had ever tasted milk more than a week old, but she could imagine! She sat patiently whilst Jeremy Bryant ate his luncheon.

After what seemed like an eternity and without being offered any refreshment, the housekeeper showed

Lost At Sea

Grace into a small room with a large imposing desk, sitting behind which was the Harbour Master in all his glory and full of self-importance. Ignoring Grace, the bespectacled Jeremy Bryant was reading a large book, the title of which she could not make out. She noted his black hair and ruddy face.

Grace stood quietly, then coughed and spoke. "Mr Bryant. My name is Grace Castle. I am the joint owner of Castles' Merchant Traders with my husband, William. I am given to understand you do not approve of women in the workplace. That is something I believe you will have to get used to. I have been waiting for some time now without the simple courtesy of refreshment."

She shook her head at the apparent lack of basic hospitality.

The Harbour Master's face changed from his normally ruddy complexion to white as her carefully selected and provocative words struck home like a hard slap from an indignant lover. He spluttered. Grace continued she had his attention.

"You do not need to apologise, Mr Bryant. I know you are a very important and busy man. I am here in search of my ten-year-old son, Samuel Castle who has been missing now since the 22nd of July. He was doing an errand for his father and was on his way home by the dockside. We have not seen him since. A second boy, one William Thomas, has also disappeared and on the same day. Can you help us? Will you help us?"

Jeremy Bryant was at a loss for words and stared wide-eyed at Grace, not knowing whether to pat her on the head and say 'there there' or throw her out for her impertinence. He recognised she was spirited, and her flushed face made her increasingly attractive. He stared at her eyes, then her mouth.

An attractive woman with fire in her eyes. Interesting.

The Harbour Master laughed out loud and shook his black curly hair in amazement. Believing he was laughing at her, Grace's eyes blazed.

"It is no laughing matter and I thank you to remember that."

"Please, Mrs Castle, I meant no harm. I admire your, what shall I say, tenacity… or is it ferocity?"

Grace smiled. "William says when I get a bee in my bonnet, I am unstoppable."

She opened her red satchel and sifted through its contents, placing a pile of papers neatly on his desk before finally removing her journal.

"Samuel Castle. Just a moment."

Jeremy Bryant got up from his chair and walked to a small bureau behind his desk. He opened the top drawer and removed a small neatly folded sack.

"Someone handed me this last night."

Opening the sack, he produced a small brass telescope.

"The telescope has a name engraved on it and I am sure that name is…" He placed it on his desk. "Yes, I am right. Samuel Castle. They found it yesterday wrapped up in a jacket and stuffed in the dock wall. How anyone found it is beyond me. It never occurred to me Samuel Castle was William Castle's son. Did your boy have a telescope with him when he was last seen?"

Lost At Sea

Grace stared open-mouthed at the telescope. So great was the shock she could not move, breathe, or even blink. Eventually, she gathered her wits. Grace picked up the telescope and handled it gently as if it was made of the most delicate glass. She had to read the inscription before she could believe the telescope was Samuel's. If it was, what was the significance of this discovery?

"Oh, my goodness, Mr Bryant! As I live and breathe, this is Samuel's telescope. As you can see from the inscription, we gave it to him on his 10th birthday. The jacket. Do you have that as well?"

The Harbour Master nodded, removed a jacket from the sack and placed it on the desk. Grace gasped and put her hand over her mouth. Jeremy Bryant opened a drawer on his desk and produced a bottle of brandy and two glasses. He poured a small amount into each glass, handing one to Grace.

"Just take your time."

She nodded and sipped the brandy, before placing it on the desk and reaching for the jacket. She slowly undid the fastened buttons before looking in the pockets.

"Is there a small carving of a ship in the bag? It is not in his pockets."

She breathed in the jacket, trying to find the scent—the very life force of her son. Grace wept silently.

The Harbour Master waited quietly to allow Grace to regain her composure.

"Mrs Castle, please, take your time. It is understandable the sudden discovery of your son's telescope and jacket has been quite a shock for you."

Grace nodded and smiled. "Thank you. I'm fine."

Jeremy Bryant turned the sack inside out and shook his head. "I am so sorry, Mrs Castle there is nothing else in here."

"Mr Bryant, can you tell me who handed this to you? I would like to talk to them, so I will better understand…" Grace's voice trailed away, and she shook her head in despair, once again trying to control her emotions.

"Mrs Castle. Grace. I do not know the sailor's name, but I know he was in the crew of the Rose. He showed me where he found it and I will take you now if you are able?"

Grace followed Jeremy Bryant to the dockside. In the middle was a capstan, around which a ship would be secured, ready for loading or unloading. Jeremy beckoned Grace to the left side of the capstan. Despite some stiffness, he got on his hands and knees alongside Grace who knelt at his side. He then leaned over. Under the lip of the top stone was a gap where a stone from the dockside was missing.

"The sack was stuffed in there." He pointed at the gap made by the missing stone. "Now whether it was just hidden there on the dockside is anyone's guess. The hole has been deliberately made; they conveniently placed it on the dockside, large enough to hide small items such as contraband."

Grace peered into the gap the best she could. She was not a tall woman and was concerned she may fall.

"It is a clever and accessible hiding place," added Grace, "therefore, whoever hid the jacket and telescope there, intended they should remain hidden until they could be retrieved."

Jeremy nodded. "It explains how the sack was found. We would not have seen this from the dock itself. It had to be from somewhere below that level. The ship was being loaded, sailors off and on, up and down from below deck. If the stone had not become loose, the sack would never have been discovered." That is why it is such a clever hiding place.

Grace agreed. "The sailor, did he give a time when he found it?"

"Yes, yesterday afternoon. The ship, the Rose, was being loaded and due to sail that evening. It was during this time the sailor noticed the sack dangling from the hole. He hauled it onto the dockside and found the coat and telescope. The captain told him to bring it to me because of the inscription. I was out, so he left it with my housekeeper. She handed it to me last night." The Harbour Master looked at his watch. "It has gone three o'clock. I have much to do, Grace. We will return to my office, and you can take the sack along with the telescope and jacket."

Grace nodded and followed Jeremy Bryant back to his office. She had much to think about. She thanked him and he offered his help, should she need it. Grace left posters describing the two missing boys.

"Give my best wishes to William and I wish you well in the search for your son. If I can help at all…" He smiled at Grace, smitten.

As she moved along the dockside, Grace instinctively walked to the side of the capstan which the Harbour Master had shown her. Something drew her there. She knelt and leaned over the side and reached into the gap provided by the missing stone. Her right hand explored inside. Perhaps Jeremy was correct? Maybe it was more than a coincidence?

Grace enquired at the Customs and Excise Office which was directly opposite. She met them regularly as part of her work. The main warehouse door was, as usual, open and so she entered and walked to the main office. Wilfred Rhodes was seated, head bowed over papers, which he read carefully before placing them onto a second pile. Grace tapped lightly on the door. Mr Rhodes frowned in irritation at the interruption, then raised his head to see Grace Castle. He smiled and waved at her to enter. She never understood the profound effect she had on men.

Smiling and nonchalantly moving the unruly wisp of her hair behind her ear, she entered. Wilfred Rhodes, a Customs and Excise Officer, pointed at the seat in front of his desk.

"Mrs Castle, Grace, this is a most pleasant surprise. I was not expecting your visit until early next month. How may I assist you?"

"I am unsure whether you know, Wilfred, our son, Samuel disappeared whilst walking home from the dockside on the 22nd of July. William and Samuel had been into Bristol calling in at the docks on the way back. William sent Samuel home because he was going to be late, but he never arrived. We also learnt William Thomas, another boy, also disappeared. He was last seen heading for the dockside after an argument with my brother-in-law, George. Samuel has just had his 10th birthday and the boy, William is a little older. You can understand how worried we all are."

Lost At Sea

Wilfred Rhodes frowned. "I heard something about a rumpus with George Castle and a boy in Bristol, and another lad was missing, but I did not connect him with you or the dockside. Did you report it?"

Grace nodded.

"Well, they should have reported it to me and the Harbour Master too. Does Jeremy know?"

"I have just come from there. He had Samuel's jacket and telescope in a sack, handed in by a sailor. Apparently, the sailor was helping to load the ship called the Rose when he saw it dangling from a gap in the dockside by the capstan yonder. He got it out and inside was Samuel's jacket and telescope."

Grace placed the sack on the desk.

"How odd," said Wilfred Rhodes who opened the sack and removed the jacket and the telescope "Ah, I see the inscription for your son's birthday so there is no mistake it is his. Will you show me where the sack was found?"

Wilfred followed Grace to the capstan at the dockside. She pointed to the side.

"You will need to get on your hands and knees and lean over."

He was a tall, angular man with rather long arms, which was fortunate, for he could examine the gap in the dockside thoroughly. He stood up.

"How very odd. The hole is large enough to hide many things, Grace."

Grace nodded. "Exactly the opinion expressed by the Harbour Master."

"Suggests contraband, small expensive items though, and they would have to be left at night. But even then, it would be risky. Unless you are desperate or in a rush," the Customs and Excise Officer frowned.

"The thing is, would you have noticed any activity from your office? Seen anyone hiding the sack?"

Wilfred Rhodes shook his head. "Did we see anyone with the sack, you mean? Unlikely, but I will ask my men. They guard the bonded warehouse day and night, and the men miss nothing. It all depends on when the sack was hidden there. I suppose one thing in our favour is that it's summer—long days and short nights, so you never know. I will have a chat with Jeremy as well, but in the meantime, I wish you well in the search for Samuel and indeed the other boy. I see it is William Thomas. He ran messages for Jonathan Jerome, if my memory serves me right."

Grace continued, "The boy, William Thomas, known as Billy Thomas, was taking a message from Jonathan to George Castle that they were needed at the dockside for the loading of the Pegasus."

They returned to Wilfred Rhodes's office. Grace handed him some of her hastily made posters, before replacing the jacket and telescope into the sack and leaving to return home to break the news to William.

Grace walked to the dockside and took a deep breath to clear her head. There was a lot to think about before she got home, not least the implications of the discovery of the sack and its contents hidden in the dockside wall. A strange place to hide anything, least of all contraband.

She frowned and walked slowly along the dockside deep in thought. Samuel would have walked this exact route on that fateful day. William had watched Samuel walk to the end of the dock before he turned left and continued the short distance home.

The sack was draped over her right shoulder; her left hand clutched her leather satchel. Grace considered. Surely if Samuel simply had an accident, they would have found him dead or alive by now, wearing his coat with the telescope and carved ship in his pockets? That they secreted the coat and telescope in the dock wall and the small carved ship was still missing was, to Grace's mind, a worrying development. Had Samuel been abducted? If so, there would have been no need for the jacket. The inscription on the telescope would have also identified him, which would explain why it had been hidden. Hiding the items in a sack in the dock-side wall suggested a deliberate or hasty act. The perpetrators would not want the sack to be discovered before they could get their hands on it.

Grace made her way home slowly and thoughtfully. William was in the study. She entered placing the sack carefully on her desk. William looked up initially with a smile, and then a frown.

"Grace, how did it go with Jez Bryant today?"

He could see from her face she was troubled. William nodded at the sack. Grace opened it, laying Samuel's telescope and jacket on William's desk. He gasped and stared at her.

"Where on earth did you find these?"

She explained the events. The Harbour Master had been exactly as William described and after somewhat of a stilted beginning, the morning went well. She explained the strange gap in the dockside wall, which was quite cavernous, and after leaving Jeremy she had gone to the Customs and Excise Office where she spoke to Wilfred Rhodes, hoping someone on duty at the warehouse had seen whoever hid it. Mr Rhodes held little hope but believed the long summer evenings and short nights may be of some help to them.

William took the telescope and stroked it gently, then opened Samuel's jacket and instinctively held it close to his face.

"The carved ship?"

Grace shook her head.

"What do you make of all this, Grace? It is just so odd."

"I just wonder if Samuel has been abducted and the telescope would identify him. As for the jacket, I am unsure. Why hide them and not simply get rid of them? Unless…"

"Unless?"

"That whoever took him simply did not have time and hid them until they could return?" added Grace. "I have gone through all this until my head is spinning."

"Perhaps," said William, "Samuel's things could be used as proof by the abductors that they had him?"

After supper, ashen-faced William and Grace sat quietly in their front parlour, deep in thought and contemplating the next step in the search for their son.

"We will need to take Samuel's jacket and telescope to Constable Norris and explain where they were found," said William. "If we went to the dockside tomorrow, I believe it would help me have a better understanding. You can show me where these items were found and then we can visit Jez and Wilfred."

Grace agreed. "They may already have given this

some thought or have more information for us. I will visit Constable Norris tomorrow afternoon."

William glanced at his wife with concern. The toll of losing their son was etched on her face.

CHAPTER SIX

25th July—Queen's Square, Bristol

Jonathan had sent a message inviting George to visit his new home. Nothing wrong with that. But George considered it strange a man who had spent most of his time speculating and trading from an office in the heart of Bristol should decide to purchase his own house. His friend had not had a home life so to speak, but simply rented rooms. He therefore pondered on the real reason for the invitation.

As dapper as ever, George wore a grey top hat, blue jacket, light blue waistcoat, white linen shirt, blue cravat, and black trousers. He wore a pair of highly polished tight black boots which reached his knees, thus making his long slim legs look even longer and slimmer.

He rushed with his silver topped black cane held in his left hand, tapping the ground. He glanced at the message with the address 32 Queen Street located just off Queen Square. George approached Queen Square, an ongoing new area in the ever-expanding and thriving city. The construction of Queen Square had begun in 1714 to commemorate 'The Reign of Queen Anne' which, despite the passing years, was still unfinished.

He wandered down Queen Street, admiring the many gleaming brass name plates of solicitors, bankers, and merchants all advertising their professions and that they were residents in such a prestigious area.

Lost At Sea

George approached number thirty-two. A plain black painted door with a brass plate simply announced: No 32 Queen Street. George laughed to himself for this was so typical of Jonathan who had the wherewithal to buy a property on Queen Square itself, but that was not his style. His friend was a man who did not like to attract attention to himself, preferring to take a back seat, picking up snippets of information and quietly weighing up his thoughts before choosing to speak. It was typical of the man to purchase a house just off the main square—less attention and cheaper.

George was the opposite, of course. He enjoyed the attention which could cause a reaction, together with the possibility of being contentious. From the reaction, he could then pick up information from any subsequent ripples. Certainly, if he had bought a house on Queen Street, it would have had the brightest front door and a large brass plate announcing with great gusto that 'George Castle, Merchant Trader' lived there.

He tapped his cane on the ground and nonchalantly walked up the steps to number thirty-two and rapped on the door with the brass knocker. He waited momentarily before a middle-aged woman wearing a plain dark blue dress and neither a white cap nor an apron opened the door.

"I am here to see Mr Jonathan B Jerome, if you please."

The woman nodded. "He is waiting for you in his study. If you would follow me, Mr Castle."

George followed her into a well-illuminated hallway. He removed his hat and gloves and handed them to the woman who then placed the items on a shiny table.

"I would prefer to keep my cane."

"Right you are, sir. Please follow me."

Her face was familiar. George realised she was in fact Jonathan's laundry woman. Mrs Thomas had scrubbed up well, he thought, laughing at his own pun. She opened the first door on the right and walked into a large, if simply furnished, dining room, with a dark blue Turkish carpet in the middle, along with matching blue velvet curtains. George followed Mrs Thomas, walking towards the oak panelling at the far side of the room. There, she reached for a discreet door handle which at first glance George had missed, and opened the door.

"Mr Castle for you, sir," she announced.

The door opened into a large study. Jonathan sat, head bowed, at an impressive, walnut table that was placed on the left side of the room and next to a large window that enabled natural light to cover his desk. George whistled; it was a fabulous room. His business partner was certainly hiding his light under a bushel.

"Thank you, Mrs Thomas. Please, George, do come in."

"Would you like any refreshments, Mr Jerome?"

"Yes, coffee and whatever you think."

Mrs Thomas nodded and closed the door.

George stood in the middle of the room, hands on hips. "Impressive!"

He glanced around the room and noted the simple but quality furnishings. To the right of the table was a fireplace, made up but not lit, in front of which was a picture of a black spaniel lying contentedly on the floor, head on paws with one eye half open, looking straight ahead; a lazy glance that followed any admirer around the room. Jonathan had rediscovered the painting only recently whilst he was moving his belongings to 32 Queen Street. He'd had the picture cleaned and found the gentle portrait to his liking, and at moments of deep concentration or frustration, looked at the dog for inspiration. By the fireplace was a small round walnut table, matching the larger one.

"Glad you like it, George. For years I have had to store my books and ledgers wherever I could; with solicitors, bankers, traders, and such. It was a real inconvenience but now everything is at my fingertips and secure. Look here."

Jonathan rose from his chair and wandered to his library, which comprised three bookcases that stretched from floor to ceiling and in which someone had placed neatly his books. Jonathan explained the first section was about tangible investments such as 32 Queen Street and ships, like the Pegasus, as well as general merchandise. The second bookcase contained documents on stocks and shares and more nebulous investments. Finally, the third contained history books.

George frowned. "History! Why history?"

"Simple. Decisions made in the past dictate what we do today. And what decisions we make today will affect our tomorrow. Choices made by governments now on trade and war will affect what happens in twenty or thirty or even a hundred years. Think of the union with Scotland and the War of the Spanish Succession, or that we now have a Hanoverian King. All these impact confidence and trade. A good trader knows his subject and where he should trade and when."

There was a knock on the door. A small girl opened it—Mrs Thomas's daughter Florence. Mrs Thomas, who was carrying a large wooden tray, followed.

Jonathan smiled. "On the table, if you please."

Florence was carrying a cloth, which she placed carefully on the table. Mrs Thomas put the tray on the table, holding an apple cake, containing sultanas and spiced with nutmeg (which had been sliced), a small blue jug of cream, and a matching large jug of fresh coffee, soft brown sugar, and spoons.

Ethel Thomas turned to her employer and asked if there was anything else. She glanced at George Castle and then back at Jonathan B Jerome and caught his eye. Imperceptibly, he nodded, but George Castle did not miss it.

"Thank you, Mrs Thomas, that will be all," he replied.

They left the room.

"Familiarity with your staff, Jonathan!" George tutted and shook his head. "Before they left, the glance and nod between you and Mrs Thomas? Poor form, old boy, poor form. Mind you, she has scrubbed up well and has manners."

"Not like you then, George." Jonathan quipped. "Manners, that is."

George frowned and was about to butt in when Jonathan laughed out loud. "I have learnt if I treat people with respect, they will work harder and be loyal as well. You should try it, George. All of Mrs Thomas's family now work for me and live in their own rooms at the back of the house. Mrs Thomas has turned out to be a real gem, and you will already know William and Noah Thomas. Come, let us eat. The coffee is fresh, one advantage of having shares in a coffee shop."

Upon finishing their light repast, George turned to his friend. "What is the real reason you have asked me here? I never swallowed that 'come and look at my new house' message I received."

Jonathan nodded and grinned. "George, you are far too perceptive for me. First, the South Sea Company stock. Please tell me you have sold your shares, or at least some of them. I have it on good authority the share price will collapse in the next week or so and when it does, it will drop like a stone, and the South Sea Company bubble will burst. People will sell and down the price will go even further. Those who have bought on credit have no chance at all. There will be a lot of angry, bankrupt shareholders, and any subsequent financial crisis may well bring the Government down. If the South Sea Company collapses, then... other questionable investments may well collapse."

"I agree," responded George, "the King may well be the governor of the South Sea Company, but they won't dare touch him. I would not want to be in the shoes of the Sub-Governor and Deputy Governor. God help them."

"You have sold some of your South Sea Company stock, then?"

George nodded, for he believed he had to simply hold his nerve a bit longer. George was a risk taker, and that is how he had become a wealthy man. However, the latest news from Jonathan was stark indeed.

All his plans to take back Castles' Merchant Traders depended firstly that the share price of the South Sea Company remains at this level or hopefully continues to rise, and secondly that the cargo on the Pegasus brings a good profit. This would enable George to buy into Castles' Merchant Traders or better still to buy his brother out. Ironically, his brother William had refused to invest in the South Sea Company, nor in George's offer to purchase a second ship and use the company's monopoly of the South Seas. George blamed Grace Castle for that. He had somehow to scupper Castles' Merchant Traders, bankrupt them, and then buy them out.

"And the second thing you wanted to talk to me about?" added George.

"When your nephew, Samuel went missing, so did Mrs Thomas's son, Billy. Similar time and, as you know, he was also last seen heading toward the docks." He continued, "It was William who delivered the message I sent to you informing you the Pegasus was loading, and we were both required at the dockside. After the boy had delivered my message, you accused him of stealing from you, and then you called the Constable and young Billy ran off. That was the day we saw William Castle and his son at the dockside and if you remember, the boy had his birthday telescope with him. It is most odd both boys have simply disappeared on the same day, having been down at the docks, albeit separately. The problem is, I feel some responsibility for Mrs Thomas who is not only the mother of William and Noah but also my housekeeper and an excellent cook. Her family likewise. None of this makes any sense to me. Why would young Billy Thomas steal from you when he knows we are partners and stealing from you would put his family at risk?"

George bristled. "I do not understand where you are heading with this. I hope you are not accusing me of…"

Jonathan waved his hand and shook his head. "Of course not, but it is most odd, don't you think? I just wondered if the young lad was under pressure from somewhere else to steal from you."

George played for time. He needed to gather his thoughts. It was in his interest for neither boy to be found, nor did he want any fingers pointing toward him, but he had to show his full cooperation regardless of his personal feelings and motives. He had to continue to be the picture of concern, not only to his brother and his wife but also to his business partner.

Jonathan continued, "It seems to me the disappearance of these young boys is linked somehow, and as you are the uncle of one and I feel I have some responsibility to the other, perhaps we can work together?"

George smiled and nodded, his expression open and honest. "What help would you like from me, Jonathan, you only have to ask?"

"Shall I talk to your brother about the possibility of collaborating?" said Jonathan.

The perilous state of his finances distracted him momentarily, George did not wish to appear churlish to his business partner whose help he may well need later. George agreed.

"Good and thank you, George. I will send a message

to William and his wife. I think young William's brother, Noah would be appropriate, don't you think?"

The two friends discussed further financial matters before George begged his leave. He needed time to think. If the news from his business partner was correct, and it usually was, then he needed to offload his South Sea Company shares, and quickly whilst the share price was high. The person to turn to was Jeremiah Sykes. He had maintained contact with Jeremiah, who he preferred to his son, Joseph. Joseph was content to act for the more ordinary and less wealthy people of Bristol and was well-regarded for his honesty and his integrity to his clients. But not regarded for his ambition.

Jeremiah had a ruthless edge and was not faint-hearted when bending the rules. The other advantage was Jeremiah had seen the opportunity in the expansion of mercantile trade and the need for legal advice, whilst his son dealt with the day-to-day matters. Jeremiah had stepped into mercantile law with gusto, for merchants were usually rich and ambitious men. So successful was Jeremiah Sykes he had become the main legal advisor to The Bristol Merchant Venturers. With that came power and influence. He had also purchased a house on Queen's Square to reflect his wealthy status.

George headed for 2 Queen's Square, the home of Jeremiah Sykes. He smiled as he approached the front door. This house was in the most prestigious part of the square and announced, 'Jeremiah Sykes and Co' with a blaze of glory by a large brass plaque, immaculate black railing, dark blue door, and large silver knocker.

So, whoever lived there was of some standing.

Whether Jeremiah Sykes was in, or whether he would see him if he was, George was about to find out. He banged on the door with the impressive door knocker. After a little while a flustered Joseph Sykes, hair untidy, jacket in disarray, and miraculously (bearing in mind his parlous state) opened the door carrying a leather bag, shouting over his shoulder.

"I will be back by nightfall, sir."

Breathless, he turned towards the open door to find George Castle calmly watching the tussle Joseph was having with his coat. Joseph blushed and thought of all the people he should meet at this very moment, it was George Castle. The irony was not lost on him.

"I am in a desperate hurry, Mr Castle, but can I be of help?"

George smiled. "If you please. It is your father I wish to see if he is available?"

Joseph Sykes considered whether to make a dash for it, but he considered his father's response if he let a client walk into their home unannounced and unguarded.

"Be kind enough to wait here, Mr Castle. I will see if Mr Sykes is available."

He returned quickly and pointed to a door at the top of the stairs where Jeremiah Sykes was standing and waving good-naturedly at George. Perhaps George's luck was about to change.

Joseph Sykes dashed out, still struggling with his coat. He was on his way to Castles' Merchant Traders.

CHAPTER SEVEN

Lisbon 5th August

It was daybreak as the Pegasus approached Lisbon Harbour. The rising sun left a cloak of haze, which seemed to make the approaching city more mysterious. Captain Fothergill was at the wheel with Caleb Joyce, watching a busy crew rushing about and preparing the Pegasus to dock.

At the prow of the ship stood an excited Seaman Wragg. Alongside him was the unnamed boy who had been nicknamed Jimmy James by the crew, in honour of the doctor, who had (in their eyes) saved the lad's life. The captain watched the two boys, pleased the young injured lad was on deck.

Doctor James was in his treatment room making a list of items he needed to replenish his stock. These included medicines and remedies, ointments and bandages, needles and twine for stitching wounds, and the replacement of items that had been used or damaged. The care of the injured stowaway had depleted his medicine cupboard, not forgetting those items that he had used on the crew.

He smiled to himself and shouted, "Augustus," who appeared from nowhere, peering around the door.

"Doctor, you called?"

Seaman Brown was grinning from ear to ear and despite one eye being covered by a patch, his face beamed. Docking was a merry time for him as he had the responsibility of restocking the Pegasus's larder and getting items for the captain and the doctor. This allowed him an element of freedom and added responsibility when they disembarked.

"Here is my list, Augustus. Who will you be taking with you?"

Seaman Brown replied, "I thought young Seaman Wragg. He is a good lad and I need a young un' to do the running about and carrying."

The doctor nodded. "Mind you, you'll need to watch him. He's sharp."

Seaman Brown nodded and disappeared.

Docking at any major port was a busy time for everyone. The crew was allowed on shore, but Seaman Mason strictly controlled this. Captain Fothergill was fair, but woe betides any drunken sailor cavorting with women who did not wish to cavort. He could be unforgiving.

Doctor James disappeared into the city to visit his preferred apothecaries who had proved the most reliable. He was also of the opinion Lisbon apothecaries were more advanced than their Bristol counterparts. They often provided remedies and tinctures that were often unavailable in Bristol and where he would discuss new methods and treatments.

Stephen James's favourite apothecary was Afonso Pereira and his wife Matilde, a backstreet apothecary the Doctor had found purely by accident when he had become lost on his very first visit. He was always made welcome and given local Portuguese specialties, which Stephen loved, before they talked about his medical needs.

On this occasion, after the usual pleasantries,

Stephen talked about his treatment of the injured stowaway. Matilde nodded and disappeared. Afonso smiled. Matilde returned with two items: a powder and a tincture in a small bottle.

Afonso clapped his hands in delight. "Perfecto Matilde."

Matilde explained the powder was to help with headaches should the boy have any, and the tincture was for the head wound to prevent infection. Stephen James shook their hands warmly. Afonso and Matilde had become close friends, always putting extra things into Stephen's satchel, which they thought would be of use to him on board the ship.

Doctor James also always visited the main Lisbon library which had an excellent medical section, and where the librarian, Mariana was very knowledgeable as well as attractive. They got on well. He would, if time permitted, visit the library.

Several days passed by, as the Pegasus was re-victualled. Despite being in the dock, the crew were busy with repairs, repainting, and checking ropes and sails as part of general maintenance. Besides replenishing his medicinal stores, Doctor James would see every member of the crew to check for injuries, sores, or other ailments.

The captain would update the ship's log as well as oversee the unloading of the ship's cargo, before reloading for the return to Bristol. It was a busy but very pleasant time in Lisbon, a most delightful city.

Captain Fothergill was on deck one morning when he noticed a rumpus on the quayside.

A voice with which he was familiar shouted, "We

have bigger rats than you on board our ship!"

Frowning, the captain peered towards the dockside and saw a group of large men, who had surrounded Seaman Wragg and Doctor James. He then saw a young black boy in chains, presumably a slave, which Doctor James appeared to be taking affront at.

Captain Fothergill beckoned Danny Johnson, Caleb Joyce, and the large and impressive Ian Darcy to follow him off the Pegasus. They walked towards the angry group of men, who had surrounded the doctor and youngest crew member who was foolishly becoming increasingly provocative. As he approached the group, Captain Fothergill made a mental note to speak to Seaman Wragg about having a calm mind and keeping his mouth shut. As he got close, he saw the young black boy was indeed a slave, complete with manacles on his feet and hands, as well as a collar around his neck. How abhorrent!

He then heard Stephen James's voice. "What use is such a young boy to you? Look at his state. Chained and shackled; what do you think he is going to do, run off? Attack you?"

A furious Doctor James was by now stepping towards a large man with a tattooed face, deadly blue eyes, a shaven head, and a gash down his left cheek. Clive Fothergill watched as Stephen James stood eye-to-eye with him, refusing to budge. Seaman Wragg was noticeably quiet. Captain Fothergill approached.

"Doctor James, Seaman Wragg, what in heaven's name is going on here?"

"These so-called human beings are taking this boy back to the slaver yonder, The Black Swan," spat

Doctor James. "Captain Jack Mac Taggert has ordered his crew," he nodded at the men, "to offload the weaker and younger slaves that would not make the crossing to be sold off in Lisbon. They have already sold off six or more, but this boy is the only one left. He is that small no one wants him."

"Saves on food, you see, and makes extra for Captain Jack," said the large, tattooed man with the shaven head. He took a leather pouch from under his shirt and shook it. "Captain Mac Taggert wants to be rid of 'em all and if we can't sell them, then over the side they go." He laughed out loud.

Stephen James turned to Captain Fothergill. "This is inhumane. The boy is already small and scrawny, and, if there is a disease or poor nutrition on the slaver, he has no chance."

The Captain presumed the large man with steel-blue eyes and a gashed face was the leader.

"Is this true? The boy has either to be sold or you will kill him?"

The leader nodded, brought a knife from his belt, and tested it for sharpness. "Don't worry, Captain it will be quick. Then the slave will be thrown overboard."

The sailor with the shaven head and tattooed face was enjoying himself. "He's up for sale if you want to buy him. He could be your slave boy then, Captain, if you have a taste for young black boys."

Captain Fothergill, fists gripped hard at his side because he was in danger of hitting him, snarled. "Do not presume to judge me and my crew like you and yours."

Lost At Sea

The captain called Stephen James over.

"Is the boy healthy?"

Doctor James frowned.

"Stephen, is this boy healthy and disease free?"

Stephen James had a puzzled look.

"I cannot allow this boy on the Pegasus unless he is disease free. Doctor, what is your opinion?"

Doctor James nodded perceptibly. He understood.

"The boy is not diseased. He is healthy enough, if thin and undernourished, but I can soon deal with that. Thank you, Captain."

Captain Fothergill walked to the man with steel-blue eyes. Eye to eye. Toe to toe.

"How much for the lad?"

He nodded to the chained and manacled slave boy. The man grinned and nodded, sticking his chest out.

"One of your English guineas."

"A guinea!"

Captain Fothergill was shocked. He nodded to Doctor James.

"Take him on board."

He then took a purse from his pocket, emptied a few coins into the palm of his hand, and dropped them on the ground. The distraction was enough for Captain Fothergill, Doctor James, and Seaman Bragg to return to the Pegasus with the boy, leaving the crew of the slaver scrambling on the dockside for the coins.

"He is your responsibility now, Doctor. Naturally, the manacles will have to be removed, Seaman Joyce will do that. I also need you to tell the crew this boy does not pose any risk of disease. Understand?"

His doctor smiled. "Thank you."

Captain Fothergill returned below deck.

Doctor James called for young Billy and Jimmy. "Now, I need your help with this boy. He is a similar age to you, Jimmy, and I think he will need reassurance. He will naturally be alarmed, and he might feel safer with you two. I am going to ask Seaman Joyce to remove the manacles and afterward, I need the boy in my treatment room to check him over."

Billy and Jimmy followed the doctor toward Caleb Joyce who was holding the slave boy.

"Caleb, will you remove the manacles and chains? Jimmy and Billy are here to help."

Seaman Joyce frowned. "I don't need help, Doctor."

"I presume the boy will have to keep still if you are to remove the tight-fitting manacles and chains. They may be useful."

"Well, one of them can get Gus. I will need some grease for the manacles, particularly the one around his neck."

Jimmy beamed, shot down the hatch, and was back in a moment with a pot full of something inedible and even indescribable. The pot stunk.

"I must address the crew about the boy."

"If I were you, Doctor, I would get Seaman Mason to call the crew together, that way you will have more authority," said Seaman Joyce.

Doctor James nodded and smiled his thanks before hurrying away, asking for the whereabouts of Seaman Mason. Seaman Joyce, whilst ignoring the young slave boy, examined the manacles he had around his feet, hands, and neck.

"Billy, go quickly now and tell Danny Johnson I

need his help. Explain how I need to remove these manacles. They are pinned. Quickly now."

Billy bolted like a ball shot from a cannon. He was back sharply with his friend Danny Johnson, who had with him a leather bag containing his carpentry tools. Seaman Johnson peered at the manacles, nodded, then ferreted in his bag and produced a wooden mallet and nails. Seaman Joyce was busy greasing the manacles on the boy's hands.

"These should do the trick. I throw nothing away. Remember that young Billy. May I, Caleb?" asked Danny Johnson.

Billy and Jimmy smiled at the slave boy which was a waste of time. The boy was peering at the deck. The young slave wondered what these men were going to do to him. Free him? No, he thought, kill him more likely. So, he closed his eyes.

Seaman Johnson picked a nail. "Billy, hold the lad's hand. Keep it still."

Nervously, Billy did as he was instructed, for the large mallet held in Danny Johnson's hand may miss and hit his. Seaman Johnson placed the nail at the top of the pin that secured the manacle on the boy's left hand. He banged the nail, and the pin moved a little. A second hit and the pin shot out. Jimmy cheered and received a frown from Seaman Joyce. The pin on the manacle on the boy's right hand was also removed swiftly and the manacles on the slave boy's hands dropped to the deck.

Seaman Joyce greased the manacles on the boy's feet. Again, two sharp taps removed each pin, and the manacles opened. The collar around the neck, however, proved to be much more difficult. The young boy realised the two sailors meant him no harm and looked at Billy and Jimmy.

"Now it gets a little tricky. We need to grease the collar," said Seaman Joyce.

Seaman Johnson nodded and stood back as Seaman Joyce took a dollop of grease and applied it to the collar. This was the turn for Billy and Jimmy to step in. They grinned at the boy. Billy pointed to the metal collar on his neck and then at Danny Johnson.

"He has to keep still. Billy, this will not be easy."

The collar was closed by a pin at the back of the neck, but it was smaller than the ones securing the slave boy's feet and hands. In addition, the collar was a tighter fit, evidenced by the abrasions on his neck. Young Jimmy stood in front of the boy placing his hands gently on his shoulders. As the boy looked up, Jimmy smiled at him and touched the collar around his neck, and then pointed at the manacles removed from his feet.

The slave boy nodded and closed his eyes. Jimmy continued to stand in front of him with his hands lightly on his shoulders. Billy, for the first time, was silent. Seaman Johnson pulled the slave boy's head forward so he could see the pin more clearly. He could not make any mistakes and he had already selected a smaller and thinner nail. The first tap made the boy stiffen, but he did not make a sound. The pin did not move. A second tap made the boy grimace but again no sound. Seaman Johnson looked grimly at the collar and then at Seaman Joyce and shook his head.

Billy said, "Try again, Danny. Please."

The slave boy gave a sob. It was as if he knew the collar would not come off and he would wear it all his miserable life.

Seaman Johnson lifted the mallet. He knew this was going to be the last chance to remove the dreaded collar, for the only other way left was to break it, which would injure the boy. He took a deep breath, stared hard at the pin, placed the nail on it, and hit it hard. The pin shot out; the collar dropped off and the boy collapsed onto the deck, utterly exhausted.

Seaman Joyce carefully picked up the boy who weighed so little it shocked him. He carried him below deck to Doctor James's treatment room, where the table had already been prepared.

"He's passed out, Doctor. The boy's neck is a mess because the collar was too tight and took some shifting."

Stephen James frowned and shook his head. "Thank you, Caleb. Could you bring me fresh water to clean this wound?"

"No need to thank me. It was Danny Johnson, Billy, and young Jimmy you must thank. I will send Billy down with the water."

10th August

Castle's Merchant Traders owned a small trading ship called the Swift, and the Pegasus docked alongside. The Swift was to head back to Bristol at first light the following morning. The captains were long-time friends and Captain Featherstone had invited his fellow captain, Captain Fothergill on board for supper.

Both men were from Bristol, and they knew each other as young boys and, as many a sailor before them, had worked on many a ship. First as a cabin boy, and then as a member of a crew. Both were experienced captains.

They discussed trading, threats by the pirates off the coast of France, and much more. Clive Fothergill eventually turned the conversation towards his two stowaways, although he had latterly come to the opinion the boys were not stowaways at all. Billy Wragg, if that was his correct name and he doubted that, had found himself by accident more than anything on board the Pegasus. Whilst the nameless boy Jimmy was a more complicated affair, for someone had clearly attacked him and, if not for the ship's doctor, would not have survived. He explained to Elliott Featherstone the circumstances as he understood it, of the two boys being found on the Pegasus. Clive Fothergill had been quite open with his fellow captain and considered asking his friend if he would take them both back to Bristol. They would be back sooner, of course, and the boys may well have worried parents, although he doubted Billy did.

However, unlike the Pegasus, the Swift did not have a ship's doctor on board. He was therefore of the opinion they, particularly the injured boy who still needed treatment for his head wound, would be better under the care of Doctor James. Captain Fothergill had prepared a long letter in which he had written, after consultation with Stephen James, the circumstances of the discovery of the two boys on the Pegasus. This described the two boys, their ages, and the injury to the younger boy.

    The envelope was sealed, and, on the front, he wrote 'Bristol Authorities'.

CHAPTER EIGHT

18th August—Bristol

William Castle closed the door and headed towards the dock. It was daybreak and there was a dull haze that seemed to stretch from the street to the sky. How strange! He shivered and thrust his hands further into his coat pockets and hunched his shoulders. He shook his head to clear his mind and then rushed towards the main dock where the Swift had anchored late the previous evening.

Rain had fallen, and he squinted hard to find his direction. The summer weather had been kind. He fervently hoped this would be the same on the journey across the Bay of Biscay from Lisbon to Bristol.

As was their wont, Grace and William always worried about the Swift as it crossed the Bay of Biscay. The sea was cold and the currents were variable. This and the brigands and pirates that sailed the coastal waters made the journey perilous. Whilst losing the Swift would not have ruined them (for the Castles had Maritime Insurance) it would still have placed their financial situation in a perilous state. The difficulty with insurance was that it took so long to be resolved, not forgetting that any documents, monies received, and cargo would have gone down with the ship. Proof of loss was made difficult. The greatest loss would be the men on board, particularly Captain Featherstone, who proved to be a first-class sailor and captain and as far as they knew, an honest one.

Lost At Sea

As the dockside came into view, William felt invigorated and alive. A big smile crossed his face like the sun crossing the horizon and illuminating everything before it, for he could see his beloved ship, the Swift, standing proudly before him.

As William approached, a voice from nowhere shouted, "Who goes there?"

This caution from the crew gladdened his heart.

"It is William Castle to see Captain Featherstone."

They welcomed William on board. The crew liked the Swift's owner as much as they liked the captain. They were both considered tough but fair. He smiled at the crew and shook the hands of their captain as he did so, whilst taking in the state of the Swift. Elliott Featherstone was naturally tired. The captain of a ship, even a small one such as the Swift, was a heavy responsibility. However, he greeted his employer and friend with a broad smile.

"How are you, Elliott? A profitable trip, I hope."

"I am about to have an early breakfast, Mr Castle. Please will you join me? We will work better on a full stomach and fresh victuals are so welcome."

After breaking their fast, Captain Featherstone explained to William the Lisbon Merchants with whom they dealt had been prompt at the dockside and consequently had unloaded their cargo quicker than normal, which meant a speedier turnaround. The weather was also kind to them and so they made good speed back to Bristol.

Elliott Featherstone added, "The Swift and the crew have done well but the main mast needs strengthening, and we have discovered two leaks, both on the prow.

Seaman Harrison, our carpenter, has made a temporary repair and helped with some spare canvas. But the winter voyages are far more unpredictable. I would not trust the repair in the winter weather."

William nodded. "The Swift is due a good overhaul, and the crew needs to spend time at home with their families."

"Also," continued Captain Featherstone, "the Pegasus, the ship owned by your brother, George and Jonathan Jerome, had docked alongside the Swift. The night before we sailed, I invited Captain Fothergill to the Swift for supper. A good man. He told me he had two stowaways on board; known nothing like it. A Captain for fifteen years without one stowaway and then two on his last trip! Both young lads it seems, and one of them was in a really bad way. Apparently, his ship's doctor saved his life."

"Maybe it is something we should consider, a doctor or suchlike, on the Swift I mean?"

It was at that point the enormity of what Captain Featherstone had just said struck William hard. Stunned, his mind in confusion, he mumbled to himself, before shaking his head to clear his thoughts.

"Are you all right? You have gone quite pale."

"These boys about which you speak must have got on board the Pegasus in Bristol, yes?"

"That's correct. You are worrying me, William."

William Castle took a deep breath. "Elliott, our son, Samuel disappeared the day before the Pegasus sailed. I was at the dockside with him and then I sent him home to tell Grace I was delayed. He never arrived, disappeared from the face of the earth so to speak.

Another boy, a young messenger who works for Jonathon Jerome and my brother, also vanished. We have searched Bristol high and low since then. Grace is distraught."

"My God, William. I understand now. Clive wrote the descriptions down for me and asked that when I arrived in Bristol, I should notify the authorities. Just a moment. I have his letter here."

Captain Featherstone opened a drawer, took out an envelope, and placed it on the desk. The envelope read: 'Bristol Authorities' and was signed 'Clive Fothergill Captain (Pegasus)'.

Captain Featherstone opened it carefully and read, his mouth moving gently in time with the words.

"It gives dates and details of how the boys were discovered. Apparently, they were not together, and they were unaware of each other."

"The descriptions, please, Elliott."

Captain Featherstone nodded and skimmed the page. "The injured boy was the youngest. About nine or ten years old, light straw-coloured wavy hair. Oh yes, distinctive pale green eyes. "

"It is Samuel. By God, it is! I am sure of it. The other boy?"

Elliott stared at his friend. "The other was an older boy, perhaps thirteen or fourteen, and said his name was Billy Wragg. Red hair, green eyes, and an earring in his left ear."

William nodded. "That description fits the other boy, William Thomas. The Pegasus, how far was it behind you?"

"Unsure. Captain Fothergill hoped to be out of

Lisbon within two weeks depending on how quickly they could load the cargo, and the weather of course."

"Before you pass the letter to the authorities, can I write the details down? I will talk to Grace and then to Jonathan and George. Grace and I will be back here first thing tomorrow morning. I promise you."

Captain Featherstone nodded to signal his agreement. "Another day is neither here nor there, and the injured boy, if it is young Samuel, is being cared for by a first-rate doctor."

William shook his head. "Is there any way we can find out where the Pegasus is?"

Captain Featherstone considered. "First, you need to find out if or when the ship left Lisbon. Start with the Harbour Master. See if Jez Bryant has heard anything. He is usually in the know. Or simply wait until the Pegasus docks."

"Your cargo manifest, is it ready? Grace will want a quick start."

Captain Featherstone grinned. "Let us see." He walked to the cabin door, opened it, and shouted, "Mr Wilberforce, if you please. Sharp now!"

William nodded. "You are fortunate to have such a capable second in command, ex-trader too."

There was a knock on the door, followed by a "Come in" from the Captain.

"Mr Castle wants to know if the manifests are complete and if they are correct."

Geoffrey Wilberforce gulped and stared hard at his captain and then at William Castle. He was not a man to mess with; tall, muscular, and good-humoured, but would not take criticism about the maintenance of his manifests. William shook his head and waved his finger at Elliott Featherstone, which produced a wide grin on the captain's face. The fire in the eyes of Seaman Wilberforce dampened when he realised his captain was playing him for a fool. The three men then got onto the serious business of checking the cargo before the inscrutable eye of Mrs Castle could.

In the late afternoon, William Castle walked home deep in thought. He called at the Round Coffee House. They had kept in regular contact with Jonathan Jerome and shared any new information they received about the missing boys. More so, oddly enough, than with his brother, George. He sent one of the many boys who lingered at the coffee house hoping for work to Jonathan's home with a message he needed to see him urgently.

Grace shrugged her stiff shoulders and leaned back against her chair. Whilst she had concentrated most of her time searching for Samuel, as the company bookkeeper there was a necessity to keep the ledger up to date as it was critical to the business. This she mainly did at daybreak before she went out distributing posters and such like. However, she had had an unexpected opportunity to do her bookkeeping. She closed the ledger for the day and glanced up in anticipation of William heading home after his visit to the Swift. The opening of the front door which creaked despite the liberal application of grease woke a heavy-eyed, Grace. She wrapped the shawl she was wearing tight around her shoulders and glanced at the fire which glowed silently as a precursor to going out.

Even during late summer, the setting sun seemed to

suck the heat out of the day to be replaced by the damp fog of the dockside. Glancing at the filled coal bucket with dried-out logs placed neatly on top, she picked one up, tapped it gently on the bucket so any insects could drop out and not come to a horrible end in the fire, and placed it gently onto the fire, hoping it would revitalise the dozing flames. Grace left the parlour and carefully closed the door to keep the warmth in and the damp out, then turned to her husband and smiled.

William had pondered long and hard on his way home about how to tell his wife the latest news.

"William, you have the oddest expression on your face. Any news from the Swift?" asked Grace.

William nodded and stared at the fire.

Puzzled, Grace frowned. "William, is something wrong?"

"I am not sure. We may have news about Samuel."

The silence spread through the small room as fast as a torrent through a breaking dam. Shaking her head as if clearing it from a bad-tempered wasp, Grace thought she had misheard.

"News about Samuel," she whispered, for she dared not raise her voice in case she broke the spell.

"Samuel…" he continued quietly after a long pause. "Whilst the Swift was docked in Lisbon, the Pegasus anchored alongside George and Jonathan's ship. Captain Featherstone invited the Pegasus's captain, Captain Clive Fothergill, for supper. Apparently, they have been acquaintances for some time and so they caught up. They share information. It appears after leaving Bristol, the day after both boys disappeared, they discovered two stowaways on board the Pegasus.

One fits the description of Samuel, the other of William Thomas. The ship had also taken on board a young slave boy, who is under the care of the ship's doctor."

In emotional turmoil, Grace gasped and whispered her son's name. William pulled his wife towards him and held her tightly as she sobbed quietly. He allowed Grace to compose herself before taking her hand and leading her to her chair. He told her as much as he could remember about the discovery of Samuel, including the news the boy they believed to be their son had been badly injured. However, they were most fortunate as there was a ship's doctor on board. William told Grace he had sent a message to Jonathan to meet them at the Swift at noon tomorrow, which would allow them to complete their business with the ship. It was important to work closely with Jonathan for the sake of their son and William Thomas.

The following morning, just after daybreak, Grace and William set off to the dockside. Grace had not slept a wink that night, spending the time going through the details of what she had been told by her husband. She had some doubts and did not want to raise her hopes too high. Some of it made little sense. Why would anyone kidnap their son? How did he end up on the Pegasus? Why and how was he injured? Why was he with another boy? Did he know him? Was the second boy the son of Jonathan's housekeeper? She closed her eyes to shut out the images. She needed a clear head.

It was daylight, and Grace and William Castle arrived at the dockside. Upon seeing the Swift, Grace fell silent. They were met on board by Seaman Wilberforce and shown to the captain's cabin. Elliott

Featherstone smiled at Grace, understanding the turmoil she must be feeling.

"The accounts and manifests are ready for you, Mrs Castle. I trust you will find all in order. We will leave you in peace whilst we see to the removal of the cargo from the hold and onto the deck."

"I would prefer to read the letter from Captain Fothergill first."

Elliott Featherstone nodded. "I expected as much."

He pointed to an envelope on the table. Grace nodded and sat in the chair proffered by the captain. Grace read the letter carefully and then read it a second time.

Satisfied for the time being, Grace removed pen and ink from her leather satchel and started work on the manifest. As usual, the accounts were in good order, and other than some slight damage and a cask of port that had been filled with cheap red wine, the cargo was as outlined in the manifest. The name of the supplier of port, Manuel Cadiz (who had been used for the first time) would be warned about supplying substandard goods. Honest traders, Grace and William were unforgiving if they believed they were being cheated. Grace noted the captain and his crew had done well, and a bonus would go to the Captain for distribution to his crew.

At noon, Jonathan Jerome arrived promptly and was shown to the captain's cabin where William, Grace and Elliott Featherstone were finishing their luncheon.

William Castle stood and shook Jonathan's hand. "I am so glad you could make it. Can I introduce Captain Elliott Featherstone?"

Jonathan nodded to the Captain. "I understand, Captain you have some information about our two missing boys."

He nodded. "Can I suggest you read this letter from Captain Fothergill? It is self-explanatory."

The letter was handed to Jonathan, who placed it on the desk in front of him. He pulled his seat closer and slowly read the letter, nodding and shaking his head as he did so. Upon finishing, he looked up at Grace and William Castle.

"A detailed letter from Captain Fothergill, typical of the man. The elder boy is my housekeeper's son, William. The younger boy..." His voice trailed as he looked between William and Grace.

William nodded. "We are sure it is Samuel. The description is perfect."

"The question is," Jonathan continued, "what are we to do now?"

"The weather limits what we can do," offered Captain Featherstone, "and it depends upon when the Pegasus set sail."

Grace added, "When is the Pegasus due back at Bristol, Jonathan?"

"They should have left Lisbon today. I checked this morning. It depends as you well know on the efficiency in Lisbon and the weather. Captain Fothergill is a first-class captain and I have every faith in him. I would expect the Pegasus would dock in Bristol by the end of the month. The Pegasus is not the fastest ship despite her name. "

Captain Featherstone said. " I suggest we notify the Harbour Master we have received this letter. I am sure he will wish to see it and it will have to be seen by the Bristol Authorities. He will also notify us when the Pegasus docks."

William said, "Agreed."

Grace continued, "I would like to make copies of the letter, if I may, before we hand it over to the authorities. I do not wish to put the cart before the horse, gentlemen, and these two boys may not in fact be ours."

Jonathan smiled. As ever, Grace grasped the nettle, even if she received a nasty sting.

"Clive Fothergill also told me," added Elliott Featherstone, "he was confused at the circumstances of the two boys being on the Pegasus. Apparently, the elder boy, William was resting by the cargo to be loaded on the Pegasus when he heard noises and hid. He saw several men carrying what looked like a long carpet. It was pitch black, you understand. The men threw the carpet; whether this was intended to land on the ship or in the water, we will never know. William believes Samuel was in that carpet. Also, Samuel had a nasty cut on the top of his head." The captain continued, "Stephen James, the ship's doctor, suggests it resulted from a blow, rather than a fall. This was a deliberate act, so it seems. You need to think hard about who might do such a thing and why? The boys are not, in Captain Fothergill's mind, stowaways. He believes Samuel was abducted and William was simply in the wrong place at the wrong time. I need to record Captain Fothergill's opinion on this matter. It may prove useful."

The cabin was in silence.

Grace shook her head. "I knew from the beginning something was not quite right. None of it made any sense then and I now am unsure…"

There was a knock on the captain's door and a seaman announced the Harbour Master had arrived on board. Captain Featherstone and William Castle begged their leave and left Grace with Jonathan.

"That was timely. We can advise him of the letter from Captain Fothergill."

Grace was silent. Jonathan glanced at her as he was preparing to leave.

"I am struggling to understand. None of this makes any sense."

"In what way, Grace?"

"Why kidnap a ten-year-old boy, beat him, change his jacket, hide him in a carpet and throw him on the Pegasus? The Pegasus would return to Bristol and the boy may well have survived and be on board. Even if he did not survive, they would identify his body on return. Then we have the discovery of Samuel's telescope and jacket hidden in the dockside. George is unaware of the discovery of the jacket and telescope, Jonathan. William and I would like it to remain that way at the moment. There is just something not quite right with George. His behaviour is all or nothing."

Jonathan agreed with Grace's summation of George. He smiled for he admired Grace Castle—her determination and sheer guts as she persevered in getting answers to the mysterious disappearance of her son. She was clever as well.

"I agree," added Jonathan. "It is odd, and in my mind, there are too many coincidences. Perhaps they had intended to throw Samuel in the water and were simply disturbed? I am still at a loss as to why young Billy was at the dock in the first place. We know he had a run in, so to speak, with George earlier that day. Perhaps he simply ran off and thought he could hide there for a while? After all the Bristol docks is a busy place."

It had been George who had called for the Constable even though he had been drunk out of his skull. As far as Jonathan was concerned, Billy was not a thief. Stealing from his employer's business partner was a foolhardy thing to do. That very employer also employed the rest of his family and was putting a roof over their heads. He agreed with Grace. Jonathan kept his thoughts to himself.

Grace smiled at Jonathan, and his heart fluttered.

She took the letter. "I will copy the letter in every detail, Jonathan and make you a copy."

He nodded and left.

Grace painstakingly copied the letter. Strangely, she felt closer to her son by doing so as if she'd lived every moment, every nuance, with her son. She understood that detail, even minute detail, may be of importance. Grace also recognised she was in no position to judge which detail or item was of relevance and which was not. Upon completion, Grace read the letter slowly to make sure she had got everything correct and then began to make a second copy.

They showed the original letter to Jeremy Bryant who believed the Justice of the Peace and Constable must also read it. Grace agreed and set to make a further copy of the letter, which she would take to the

Constable herself, along with a letter by Elliott Featherstone detailing the conversation he'd had with Clive Fothergill, and the suspicions both he and Doctor James held.

The investigation began.

Jonathan left the Swift, leaving the Castles and the captain to continue their work of unloading the cargo and completing any payments that needed to be settled. These were private matters. He fastened his coat and wrapped his scarf carefully around his neck to keep out the unseasonal wind and cool weather. Jonathan clenched his gloved fists tightly and pushed them deep into his coat pockets.

An interesting morning, now that was an understatement. Jonathan plodded through the damp and wet streets. A conundrum, in fact, a few conundrums! The saga made little sense. Samuel Castle seemed to be the key to this mystery but why was young William at the dockside so late? Why did he stay there so long? If there was a connection, he needed to find it. First, he needed to speak to Mrs Thomas, his housekeeper, about her son and then to George about his missing nephew and the Pegasus. It would be interesting to see George's reaction.

Trudging his way homeward, Jonathan saw a familiar blue light that swung ferociously in the prevailing wind. The Ship Inn was a welcome sight. He had had little time to himself recently and so he pushed the heavy door, which reluctantly opened. It was quite busy for such a miserable afternoon. The gentle humming of voices stopped as heads turned to see who had entered. Recognising Jonathan, many nodded before continuing their quiet chattering.

The Ship Inn was a calm place compared with some of its noisier neighbours such as the Anchor or the Rat and Barrel which were further down the street, for they were raucous places notorious for drunkenness and disorderly behaviour. Ironically, George frequented both premises.

The Ship Inn simply did not have such problems. As he entered, the innkeeper, Harry Wetherall, walked from the kitchen at the rear.

"Hello, Mr Jerome. A damp day. Get yourself by the fire. There's an empty table there."

Jonathan removed his gloves and scarf and then his coat, placing them over the back of his seat to dry.

Harry's wife, Gem was a fair cook and Jonathan realised, as tempting smells wafted from the kitchen, he had not eaten since he had broken his fast at seven o'clock that morning. He was hungry. He ordered a mug of porter and beef broth, fresh bread and a warm cheese pasty. Jonathan stretched his legs and relaxed.

He watched as Harry wandered about the room, a word here and a slap on the back there, laughing at a joke or showing concern for the wellbeing of a customer. He was a natural. A giant of a man, whose very presence kept a calm atmosphere. Harry would not truck any inappropriate behaviour and was very good at knowing when to step in to diffuse any fallouts between his customers. Crucially, he could handle himself if riled.

Jonathan's drink and meal arrived promptly, and he ate hungrily. Finishing his meal, he relaxed with a second mug of porter and contemplated the events of the day.

However hard he tried to work out the saga that had unfolded, it still made little sense. Two boys, who barely knew each other had found themselves at the Bristol quayside at the same time and at night. They both ended up as stowaways on the Pegasus. He shook his head. Something was not right, not right at all. Harry broke the spell, sitting next to him.

"Deep in thought, Mr Jerome?"

Jonathan looked at the innkeeper, wondering if he could take him into his confidence. He decided he could. Harry was a sensible chap and if anything unsavoury had happened on the dockside, then an innkeeper would be knowledgeable.

"Can I talk to you in confidence, Harry?"

"You know you can. I would be a poor innkeeper if not."

Jonathan continued. "You will be aware of two boys who disappeared a few weeks ago, young Samuel Castle and William Thomas?"

He nodded. "Yes. Mrs Castle has been in here a few times bringing posters and descriptions of the missing boys."

"We may have information about their whereabouts. Two boys fitting their descriptions ended up as stowaways on the Pegasus when it left Bristol on the 23rd of July, heading for Lisbon. The boys were discovered during the journey, and apparently, neither knew the other was on board. The young boy believed to be Samuel Castle had been badly injured and if the Pegasus had not had a ship's doctor on board, he would not have survived. It is a genuine mystery. We believe they arrived safely in Lisbon and are due to be back in Bristol by the end of this month. I would ask you to keep this confidential until we know more, and the appropriate authorities have been informed. I would be grateful for any information you may pick up. It really is strange and I am unsure of the truth of it. You understand?"

Harry nodded. "I understand, and I think I can help. Something was said to me about an incident down near the docks, which I thought was odd, but I thought little about it at the time as it didn't make a lot of sense. It was the day George Castle called the Constable saying William Thomas had robbed him. Give me a couple of days. I'll send a message."

CHAPTER NINE

20th August—At Sea

As the Pegasus sailed out of the harbour and into the Atlantic Ocean, the sun was shining, and seagulls shrieked and cried in the clear blue sky above. The ship was at full sail with Captain Fothergill at the helm in his element at the thrill of being at sea. The Ship's doctor was busy updating his log and cataloguing the medicines and various remedies he had got in Lisbon—a most sophisticated city of which he never bored, and as ever he looked forward to his return.

Stephen James was in deep concentration; pen poised over his small ink well, he turned yet another page of his ledger, the lifeblood of his career, and as a doctor, its very heart and soul. He leaned back into his chair, wincing with pain in his lower back, the result of a chair that was too high and a desk too low. He laughed out loud at the irony of a man of medicine with cures for many things, but not back pain.

Stephen was concerned about the health of the young slave boy, but from time to time his mind would drift to the young boy who had been at death's door and who was now well on the way to recovery. He was a lucky lad. Thankfully, his memory was still improving if a little patchily. But who his parents were, where he lived, or how he had ended up on the Bristol Dockside, was still a mystery. With a bit of luck and a good headwind, the Swift may have arrived in Bristol by now and possibly, some of his questions may have been answered.

The Pegasus was making good headway, courtesy of a strong south-westerly wind, which filled the sails that sighed with gratitude, sending the clouds gleefully scudding across a clear blue sky. All hands were at full stretch on deck. The captain was determined to take advantage of the gift of pleasant weather. The anonymous boy, nicknamed by the crew as Jimmy after the doctor who had saved his life, stood in his normal position on the foredeck facing the wind, straw-coloured hair flying, and his face in ecstasy.

Billy Wragg skipped up the stairs from below deck after delivering a message to the ship's doctor. He stood close to the captain awaiting any further errands when he noticed Jimmy. Billy had found his young friend an oddity from the very moment he saw him. He thought he recognised Jimmy but could not quite place where from. His clothing was not quite right, either. For a start, the jacket Jimmy had on when he was found on deck did not fit. It was too big. In fact, if truth be told, the jacket was too big for Billy, and he was taller and larger than Jimmy. It made little sense.

"I know you. I know you," he muttered.

Then, he realised. His brother Noah had pointed him out one day. It was the boy with the telescope. Samuel Castle. His father was William Castle, brother of George, and his mother had sent food with Noah for the family. Billy cursed himself for being a fool. He would keep this revelation to himself and talk to Doctor James who would know what to do.

Captain Fothergill signalled Billy and told him to tell the cook to prepare for the first supper sitting at six o'clock. Determined to please, he scurried below deck and passed the message to Gus.

On his return, Billy passed the open door of the doctor's treatment room, which was empty, and where Jimmy's cot was located. Glancing behind him, he slid into the room and quietly shut the door. Quick as you like, he found Jimmy's jacket and trousers folded neatly under his pillow. They were encrusted with salt and smelt of the sea like everything seemed to. Billy unfolded the jacket carefully.

"Just too big," he muttered, "too big. Just not right!" He then unfolded a pair of dishevelled trousers and a shirt. "Now these fit him," he muttered to himself, "but the jacket won't."

As he folded the trousers to put back under the pillow, a small ivory-coloured item dropped to the floor. A miniature carved ship. Billy picked it up and examined the intricate carving and was tempted momentarily to keep it. He smiled thinking of Gus's words about crew members depending on each other. He carefully placed the carving into one of the trouser pockets.

Billy went back on deck and returned to stand close to the captain once again. He was still bemused and unsure of what to do. Should he tell the captain? Billy shook his head. He would talk to the doctor. Something was not quite right. What was it?

"The jacket wasn't his, that was obvious, but the trousers and shirt were Jimmy's or Samuel's, that is. So, what did it mean?"

In deep thought, Billy realised whoever kidnapped his new friend had changed his jacket. There must be a reason for that, and somehow this was important. What that was, he did not know, but he needed to speak to Doctor James.

After supper, Billy approached the doctor's cabin and tapped lightly on the door. The doctor's distinctive voice answered, and the boy entered. Billy explained he had always thought not all the clothes young Jimmy was wearing when he was found were his own. He then confessed to finding his clothes in his cot, then laying them out and checking the pockets. He also mentioned the small carving of a ship.

"I am sorry, I shouldn't have looked at his things but…" Billy stopped and said quietly, "I think I know who he is, Jimmy that is. When I first saw him, I knew him somehow, but I couldn't quite…" his words drifted off. "I have just remembered where I have seen him and think he is Samuel Castle. Son of William. His uncle is George Castle."

Doctor James stood quietly. "Are you sure?"

Stephen knew that, along with Jonathan Jerome, George Castle was part owner of the Pegasus.

"Go on," encouraged the doctor.

"I thought when I saw him below deck after you and Seaman Gus had cleaned him up his face was familiar, but he had all those bandages around his head and his face was bruised. When I stayed with him to help him drink, I kept looking at him, sure I knew him, but I could not remember where I had seen him. Then I realised on deck today. Jimmy was not wearing a hat and his hair was blowing about and it was then it dawned on me who he was. My brother, Noah took messages for Mr George to his brother Mr William and that's where he met Samuel. Noah really enjoyed going there as he got well fed by Mrs Harper and Mrs Castle was kind to him. Noah saw him a few days later before we ended up on the Pegasus. Samuel was walking with his father. He had a telescope and was pointing it everywhere and it was then Noah told me who they were. The thing is, Samuel was not wearing a hat."

"Billy, you have done right to confide in me. Now not a word and leave this to me. I need to talk to the captain and then to Jimmy and see if any of this rings any bells with him. Understand?"

Billy nodded and left.

Stephen James considered. When he first saw the boy and the state he was in, his last thought was of clothing. After all, as was to be expected, they were dishevelled and coated in salt. Clearly, it had not occurred to anyone else either. Fresh clothes, more appropriate for being on board a ship, had been given to him. If what Billy reported to him was correct, then the young boy was Samuel Castle and who would wish the boy harm or even death? But why let him keep his own shirt and trousers and not his jacket? The jacket they found him in was clearly not his, which begged the question… why?

So many unanswered questions. Why change his clothes at all unless it was intended he would not be found, or, if he was it would be assumed he was someone else. They had taken a lot of effort to keep the identity of this young boy a secret. Perhaps the identity of the perpetrator was someone of standing or importance.

Stephen made his way to the captain's cabin where

Clive was having his morning repast. Clive beckoned his friend to enter his cabin and share what was left of his meal. Shaking his head, the doctor explained the reason for his visit, leaving Billy out of the equation. Looking through a shipmate's belongings was a disciplinary matter. He explained moving items in his treatment room, he had realised the boy's jacket was far too big for him.

Stephen James continued, "There is more. Seaman Wragg has been to see me. He said he had recognised the boy but could not remember how he knew him or where he had seen him until today. He believes the boy is Samuel Castle. Son of William and nephew of George."

Clive Fothergill raised his eyebrows in surprise. "Really! Is the lad sure?"

"My question exactly. But Seaman Wragg insists he is. Apparently, his younger brother Noah has taken messages between George and William Castle, and it was whilst he was at William Castle's home awaiting a reply, he met Samuel. Sometime later, Seaman Wragg was with his brother when he saw William Castle with his son, Samuel. It was then Noah pointed them out to him. He says he only saw him once, but his view was clear. Also, the boy was without a hat. I think it has taken Seaman Wragg some time to recognise Samuel because of the boy's injuries. It was today whilst they were both on deck he recognised who he was. It was, believe it or not, all down to Jimmy not wearing a hat."

"Nothing I can do until we return to Bristol. I believe you are the person to speak to the boy as he trusts you."

Stephen James nodded and agreed to speak to young Jimmy. This saga was changing quickly before his very eyes. Whatever next? He shook his head in despair.

The doctor went on deck and there staring out to sea, with his straw-coloured hair, billowing was the young boy. Stephen James now understood Seaman Wragg's certainty this boy was in fact Samuel Castle for the lad's hair was quite striking. He walked up to him.

"This seems to be your favourite place on deck."

The boy said nothing.

"Does it help you up here on deck, facing the wind? Clear your mind."

The boy nodded.

"Does it help your memory?" continued Stephen James. He then carefully removed the small carved ship from his pocket. "This was on the floor next to your cot. Does it belong to you?"

Jimmy smiled. "I found it in my trouser pocket. I know it is mine and that a girl called Alice gave it to me. I think it was for my birthday." He pondered a moment. "I remember her mother was our cook, and they worked for my mother and father. Mrs Harper! I remember they called her Mrs Harper."

Doctor James patted the boy on his shoulder and shook his head in amazement. "Anything else you can remember like your family name, for example?"

"No but I remember I had a telescope for my birthday, and it had my name on it."

"Go on," Stephen James resisted the temptation to prompt him.

The boy frowned. "I can remember going to the docks with my father and looking at the ships through the telescope."

"Can you remember what the name was on the telescope?"

The boy looked at the doctor, nodded, and then closed his eyes in deep concentration.

"There was a date and then my name." The boy shook his head. "My head really hurts."

Stephen James placed an arm around his shoulder. "That's enough for now, but well done. You need to rest."

The boy smiled and obediently went below deck to his cot to sleep.

As dusk fell, Stephen went to check on the young boy who was sitting up in his cot, holding his carved ship.

He grinned at the doctor. "Alice told me her father carved this from a whale's tooth. Can you believe that? She also called me Sam. I remember the name on the telescope. It was Samuel Castle. That is my name, isn't it? Samuel Castle."

Stephen James went out of the room and shouted for Seaman Wragg who he was told was doing an errand for the captain. A short while later, breathless, he appeared.

"Yes, Doctor."

Stephen James nodded to the boy holding his carved ship.

"Tell Seaman Wragg who you are."

Grinning from ear to ear, he said, "Billy, my name is Samuel, Sam Castle."

"I knew it. I told you, didn't I, Doctor?"

Billy continued, "I also need to tell the truth now.

Lost At Sea

My real name is Billy Thomas. And I have a brother, Noah."

Samuel frowned. "I know that name."

"Our Noah took messages between your father and your Uncle George. My family work for Mr Jonathan who is buying a house and my mother is to be a housekeeper."

It dazed Samuel. He looked like a startled rabbit facing a shotgun. "Uncle George? I know that name."

Billy added, "Mr George and Mr Jonathan own the Pegasus. The day before we both ended up on board your Uncle George accused me of stealing and he called the constable. He said nobody would take my word against his. But I did not do it, I swear. I had no chance. So, I ran off to the dockside and ended up on the Pegasus by mistake. When they found me, I thought if I gave my proper name, I would be in real trouble."

"Do you remember anything, Samuel? About being at the dockside," asked Billy.

"It still seems so muddled. I close my eyes tight and try hard to remember. I get flashes and noises. My head seems to spin as if everything was happening quickly. Yes! I remember there was a light and voices... different voices, men arguing. The strange thing was one voice seemed different to the others. He was giving orders and it seemed familiar somehow."

The boy frowned.

"Do you remember being struck on the head, Samuel?" asked Doctor James. "Your wound, I mean."

The boy pondered. "I was dragged along and then I was hit."

"Were they wearing masks or hoods?"

"Masks! One of them lost his and then everything blacked out."

The boy rubbed his head and then grimaced.

"Well done, Samuel. That is enough for now," concluded Stephen James.

Later that evening, Stephen was in the captain's cabin having a nightcap, both sitting amicably, legs stretched out with a glass of brandy in hand. Clive Fothergill was swirling the amber liquid in his glass to warm it through before taking an elaborate sniff, mimicking his friend who had earned a reputation for smelling everything and anything.

"I so enjoy French brandy," laughed the captain, "even more so when seized from a French captain!"

Stephen smiled, and after sniffing his brandy, took a sip. "Delightful."

"Tell me about the boy. Young Samuel Castle. Then about Billy Wragg or Billy Thomas as we now know him."

"The memory of young Samuel is coming back, but there are still a lot of gaps. It is possible his memory will not recover totally. Partly the injury and partly because of the trauma of being kidnapped," replied Stephen." He has flashes of memory, of noises, smells, sounds and such but he cannot make sense of all of it. He remembers a group of men and believes he recognised one voice. Therefore, one of his attackers will probably be known to him. He remembers also they were all wearing masks, but a mask came off one man and it was then Samuel was struck hard on the head. This may well explain the nature of his injury and suggest he may have recognised one of his assailants. Maybe even the ringleader. "

Clive Fothergill added, "It may well be young Samuel never actually saw the face of the man. The man would not have known and perhaps the risk was too great to let the boy live. That does not explain why they did not kill him or dispose of his body. Weighted down and thrown in the river. Not too difficult. Something went wrong, and they panicked."

"As for his clothing," added Stephen, "his shirt and trousers fit him, and I believe they are his. Whilst his jacket is much too big. It begs the question why bother to change some clothes and not all of them? Whoever they are, they seemed to take a lot of trouble. It makes little sense."

Captain Fothergill nodded, and then paused for a moment, deep in thought. "Could it be his captors originally intended to hold the boy for ransom? They must have believed Samuel's family could and would pay up."

"Makes more sense. It would have to be someone close to them to know about their ability to pay and their movements," said Stephen.

"Then during the kidnap, a mask comes off one of them. Someone the boy would recognise. They then must hastily change their plan, kill him and get rid of the body," concluded Doctor James.

"A family matter, perhaps! Now there is a thought," added the Captain.

"There has to be a link between Billy and Samuel."
Clive Fothergill frowned.

Stephen James continued, "First, Billy Wragg is not

his proper name. It is William, Billy Thomas. He has a younger brother, Noah who delivers messages between George and his brother, William. Noah has met William and Samuel Castle. Second, it was Noah who pointed out William and his son Samuel to his brother. Billy and Noah work for Jonathan Jerome and Mr Jerome and George Castle own the Pegasus and are our employers. Apparently, George Castle accused Billy Thomas of theft and called the constable. Now, the young Billy knew he had no chance and ran away to the dockside and hid. The rest we know."

Captain Fothergill stared at his friend in astonishment. "You could not make that up. This sorry episode, it seems to me, is about money and settling scores. I dare not ask about the slave boy. How is he fairing, or is there something else I need to know?"

"Timid and withdrawn as you would expect. You can remove the chains from the boy but not the boy from the chains. At least he is safe and well fed, and disease free. Billy and Samuel are the ones who look after him, but mainly Samuel. His head injury makes him vulnerable and so the slave boy is more akin to him. We will have to give the lad a name; we cannot keep calling him the slave boy."

August 24th

It was dawn, and the sun peered over the horizon like a sleeping giant awakening from a deep slumber and giving the sailors on board the Pegasus a heartening glimpse of daylight and warmth most welcome. The colour of the sky changed slowly from black to yellow and red, before reflecting onto the sea, making it look like liquid gold.

The captain was standing at his normal post on the raised deck behind the wheel, from where he had the best view of the sunrise. His favourite time of the day. His head bare, and with legs apart and his feet firmly rooted to the deck, he slowly passed his fingers through his hair in a casual, contented manner.

Mesmerised by the rising sun and the magnificent scene unravelling before his very eyes, it moved him to tears—the simplicity and beauty of it all. The more times he watched the sunrise, it never failed to give him such joy. It made him glad to be alive and sometimes he needed to be reminded of that, for nature was cruel as well as a creator of great beauty.

There was a cough from behind and there Gus Brown stood with the captain's hot chocolate. He pondered the steaming mug.

"The milk still…?"

"Fresh as a daisy, Captain, well a drooping daisy that is. Should be fine for a day or so yet."

Gus asked, "Don't you get fed up, Captain?"

"Fed up with being pestered, certainly." He smiled at the sailor come cook come doctor's assistant.

"No, Captain; fed up with watching the sea, sunrise, and all that."

"Ah, I see. This ritual of mine, for that is what it is, reminds me at the beginning of each day of the wonder of it all. The wonder of nature; its beauty but also its terror. I need to be reminded for all our sakes; complacency is a harsh taskmaster."

He turned towards Seaman Augustus Brown who

was staring at him.

"I never thought of it like that, Captain. Doctor James would have a big word for that."

"I reckon you are right. Thank you for this." Captain Fothergill lifted his mug in acknowledgement. "Simple things like hot chocolate make my life bearable, easier if you like, and I appreciate it."

Seaman Brown smiled his soppy grin, for he liked the captain and thought any sailor in his right mind would agree.

The captain watched the sunrise and with it the light and warmth it brought. A familiar sight. He glanced upwards at the billowing sails. After leaving the Port of Lisbon, progress had been fair. Variable winds and his preferred circuitous route to avoid pirates who peppered the Spanish and French coastlines had made progress less than he would have liked.

Whilst taking a wide berth may well leave the Pegasus at the mercy of the elements, it would still be safer than meeting the brigands and pirates that blighted the coast. Really it was a simple decision for him to make.

He knew he could not fight the marauding brigands but, as an experienced captain, he could navigate and out sail them and therefore the odds were more in his favour.

Clive Fothergill glanced upwards to the top of the middle-mast and to the crow's nest. In his experience, not the most popular place for a sailor to spend his time. It was cold, miserable and dangerous but crucial to the safety of any ship. After losing one of his sailors overboard, he had his second-in-command, John

Mason—a clever and astute sailor who it seems could turn his hand to anything which involved intuition and a rope—devise a sling to attach a man securely to the mast.

Ironically, the crow's nest was now a popular place, for even as he looked up at the mast, one tall and one smaller figure were scrambling up the rigging at a pace, with slings over their shoulders. As they reached the crow's nest, he could see Johnny Mason secure his young charge before himself.

Young Billy had the eyes of a hawk and with the experience of Mason, they were an ideal partnership; a partnership that the captain had every faith in. Captain Fothergill shook his head and smiled. The transformation of young Billy from a disrespectful and unruly boy to something coming up to mature and sensible was astonishing. Even his change of name suited him!

He then shouted for the ship's carpenter, Danny Johnson, whereupon a blonde-haired, tall man with muscular shoulders, powerful arms and steel-blue eyes appeared quietly for such a big man, knuckle to forehead in salute.

"Aye, aye, Captain."

Nodding towards the middle-mast, he said, "Mr Johnson, the middle-mast, how's it bearing up? Will it do us? Get us back to Bristol?"

"Should do, sir, as long as the weather doesn't turn nasty. The work by Richard Hardwick. Well, words fail me, Captain, they really do."

Able Seaman Johnson shook his head in dismay.

Captain Fothergill nodded. "You've done a fine job,

Mr Johnson. Indeed, you have. Forecasts are good and we will be in Bristol afore too long. Monitor it for me and report directly to me if there are any changes."

"Aye, Captain."

Content the ship was making progress, he signalled to Abel Joyce his intention to go below deck to break his fast, which he normally took in his own cabin before starting the ship's daily log. His routine was well established.

Passing by the galley he would shout, "Break-fast if you please, Mr Brown."

A voice from the galley would reply, "Aye, Captain."

The captain made his way to his cabin, removing his jacket with care before placing it gently on his cot like a devoted father would place a sleeping infant in his bed. He sat behind his large desk and opened the ship's log. He picked up a pen in his left hand, dipped it in the ink, and wrote:

24th August 1720. At sea. Wind from the southwest now enables the Pegasus to make progress. Urgent repairs to the middle-mast undertaken in Lisbon holding up well. Shoddy work by Richard Hardaker and Sons, the chandler's at Bristol.

Captain Clive Fothergill.

The condition of the main mast was a worry. In fact, it had been clear on the outward journey from Bristol to Lisbon that all was not well. They evidenced a split from the base of the mast where it was fitted to the deck, and where a repair had been made by Hardaker and Sons when the Pegasus had been in dry dock in May.

Small initially it may have been, but Billy Thomas well spotted it as the Pegasus entered Lisbon harbour. Clive Fothergill thought himself fortunate at the time as the ship's carpenter, Danny Johnson undertook emergency repairs and had extra support built into the mast, along with a metal ring around the base for the homeward journey. However, the split had in fact extended further up the mast. It was a worry indeed and much depended on pleasant weather.

There was a sharp rat–a–tat–tat on his door. Captain Fothergill opened the door to reveal Gus Brown holding a tray. As ever serious over his cooking, Gus Brown walked solemnly into the cabin and placed the wooden tray, heavily laden with food, onto the desk.

"Best cut of beef, Captain and the bread is weevil free. I promise."

The captain stared at the bread. "You said that yesterday."

Shaking his head in dismay, he replied, "The little buggers get everywhere, Captain. Ale is safe, though."

The captain sat at his desk and ate the thick slices of bread and salted beef, knowing that whatever the quality of the food on his tray it would be better than that which his crew would be having.

After his meal, he took a key from his inside jacket pocket and opened a locked drawer in his desk where he kept the ship's inventory and key to the hold. He then went down into the ship's hold to look at the cargo the Pegasus was carrying.

Clive Fothergill was a quick learner. On his first

voyage as the captain ten years ago, he had allowed the Cargo Overseer, a certain Malcolm Harrison to keep the inventory to check the cargo. However, Harrison had indulged himself on fine wines, which he had replaced with seawater, along with some fine leather boots replaced by his own. The inventory had tallied of course and only when he was back at sea were the discrepancies identified by an angry vintner and boot maker, as well as angry owners, George Castle and Jonathan B Jerome. Clive Fothergill understood without access to the inventory, the Overseer had little idea of the exact amount of cargo a ship was carrying, nor could the inventory be forged.

Whilst he trusted his Cargo Overseer, Jonah King, as much as you could trust any sailor, the temptation was a wondrous thing. A bottle lost here, a bolt of cloth there would cause an angry Bristol vintner or merchant, or a well-dressed and drunken overseer.

Fortunately, the journey had not been arduous and so he expected the cargo would not have had any breakages and the inventory would be the same. Jonah King was at his post, a small desk with a lamp upon it, at the entrance of the main hold. Seeing the captain approach, he stood, swollen knuckle to his brow in salute.

"Morning, Captain."

"Let's take a look, Mr King."

He handed the Overseer the keys and waited for the heavy wooden door to be unlocked. Picking up his lamp, the Overseer led the way.

"I could save you all this time, Captain. Honest, I could. I'd do the checking and you need not worry about me being tempted like, sir. Wouldn't let you down."

Clive Fothergill looked his Overseer in the eye. "An enormous responsibility, Mr King, a captain's I think."

The checking of the cargo by Captain Fothergill was quickly done.

"I will give some thought whether to give you more responsibility. You will let me down but once, I warn you."

"Aye, Captain."

Clive Fothergill, pondering whether to give his Overseer more responsibility, returned to his cabin. He replaced the inventory and cargo hold key in his top drawer, locked it, and then placed the key into his inside coat pocket tapping absent-mindedly.

Clive Fothergill walked slowly up the wooden steps to the door leading to the deck followed by Mr King. As he did so, the ship shuddered, and it threw him backwards, landing on the hapless Overseer with a thud.

Stunned momentarily, he got to his feet, grateful for the thick-set Overseer who cushioned his fall and who remained prostrate and winded on the floor. Cautiously, he climbed the stairs and grabbed the door handle for some stability as the ship once more shuddered. He opened the door to be met with darkness despite it being midday and wind that howled and snarled with such ferocity he stood quietly to get his breath and regain his composure. He could see Abel Joyce was at the wheel. It was a relief to see his best man in such a key position and tentatively he made his way to him.

"Why didn't you call me, Mr Joyce?"

Caleb Joyce was straight-faced. "Came from nowhere, Captain. Wind was getting up a bit, clouds flying but nothing to worry about, then this from nowhere. Never seen such like afore. The mast needs looking at, Captain. Serious."

Caleb Joyce nodded at the middle-mast swaying in the wind like a drunken sailor.

"I hope Mr Mason and young Thomas aren't still on the lookout, Mr Joyce."

"No, Captain. They could see something was coming, so they got down sharpish like, and they just made it. He sent Billy to look for you, Captain."

As if by magic, a dishevelled and out-of-breath John Mason, blood pouring from a head wound, appeared with Seaman Johnson and Billy Thomas behind.

"Below with you, Mr Mason. See the doctor as that looks nasty."

"But, Captain," replied his second in command, "all hands are needed on deck. We need..."

John Mason's eyes glazed over, and slowly he slumped to the deck. Captain Fothergill turned to the now-named Seaman Thomas.

"Hurry now, fetch the doctor."

Without a second word, the lad bolted like a catapult shot, quickly disappearing below deck.

Snapping orders, the captain turned to the ship's carpenter, Seaman Johnson.

"Can you do anything? The mast may well be the death of us all."

The words were barely out of his mouth when a wave crashed over the bow running amok on the deck like marauding pirates, scattering the crew to different corners of the beleaguered ship. Only Caleb Joyce, hands secured to the wheel, remained at his post. It was fortunate there were no injuries or men lost overboard. The captain got up and walked slowly to stand behind Seaman Joyce, who was in a more sheltered position. His mind raced with the dire position the Pegasus was in. He glanced up at the dark and angry sky then at the raging sea below. The waves towering above the ship were throwing it about as a cat would play with a mouse.

Whipped up by the angry wind, a wave—foaming like a deranged man frothing at the mouth—plucked the Pegasus from the sea, turning it this way and then that as if examining its prize before dashing it down in disdain. The ship shuddered and groaned. Captain Fothergill grimaced. In all his years at sea, he had seen nothing like this. It was terrifying. Mast or no mast, the ship was in trouble.

Below deck, Doctor James was in his treatment room. Billy knocked on his door.

"Yes," said an impatient Doctor James.

Stirred from his lapse, Billy shook his head to clear his mind.

"You are needed on deck, Doctor. Now!"

Frowning and annoyed at the disturbance, he responded, "Can't it wait? You can see I am with a patient."

His eyes moved from the doctor to the young slave boy, then back again.

Eyes like a fish floundering on dry land, the boy spluttered. "But the storm! The Pegasus; the mast it is..."

Words failed him. He was rescued as the ship, battered yet again, shuddered and groaned. Doctor James, Billy and the slave boy were hurled against the door with such force it shattered. Momentarily stunned, they lay badly winded but miraculously uninjured.

As calm as ever, Doctor James got to his feet, helping the two boys and as he did, so a thought came to his mind.

"Billy, where is young Sam? Is he safe? Just stay there." Stephen James pointed at the slave boy before following Billy Thomas up the steps to the door leading onto the deck.

The heavy wooden door would not budge and so together the doctor and boy threw all their might as best they could in such a confined space to batter it down. As they did, it opened suddenly, and it hurled the two out. The Pegasus poised precariously on top of a wave tipping over the edge, heading downwards into the swirling mass below and throwing anything not tied down towards the prow of the ship or overboard.

In the resulting melee, Doctor James and Billy got separated. The doctor, shocked by the sheer noise of the storm that by now had engulfed the ship and the chaos it had left in its wake, leaned against ropes that were still coiled and secured in place on deck. He squatted on his hands and knees and took a deep breath to calm his mind.

He needed time to think about what they needed from him. Gradually getting to his feet, he headed in the wheel's direction and therefore to Captain Fothergill. After what seemed a lifetime (but in reality a few minutes) he found him next to Caleb Joyce who was still at the wheel. Stephen shouted to his friend, but his words seemed to be hurled back at him by the wind. Moving closer, he tapped the captain on his shoulder and as his friend turned, he saw anguish etched on his face.

"Thank you for coming so promptly, Stephen. Mr Johnson needs your help. You must get him below deck."

The doctor followed his friend's nod to a figure slumped on the deck a few feet away. At that moment, a wave crashed over the bow smashing into the middle-mast, plucking it up and hurling it over the side. Mr Johnson went with it.

The Pegasus was doomed. Oh, for a pair of wings to fly the stricken ship away from this hell on earth.

Billy had become tangled amongst fallen rigging that had saved him from being dragged overboard. He cursed as he disentangled himself from the ropes before going to help young Sam, who had the body of a dead Gus Brown resting on his lap. The relief at company amongst the chaos was clear in his expression.

"Captain Fothergill wanted the rigging cut free lest it drag the ship down, so Gus and I set to it and then a wave as high as heaven came crashing down on to us and..."

At that, tears welled up in the young boy's eyes. A sob wracked through his body.

Gently, Billy placed an arm around his shoulder. "We must find the captain. He will need our help. Gus would expect us to do that."

Samuel nodded solemnly and with care, he placed

Gus's body on the floor and unravelled himself from the rigging, and Billy made his way slowly on hands and knees to his captain, who was at the wheel. The Pegasus was battling hard against a mighty foe, for the ocean was unforgiving and had surrounded the ship, howling and screaming.

Arriving at the wheel, there was no one to be seen other than a lifeless Caleb Joyce, hands still tied to the wheel.

"Billy, the mast it's gone," stated Samuel, now staring at where the mast should have been.

The ship groaned and shuddered like a mortally wounded animal fighting its last fight and gasping its last breath, whilst waiting for the last attack. There was a rumbling noise from below deck, a terrifying pounding of feet and a humming. Both boys stood still mesmerised, unable to make it out. The noise became louder and louder and reached a terrifying pitch, when the door to below deck exploded, and out poured an army of rats heading in their hundreds from the bilges below.

The boys were horrified, stood frozen to the spot, as rats in sheer panic ran by them, round them, and over them—anywhere rather than be drowned in a sinking, stinking ship. Following a large black rat, which appeared to be the leader of this horde, they all headed towards open space and open air and over the side.

Despite their young ages, the two boys realised the enormity of what they had just witnessed. Rats were leaving a sinking ship. The boys looked around them and there was not a soul in sight. The storm had calmed a little and with it, the noise.

"We have to jump ship, Sam."

Sam nodded. "We need to grab whatever we can to take with us."

They opened the door to below deck and stood back, lest there were any more rats.

"Two minutes to grab what you can and meet me here."

Sam said, "And the doctor, Billy?"

Billy shook his head. "The doctor was with the captain when I last saw him, Sam. He left the slave boy below deck. We have to find him."

Billy continued gibbering and not making much sense. Sam nodded and went into the galley as quickly as he was able. He grabbed a bag and food, and anything else he could find. He knew they had little time.

Billy went to the treatment room to look for the slave boy. There was no sign of anyone and he knew what they took was important. He grabbed knives and bandages before thrusting them into a small canvas bag he found. He hurried out of the treatment room and saw Sam. Together, they entered the captain's cabin. Grabbing what they could, including a telescope, they wrapped it all in an oilcloth.

Underneath the desk they found the small slave boy huddled in terror.

The Pegasus groaned, awakening them from their revelry for, momentarily, they had forgotten the peril they were in. Together Billy and Sam scrambled under the table, both grabbing one of the boy's hands. They ran down the corridor and to the stairs, dragging the startled boy in their wake. The parlous state they were in stared them starkly in the face. It was being battered to death. The starboard side was nearly touching the sea and so they decided that was the point from which they should jump. The ocean was full of debris from the Pegasus like leftovers from a banquet: wood, ropes, floating barrels, rigging, canvas, and bodies. The waves were a floating, deadly graveyard.

Hand in hand, the three boys stood, terrified to jump, but too terrified to stay.

CHAPTER TEN

24th August

The battered Pegasus was perched precariously a-top of a giant wave, oblivious to the imminent catastrophe it was about to face. Wind howled and shrieked, haranguing the beleaguered ship to dare to topple over into the sea below. The three boys stood on what was left of the deck, the sole survivors. No captain, no doctor, no crew, not even a rat.

Billy Thomas stood in the middle of the three boys as they teetered on the edge of extinction. He was, he believed, the leader of this tiny band and was the captain, and these two boys were his responsibility. Standing to his full height, red hair blowing in the wind, his boy's body now tanned and muscular with his cloth bag over his shoulder, he peered over the deck side and turned first to Sam, then the slave boy and grinned.

"We're in a lot of trouble. We are going to have to jump. Do you understand? All of us together."

The slave boy stared in terror at the heaving menacing sea, wondering what he had done in his miserable life to deserve such pain and sorrow. Sam had his eyes tight shut, praying, something he had instinctively done. His mother had taught him, he recalled. He smiled to himself at another memory.

Billy took hold of the hand of each boy and stepped forward.

"Now," he shouted, but the words disappeared with

the wind and flying foam.

He tugged the two boys and pulled them with him into the abyss below. They fell for what seemed an eternity before they hit the sea beneath. The shock of the impact stunned them whilst the cold sucked their very breath away.

The slave boy was sucked beneath the waves. Unable to swim, he resigned himself to death, for what alternative was there? His meagre life flashed before his eyes.

Their village had received news that slave traders were attacking the coastal villages, but the elders believed their village was sheltered and therefore safe. Complacent, perhaps! His father talked about the slave traders as snakes creeping through the grass to catch people unawares and some of the biggest snakes were close to their home. How would the slave traders know where to attack? This, he found confusing.

The second confusing thing was the men who attacked the village were black. Their own people captured them and then sold them to white men! Yet, here he was at death's door, with two white boys at his side.

Closing his eyes and wishing to die, he felt a sharp tug on the back of the coat he had been given and was being dragged to the surface by Billy Thomas. Swallowing mouthfuls of water, he gasped and writhed like a floundering fish, arms and legs in every direction. Billy had spied one of the ship's rowing boats they used as transport to and from the shore and between ships when docked in the harbour. Their first bit of luck—the boat was unscathed. He then dragged the slave boy onto a large piece of wood which had a rope tied to it. Quickly, Billy wrapped the rope around the boy to secure him to the wood next to Sam, who had a gash to his forehead but other than that was cheerful considering he had nearly drowned.

The slave boy stared at his rescuer and the bloodied boy who grinned back at him. Perhaps he was not bad after all. Perhaps it was his fate to survive. At that moment, he decided he would make his parents proud of him. He nodded his gratitude to Billy and smiled at the bloodied Sam. Having clambered onto the rowing boat, Billy dragged the slave boy, who he knew was in the worst state of the three of them, in before finally dragging Sam on board.

Survival was at the forefront of Billy's thoughts, and he wondered how his young charges would cope with the perils they faced. He need not have worried. Sam and the slave boy were re-invigorated and there seemed to be an understanding between them. Billy's first job was to make their meagre craft secure, to provide some sort of cover and ensure none of them could be washed overboard. They had some more good fortune. The storm dissipated as quickly as it appeared. The sea seemed to have lost all its might, fight and anger, which meant their boat was becalmed along with debris from the Pegasus.

There was plenty of wood, canvas, ropes, barrels and such floating on the surface. Billy recognised they had to make use of whatever they could but also needed to know the debris was a danger to their small craft, which was already struggling underneath the fallen ropes, useful when they clambered on board. Although the boat was small, it was about the length of three sailors placed head-to-head, and one sailor wide was just about sufficient for three boys.

Shelter was a priority to protect them from bad weather and the heat of the day.

Sam and Billy had knives in their belts and with the help of the slave boy, they used the ropes already lying on top of their craft to secure and strengthen it, and give them grips to hang onto should it be needed. Canvas floating on the sea was cut and shaped, before being brought on board. They made a rough shelter to protect them from the weather. The slave boy pointed to the knife in Billy's belt and held out his hand. Wide-eyed, Billy shook his head having heard stories of African savages. Samuel calmly placed his hand on his friend's shoulder, smiled at the slave boy, and offered his own knife for he knew if they were to have any chance of survival then it would take all three of them to work together. He and Billy had to trust the boy, and he had to trust them. Despite his young age, Sam understood this was a crucial point in their relationship. The alternative was unthinkable.

Billy glared at him. He was the leader, was he not? So he considered what Captain Fothergill would have done; he was a disciplinarian, and yet still gave his men the opportunity to prove themselves. Had he not helped him, giving him a chance when he had not deserved it?

Billy smiled at the slave and nodded his head at Samuel. Billy placed one hand on Samuel's hand in which he held his knife, before passing his own knife to him. He then turned his back on the slave boy to

Lost At Sea

recover a barrel floating gently by, but ever alert.

The boy was a revelation. Using the knife quickly and with great skill, he cut off pieces of rope before separating individual strands. He made holes in the canvass, then cut a piece of the canvas off, making holes before threading the strands through. Sam then helped him secure the canvas over the boat, overseen by Billy who then made the ropes secure as he had done so many times under the watchful eye of John Mason.

The slave boy handed the knife back to Billy and smiled shyly at him. Billy, hands on hips, struck a serious captain-like pose and nodded at the boy. They then looked at what they could make of the debris that surrounded their boat. They carefully examined the smaller barrels one at a time. They made a small hole in the barrel's top so they could check the contents and if necessary, make a bung to secure it, and even salvaged a small barrel of salted fish, barrels of brandy and sherry, and a barrel of biscuits, securing them all on the side of the boat.

Wood passed them by alongside drowned sailors who were becoming bloated and turning from blue to black. Gruesome. Despite the overwhelming stench of seawater and decay, Billy insisted checking the bodies of their fallen comrades was his job. He removed from their bodies what he thought could be used: belts, buckles, jackets, a knife, a pistol, and a bag of coins. Billy patted the two boys on the back and nodded.

"Well done. Well done."

The shelter was basic but would suffice. The last task was to give the slave boy a name unless he had already got one. Billy was unsure about darkest Africa and whether people had names. Sitting quietly after their exertions, he patted both boys on the back and turned to Sam.

"We have to give our friend a name."

Billy nodded towards the slave boy who was seated opposite. Samuel grinned and nodded. He was an odd sight. They had bandaged his head within an inch of its life with a piece of coloured cloth from Billy's bag, which made him look quite sinister.

Samuel turned to the slave boy. He pointed at Billy. "Him, Billy." He then pointed at his own bandaged head. "Me. Sam. You?"

He pointed at the slave boy who grinned and pointed at his own head.

"Ottobah."

This was the first time they had heard Ottobah speak. In fact, it was the first word Ottabah had spoken since his capture many weeks before. The sound of his voice was a pleasant surprise to his own ears and a shock to his two friends.

He had been fearful of looking into the eyes of these boys for he had been told by the village elder that their eyes could penetrate your very soul. Eyes cast down was the best way to avoid such a disaster. However, Ottobah was still alive and whilst with these two white boys, he had in fact looked into their eyes several times. He had not shrivelled as he had been told.

Taken aback by Ottobah's strong accent and rich voice for such a small boy, Billy smiled.

"Otto it is."

"Otto?" questioned Ottobah, shaking his head. "Otto

bah." The sound of his own voice shocked and pleased him. He laughed and shouted at the top of his voice. "Otto bah. Otto bah. Otto bah."

Samuel and Billy stared at their new friend, shocked he could speak and shocked he had a name. Sam started laughing and joined his new friend in chanting out loud.

"Otto bah. Otto bah."

Somehow, Samuel seemed to understand having not spoken a single word for so long, Ottabah had found his voice again and more than that, he needed to hear himself chant his name, as if doing so made it more real and Ottobah more alive.

Staring at his two friends, Billy shook his head.

"Ottobah it is."

The sun was at its zenith and hence at its hottest. The wind was soft and the sea gentle. Billy and Sam sheltered under the canvass whilst Ottobah sat at the front of their boat. Each boy sat alone with his thoughts. Ottabah had the freedom to breathe fresh air, smell the sea and sit with his head upturned with the breeze fully in his face.

Billy was considering what they would eat and drink. How would they catch fish? If it should rain, how would they collect water?

Samuel simply wondered about his family. During those dark moments when the three of them had jumped from the sinking Pegasus and into the sea, his short life flashed before him. It had not only been quite frightening but also confusing. He had odd feelings of familiarity. Like somehow knowing how to pray.

As the heat of the day passed, Billy and Sam crept

from under the canvas and sat one on each side of Ottobah in companionable silence, staring out to sea. As they did so, the sea seemed to change before their eyes with flashes of light that meant they had to shield their eyes with a hand. Then came a noise, a strange noise, a terrifying noise, that none of them had heard before. A bubbling. Their boat seemed to move at greater speed as if carried by a torrent of water, and then it happened.

Large fish in their hundreds leapt from the ocean and the entire sea appeared to come to life before their very eyes like a boiling, writhing cauldron. The expanse of ocean as far as the three boys could see was alive with fish that seemed excited and joyful to be travelling on a long journey to God knows where. The small boat was buffeted about and sent spinning, and in that moment of great wonder at what was unfolding before them, the three friends cheered until their lungs would burst, or the boat would collapse. Then a second miracle happened for one fish mistimed its leap and landed on the boat. Billy, quick as lightening, leapt on the biggest fish he had seen in his life to hold it down.

He shouted at his friends, "Hit it with something, quick!"

Sam grabbed a spare piece of wood, which was as long as a man's arm and which they had fortunately scavenged for what purpose he did not know. He raised it above his head.

"The fish, not me, Sam."

The fish was not giving up without a struggle and Billy was floundering and sliding on the slippery creature. Ottobah grabbed its tail, and was hurled over the edge of their boat, hanging on for dear life to one rope securing the canvas roof.

Without hesitation, Sam brought the wood down onto the fish's head with all his strength and then he dropped onto his hands and knees for fear of falling overboard. By this time, Ottobah was becoming tired as he grimly hung on.

The fish was stunned momentarily. Billy grabbed his knife from his belt and rammed it into the throat of the fish to kill it. Shattered and slimy, Billy collapsed.

Meanwhile, Sam grabbed one of Ottobah's hands with both of his. However, the boat had become treacherous with the slime from the fish and Sam could not keep a firm grip of Ottobah's hand. He was in danger of falling overboard himself as well as losing his new friend. Distraught, Samuel looked into the pleading eyes of Ottabah. He gritted his teeth for one last pull when two hands came over his shoulders and grabbed both arms. Together, Billy and Samuel dragged Ottabah back on the boat and the three boys fell unceremoniously on top of the fish.

They lay exhausted. The shoal disappeared into the sunset and the sea calmed. Billy, who was the strongest of the three boys, was the first to recover and sat with knees under his chin, staring at the goggle-eyed fish.

"We need to gut the fish and cut it into small pieces to last us. Can you do it with me?"

Sam shook his head and in a whisper. "No."

He was exhausted and felt a wet patch on his head. His head wound had reopened.

"Ottobah!"

Billy nodded at the fish and removed his knife from

the back of his trousers. Understanding immediately, Ottobah grinned and pointed at the knife and then at himself. Sam handed him his knife. Between the two, the fish was gutted and cut into small portions. Hopefully, thought Billy, it should last them a little while and give them a chance of survival.

"All we need now is water," Billy said to no one in particular.

Ruefully, he glanced up at the cloudless sky. Not much chance of that, he thought.

"And we need to be prepared."

Billy considered what Danny Johnson would have done in his position. Danny could construct anything from nothing and would have made a container of some sort from what they had in the boat. With the help of Ottabah, they cut a piece of canvas, folded it in two, and placed it into a small empty barrel they had salvaged. Billy scooped sea water into the barrel, and it did not leak. A relief. Until there was some rain, they would have to make do with the moisture from the fish.

The days at sea dragged slowly by. Sam watched as Ottobah bent a thin piece of metal into the shape of a hook which he then tied to the end of a piece of twine and dangled into the sea. Billy was staring into the distant horizon deep in thought.

The Pegasus had been at sea for several days on its journey back to Bristol and the last time he had been in the crow's nest, Seaman Mason thought they were well up the French coast and heading towards the English Channel. How far the ship had been blown off course by the storm was anyone's guess.

Billy had learned basic things from Danny. He knew

the sun rose in the east and set in the west, but that was about it. He could not see land.

"Sam, pass me the telescope. We need to work out where we are."

The telescope, wrapped in oilcloth, was salvaged from the captain's cabin. They had placed the telescope in a barrel that had been found amongst the debris and which had contained a small leather-bound book. They then placed the telescope in the barrel alongside it for safekeeping. Amazingly, the book and the telescope stayed dry.

He removed the telescope, carefully replacing the bung to secure the barrel, before handing it to Billy.

The book had intrigued Sam and so a little while later, giving in to curiosity, he removed the bung and opened the barrel. He lifted out the book and unwrapped the oilcloth. Resting the small book on his knee, he pondered a while. Why had the small book been placed in the barrel and why was it so carefully protected? It was as if someone had hoped the barrel and the book would be discovered. He shook his head in wonder at the likelihood the barrel would be discovered on the high seas and by the only survivors of a shipwreck. It was as if someone was watching over them.

Sam removed the covering which revealed a small book, a diary, in fact, belonging to Doctor Stephen James. It was not what he expected. The ship's log, fair enough, but not this. He opened the book. However, he closed it gently, thinking the writing was something personal to the doctor, who he had admired so much, and who saved his life.

But then! But then! The book was supposed to be found and if that was so, then it was his responsibility to read it. Reverently, Sam opened the pages. The first one listed the names of the crew which he read slowly one by one, a finger following each line. Familiar names, some of whom he knew well, were written there. The doctor had recorded the condition of each sailor along with observations about their health. It showed the last two entries as 'two stowaways.'

It described one as fit and healthy if a little thin and about thirteen years of age. The second younger, about ten years of age, well fed but badly injured about the head. A note was added: 'The injuries to this boy were severe, deliberate. Indeed, he has been lucky to have survived at all.'

"Billy, look what I have here. It's the doctor's notebook—a diary from the Pegasus..." His voice trailed away.

Billy tilted his head and frowned as if trying to recall some distant memory before staring at his friend.

"You sure?"

Sam nodded. Billy, rather than standing and stepping across the raft which was still slippery underfoot from the left-over fish slime and seawater, slithered across on his backside to sit beside him. Carefully placing the telescope to one side, Billy sniffed at his hands, and grimaced before wiping them on his already stinking pants.

"How do you know?" asked Billy.

"It says so here."

He read the first two pages out loud whilst Billy gawped at his friend, mouth wide like an upturned

Lost At Sea

barrow of apples tumbling to the ground.

"You can read!" said Billy in astonishment.

"Yes. It appears I can," was the shy response.

"Well, see if there is anything about us. About how we ended up on the ship. We had to have come on the Pegasus at the same time. Somehow! You and me. It makes little sense otherwise. Look for the Pegasus docking in Bristol the last time. June or July. Understand?"

Sam nodded, but he had doubts. "But this is the doctor's diary, not the ship's log."

Billy shrugged his shoulders.

"It says the Pegasus arrived in the Bristol Docks on the 30th of June but..." Samuel continued to turn the pages. "What was the date the Pegasus left Bristol? I have no memory of it."

"23rd July."

"Here we are." Samuel read the words, muttering to himself as he did so.

"Just before midnight on the 22nd, the night watch reported suspicious noises on the quayside. Whispering, then a loud thud. But there was no sound of a splash like someone falling into the water. How odd. The captain then ordered the crew to make a search of the dockside to ensure no one was attempting to get on board or had been hurt. They found nothing."

Tears welled in Sam's eyes at the confusion of everything. "I can read, I don't know how. I say my prayers, I don't know why. There is a carved ship in my pocket. And... I feel someone is looking out for me." He wiped his eyes and turned to his friend, Billy. "What about you? Will you have any family looking for you?"

Billy shook his head, his red unkempt hair blowing in the wind. He shrugged his shoulders.

"Depends! My mother worked for Mr Bernard doing his washing and such and that was how I met him, and then I started running messages. He was a fair man if you understand, few about, and he said we could have a room in a new house he was buying. If she is living there, he might miss me, or my mother might, and tell him. So, maybe!"

CHAPTER ELEVEN

Bristol 26th August

Harry Wetherell, the innkeeper of the Ship Inn was true to his word. One of his customers was a local man called Edward Champion and Ned for short. Ned worked at the Customs and Excise Depot at the dockside. On the 22nd of July, he had been at the depot at first light and was rewarded by an early finish if he deposited letters at the Martin's Bank in Bristol.

At noon he took his leave, arriving a little later in the town centre. It was then he came across a crowd of people, in the middle of which was a young lad and a very drunk man. The drunken man had accused the youth of theft, which he hotly disputed. Ned thought the debacle was getting out of hand as by now the very drunken man was increasingly irate and kept shouting at the young fellow.

"Do you know who I am?"

He insisted on calling for the Constable to deal with the young thief. Sharply, the lad ran off toward the docks.

Ned shook his head at the palaver and continued to the bank where he deposited the letters. He then went to a local high-class tailor's shop where his wife, Elizabeth worked. Later that afternoon, Ned and Elizabeth were on their way home when they witnessed an incident involving a group of men.

However, at this time of year, they travelled to the farm owned by Elizabeth's parents, which was called

High Gate Farm. The farm was located south of Bristol. So, the next morning they left for the farm. This was their annual holiday where they worked hard and were well fed, returning home with enough provisions to keep them going over winter.

On the 22nd of August, having returned home to Bristol, Ned visited the Ship Inn—his local. Upon entering the Inn, he read the two posters about the missing boys. The description of the older of the boys seemed very similar to the lad accused of theft and if truth be told, the incident had prayed on his mind somewhat.

He told Harry Wetherell about the two events he had witnessed. The first one involved a drunken man and youth accused of theft. The second one took place a little later that same afternoon when he was with his wife. A group of men had been acting oddly. In fact, Ned actually doubted what he had witnessed for one man seemed to be the same drunken man he had seen earlier, and who had miraculously sobered up. Even then, Harry had not understood the significance of these chance encounters until Jonathan's recent visit. True to his word, the innkeeper sent a message to Jonathan to say Ned Champion would be at the Ship Inn the following day at noon.

Jonathan sent young Noah Thomas with a message for Grace and William Castle to meet him there.

William and Grace set off in plenty of time to give them time to consider the implications. They pondered the news Jonathan had mentioned. They had a new witness, a man named Edward Champion.

At noon, Grace and William arrived at the Ship Inn.

As they entered, the customers turned together, nodded, smiled, and then continued their quiet chatter. Jonathan, who was already there, was seated at the back of the room and waved at them to join him. The innkeeper efficiently appeared and wandered over to welcome the Castles.

Harry nodded at Grace and smiled.

"I am glad to see you, Mrs Castle. All your hard work circulating posters and doing the rounds knocking on doors has had some success."

He placed a jug of ale on the table for the two men and reappeared shortly with a smaller jug for Grace.

"Madeira wine for you."

They had barely sat down when Edward Champion walked into the inn—a short, stocky man with long black curly hair, which deserved to be unkempt but strangely was not, and a tanned face. Ned smiled and nodded to Harry.

"I'm here as I promised."

The innkeeper grinned. "Thank you, Ned. Over here. Mr and Mrs Castle and Mr Jerome need to hear what you have told me. It will soon become clear to you why."

Ned sat at the table. They brought a mug for him to share the ale.

"I understand, Mr Champion," said William Castle, "that on the 22nd of July, you witnessed two events. One involved a young boy, William, and the other possibly our son, Samuel. Is that true?"

"It's Ned. Look, I am not sure whether who I saw that day was in fact the missing boys. The first incident was about twelve noon. I was on my way to the bank when, as I got to the main street at the Round Coffee House, a crowd had gathered in the street and in the middle was a young lad. There was a man who was very drunk; I understand that was George Castle. He accused the lad of stealing from him, which the lad denied. George Castle insisted that a Constable be called saying something like, 'Let us see who he believes. Me, or a guttersnipe like you.' The lad panicked and shot off past me. I thought little more about it then. I did my errand at the bank and called for the missus who works in a tailor's shop, and we set off back home. We walked towards the docks the long way round."

"Ned what time was this?" asked William.

"Good question. I picked Eliza up at three o'clock. So well past four, maybe half-past."

William glanced at Grace.

"It was the missus that spotted them at the head of one of those alleys that lead to the docks. There were five or six men with what looked like a rug that was rolled up and lying on the ground. They were arguing over something which we couldn't hear but one of them looked familiar. I thought to myself, where have I seen him before? Then I realised it was the man who was accusing the young lad of stealing. It was George Castle as I live and breathe. He was jabbing at the chest of one other. Four of them picked up the carpet. Eliza said to me, 'How odd. I thought I saw a pair of feet sticking out of the carpet.' I told her not to be so daft. They walked off down the alley and we returned home. That's it."

William and Grace were stunned by this revelation.

"Ned, are you sure about the day and time of the men with the rug?" asked Jonathan.

"Yes. Banking day. Mrs Champion will tell you the same. She says you can talk to her too."

"Ned, how far away from these men were you? Could you be mistaken at all?" asked Grace Castle.

"Fair question." Ned pondered a while, sucking his teeth in concentration. "We noticed them because they were arguing, a real ding-dong. So, we stood watching them for some time. They were sort of not interested in anyone else and didn't notice us, or so it seemed. How close were we? Now that is difficult, but close enough to recognise George Castle, and close enough to see the rug. Now the missus has eyes like a hawk and can see through walls if you get my drift? She said to me only yesterday she is sure she saw something sticking out of the carpet and she believes it could only be a foot."

Grace tapped the leather bag at her side. "Ned, would you repeat all this for me so I can write it all down in my ledger? I would be most grateful if you would. Sometimes pieces of information we get make little sense. But, then other snippets, such as what you are telling us now, come along and by adding it to what I have already, it makes more sense. A bit like finding the missing piece in a puzzle."

Ned grinned. "Aye for you, Mrs Castle, if the Landlord here will fill this jug up talking and thinking is thirsty work."

Grace Castle and Ned Champion moved to a table at the rear of the inn and out of hearing of other customers. Grace had become good at talking and listening to people and good at being able to glean every bit of information and detail from people that they did not think they had.

Jonathan and William huddled together. The subject of both their concern was George Castle but how and where to start? Ned Champion was an excellent witness, and they believed him. The witnesses Grace had already spoken to had provided sufficient information about the initial incident of a drunken George Castle, and accusing young William Thomas of theft. Ned's explanation of that altercation simply supported what she already knew, which Ned would be unaware of. They knew from Ned's explanation of the first incident involving young William Thomas and George Castle, that his memory of the incident involving the men and the rug was also true. Significantly, because he had seen George Castle earlier that day, he had identified him as one of the men. George Castle was involved.

Jonathan was the first to say what they were both thinking. "William, I realise somehow George is up to his neck in this. I know he is my business partner, but he is your brother and Samuel's uncle."

William shook his head and shrugged his shoulders, dismay etched on his face.

"I suppose we have to be sure and understand how and why George is involved, and I also think we need to wait until Grace speaks to Ned's wife. We either confront George with this information or go to the authorities."

Jonathan nodded and frowned. "What we could really do with, is one of the other men with George to turn coat and tell us. Then that would make it very difficult for George to deny his involvement."

"But I still do not understand why George would get rid of Samuel. What has he to gain?" said William.

"I know George was bitter your father left the family business to you and then to Samuel. He was incandescent with rage when you sent him the letter in which you had decided that, on Samuel's tenth birthday, he was to join the family business. I have rarely seen him so angry. I was quite shocked."

William was horrified. "I knew George was furious at being left out of our father's will, but we did not have any choice in the matter. I now understand because Grace was mentioned in the will, it simply fuelled his fury. George was, however, left a goodly sum in his inheritance and he has done well for himself, thanks mainly to you. I really believed his desire to put this all behind us was an honest one. "

Jonathan contemplated how much he should tell William. In his mind, George had never gotten over the humiliation, as he saw it, of what he believed to his being cheated out of his inheritance, and he had never forgiven his brother, even though the decision was not his to make. Much of his hostility and hatred was directed at Grace, and now onto their ten-year-old son.

Jonathan believed William's father had made the correct decision in leaving the business to the younger more level-headed son and his very competent wife and however hard he, Jonathan, had tried to convey this sentiment to George, he had turned a deaf ear. Jonathan now believed it had gone past the pale.

First, a drunken George had tried to abuse and bully young William Thomas by threatening him with the

Constable and arrest. Who would believe the young boy's word against that of George Castle, a well-to-do figure in Bristol? Second, Mr and Mrs Champion had implicated George in the subsequent abduction of Samuel Castle, who was badly beaten and very lucky to have survived. Jonathan pondered whether George was settling old scores and having his eye on Castle's Merchant Traders. He did wonder if George's real intention was to become a partner by investing in the company, or even buy the company. It was a mess. Jonathan also hoped George had sold his South Sea Company shares as the share price had started to fall as he predicted.

"William, I believe we have to tread cautiously with George," said Jonathan. "I know he has never forgiven your father for leaving Castles' Merchant Traders to you and your wife and now to your son. He felt cheated and betrayed, I know that for a fact. But frankly, like you, I had believed his success with his inheritance had to some extent quenched that fire. On seeing these recent events, I think not."

William nodded. "We need to speak to Ned's wife, which Grace will do, and then see if we can find and persuade any of these men who were with George that day to confide in us. Perhaps Harry, the landlord, may help us."

"Harry… we need your help!" shouted Jonathan.

The following morning, Grace Castle visited Elizabeth Champion at her home—a friendly woman who confirmed what her husband had said. She recalled it was a pleasant day and a treat for Ned and herself to have an afternoon together and so she remembered it well. The walk home, the chat, and the group of six men who seemed to act oddly.

"You know that feeling when something isn't quite right, but you can't quite put your finger on it? If you get me?"

Grace nodded. "What exactly was odd, Eliza?"

Eliza pursed her mouth. "Men don't always get it, do they? But they were furtive, furtive I think that's the word. Huddled together like. One, the one Ned says was George Castle, seemed really cross, prodding his fingers into the chests of two of them. They didn't see us; they were so intense on what they were up to."

"How long were you watching and what about the carpet?"

"We watched them for a few minutes. Ned was telling me the tale about the previous thing with George Castle and the other lad. He said something like, 'That's him, the tall well-to-do man, long boots to his knee, dark curly hair.'"

"And the carpet?"

"Ah, yes. The other man with the rug was quiet and kept looking at the floor as if not happy. It was when the well-to-do man, George Castle, stopped jabbing the other two, they then lifted it onto their shoulders with the quieter one at the front. As they were shuffling it onto their shoulders to get it right, so to speak, that is when I saw something sticking out of the front. Looked like shoes to me. But only for a second. By the time I said to Ned, 'Did you see that?' 'See what?' he replied. I said, 'Shoes out of the rug yonder'. He called me a daft woman. I then doubted for a moment what I had seen. But I am sure."

"Then what happened?"

"They walked down the alley, with the well-to-do man at the back."

"And the time, Eliza?"

"Ned picked me up just after three, we walked around then to home. So, half four, maybe five but no later. We were home by half past."

"Thank you, Eliza, this has been so helpful."

"Do you believe they rolled your boy up in the rug? I wish I had said…" Eliza's words failed her, and she shook her head in dismay.

Grace smiled. "It is possible. We had not even realised Samuel was missing, and it is only recently we have learnt that they had found two boys on the Pegasus. The boy we believe to be Samuel was badly injured, which fits in with what you and your husband have said. Can I ask you and Ned to keep this to yourself? If you see these men again or think of something else, can you let us know or even Harry Wetherell? He knows how to find us."

Grace made her goodbyes to Eliza Champion who she liked because of her straight talking. Like her husband, Ned, no frills, just straight to the point.

Grace believed the Harbour Master had been a great help to them and had decided to visit Jeremy Bryant once more. The following morning, she walked on the dock front. As she got about halfway, she could see a new ship had recently docked.

There were men on the dockside who were talking animatedly and in the middle of whom was Jeremy Bryant. Grace walked towards them but as she approached, she could see the source—an animated

Lost At Sea

Harbourmaster. The ship that had docked was the trading ship, the Kite, which was in a sorry state. One of its masts was lying across the deck, the rigging was torn down, and the prow was battered. Splintered wood was strewn across the deck along with smashed barrels and decking.

Grace stared in dismay. In fact, all honest traders and merchants would have sympathy with the crew and the Kite's owners. Grace was well known and so she walked towards the gathered throng of men to offer her sympathies. She listened to the captain, Nicholas Hibberd who was talking to the Harbourmaster.

"A storm like no other came from nowhere and battered us witless. We are lucky to be alive. As for the cargo, I dread to think what state it is in. A ship caught in the middle of that storm would have had no chance."

"Where have you sailed from?" shouted Grace.

"Lisbon," answered the captain.

The Harbourmaster saw the distress on Grace's face. He knew what she was thinking, for the Pegasus would not be that far behind the Kite.

Grace quickly composed herself and listened intently to the conversation between the sailors and the Harbourmaster.

"Anybody injured?" asked Jeremiah Bryant.

"We have been lucky to have only one man overboard and lost at sea, and another one with a badly injured leg, which might have to come off," replied the captain.

"Any other ships about in the storm?" asked Grace.

Captain Hibberd shrugged his shoulders. "We didn't see any other ships at all. The storm was on us before we could blink. Seen nothing like it. We were lucky to get out alive."

Grace understood it would occupy the Harbourmaster and so she returned home. She needed to talk to her husband and discuss with him the possibility the Pegasus may have been caught in the storm and sunk.

She walked home and pondered the news. It may well be the Pegasus had avoided the storm as described by Captain Hibberd, but the timing was ominous as the ship would have been only a day or so behind the Kite. Either way, the ship would be due now. The feeling Samuel was still alive remained strong.

William was in the office completing the cargo of the Swift along with the delivery to the various merchants in Bristol. Aware that Grace intended to visit Jeremy Bryant, William had not expected Grace to be back in the office until much later. He knew from her expression that something was amiss. Grace sat down opposite William and explained the reason for her being back home sooner than expected.

William's first reaction was that the news was not good. He had long since learned it was no use patronising Grace and so he said what was in his heart.

"If the Pegasus is on time, then this news is not good."

She nodded. "Not good at all. I hope the ship was delayed in Lisbon."

"Or," continued William, "that the Pegasus avoided the storm somehow. Captain Fothergill is a fine captain. We must send a message to give Jonathan our news."

"We need to speak to Jez Bryant as well."

"Yes, but he knows the position concerning the two boys, and that they are on the Pegasus. If there is more information that comes to light or another ship docks, he will let us know, I am sure. By the way, we have had a message from Jonathan. The boy, Noah is waiting in the kitchen to take our reply. Apparently, Jonathan also has some information, and he has suggested we meet him at his home address. He will be at home all day tomorrow. It is about the day the boys disappeared."

"About the group of men and George perhaps?" quipped Grace.

"I will send a message to say we will be with him at noon tomorrow and we also have information that may affect the Pegasus. Knowing Jonathan, he may already know."

Grace left William to reply to Jonathan and went into the kitchen to find Noah helping Alice peel apples for a pie.

The next day, Grace and William Castle arrived at 32 Queen Street, Bristol by horse and carriage. Grace noted the unassuming nature of the modern stone-built property. Typically Jonathan, she thought. William gripped the door knocker and rapped three times. As if waiting behind the door, Mrs Thomas opened it, with Noah peering around his mother.

Mrs Thomas welcomed them inside and said Mr Jerome was waiting for them in his study. Grace asked Mrs Thomas if she could spare a moment. Noah took William to Jonathan Jerome's study. William was astounded by not only the size but that there was such a vast collection of books that could only be described as a library.

"Jonathan, I am in admiration of your study, or should I describe it as a library?"

Jonathan laughed. "Before I purchased number thirty-two, I lived in a variety of rental accommodations. My accounts, ledgers, books, and what have you, were secured in a variety of places. I spent a lot of my time going here and there collecting this book or that ledger and often not having the right ledger at the right time. I vowed if I ever bought my own house, then I would accommodate all of them in one place, hence the extensive study. But the time this has saved me is beyond comprehension."

William nodded and looked at different shelves. "I see you have history books."

"Of course, trade does not exist in isolation." Jonathan added, "We must adapt to circumstances here and on far shores, and trade accordingly. The most successful traders are the ones who can foretell the future."

William laughed and nodded. "Quite true. I am impressed with so much information at hand, so to speak. Your study area is well thought out as well. Impressive. I wish Grace and I had this amount of room."

"My library did not impress your brother, George. That these houses are newly built means you can have a say in the construction. I said I wanted one large, airy, well-lit room for a study and library. They are still building, William so I can help reserve a plot for you."

William nodded. "I need to talk to Grace."

William and Jonathan continued their discussions

whilst Grace followed Mrs Thomas into the kitchen.

"What can I do for you, Mrs Castle?"

"Grace, please, Mrs Thomas. May I call you Edith?"

Edith nodded.

"We are two mothers who have sons that have disappeared into thin air. I just wondered how you are, and how you are doing. Whether it would help both of us to talk?"

Edith sighed. "I keep scratching my head over it. I know Billy is a strong-willed lad, even stroppy, but with my husband away at sea so much or may never be home, Billy has really had to step up and he has, truly he has. Honest as well. I do not believe this rubbish he has stolen from George Castle. Not for one minute, and begging your pardon, Grace, George Castle is both a wastrel and a liar and I dislike him. Got it off my chest, it needed saying."

Grace laughed. "I'm not all that fond of him, Edith and I do not trust him either. That is for your ears only."

"You see it makes little sense. Billy stealing from George Castle, that is. He is Mr Jonathan's business partner so he would tell him if Billy had thieved from him, wouldn't he? Mr Jonathan has put a roof over our heads and been kindness itself to our family. Billy wouldn't put that at risk."

Grace nodded. "Nothing makes any sense. Has Billy said anything about George Castle?"

"Well, not as much as Noah. Billy does not trust him, that is for certain, and he tried to make sure he did all Mr Jonathan's messages to Mr George Castle but sometimes he couldn't. Noah has mentioned a reply from Mr William back to Mr George, something about Samuel following in the business. He went mad so Noah said, something about it should be him. You need to speak to Noah. Really, you do. He will be home soon."

Grace nodded her thanks to Edith Thomas and followed her daughter, Florence to the library where she found the men in discussion over trade and financial matters.

"What do you think of this library, Grace? Everything in one place and a good section on trade and even history. I am envious, indeed I am. Accounts, records, and all business transactions."

It impressed Grace that everything was at hand and easily found. Jonathan had the advantage, however, of a large room combining both business and research. Jonathan led William and Grace to three comfortable chairs surrounding a walnut table.

"Jonathan, are you aware of the news about the docking of the Kite and that it had just returned from Lisbon? Apparently, the ship was fortunate to have survived a terrible storm," said Grace. She continued, "The Pegasus would not have been that far behind. According to the ship's captain, they had been lucky the Kite was not at the bottom of the Atlantic, and he was unsure whether the cargo was salvageable."

Jonathan smiled. "I knew the Kite had docked. I went to the dock first thing this morning. The ship has been lucky, of that there is no doubt. As for the cargo, I hope they are well insured. I fully understand the implications for the Pegasus." He shook his head. "We can only hope and pray for the ship's safe return."

Lost At Sea

"You have some news for us about Samuel and William?" said Grace.

"Yes indeed. It makes for grim telling I am afraid and that is why I suggested we meet in private. Grace, you may remember the description by Ned and Eliza Champion of the group of men with a rug and that Eliza thought she saw a foot sticking out of it?"

Grace nodded.

"You may also remember them commenting about one man, the one at the front who looked ill at ease. It is that man who has not so much come forward as having been found by one of Harry Wetherell's customers. Now he will put nothing in writing because he is terrified of George and this gang of men."

Jonathan looked at Grace and William.

"By now, you know that George never forgave your father for leaving Castles' Merchant Traders to you instead of him. His resentment has been burning ever since. He was furious. In addition, George is desperate to shore up his finances. I had warned him to get rid of all of his South Sea Company shares, but he did not, as he felt if he could just hold his nerve, he would make a small fortune. We know that will not happen." Jonathan continued, "Also, George needs the Pegasus to return to Bristol with a profitable cargo. If the cargo on the Pegasus was damaged, or God forbid it sinks, the Maritime Insurance takes time to pay out. George does not have that time. Apparently, he has been on the lookout for someone to be paid, professionals that is, to kidnap Samuel and then send you a ransom demand of something like £15,000 or more."

William gasped. "That amount may bankrupt us."

Grace shook her head in dismay. "Not quite, but we would have to sell the Swift and reduce our trading."

"Precisely," added Jonathan. "And you would do that. Sell the Swift, that is?"

Grace and William looked at each other and nodded.

"Of course," said William.

"Now I don't know for sure, but I think George would borrow enough to buy the Swift, and when the ransom was paid to him, he would pay the mercenaries and then settle the amount he had borrowed. By doing so, he would also become an investor. That is not the end of it I am afraid. If George becomes a substantial investor in the Company, then this may of course result in him being a partner. He has asked his solicitor to look at his legal position in what *is* a family business. He would not admit this I suspect, but insist he was simply supporting the family business which, as a partner, he would be entitled to do."

William and Grace were shocked.

"What happened next?" asked William.

"George hired six mercenaries to capture Samuel by some subterfuge or other which would leave George with a clean pair of hands. William, do you remember that day on the dockside when we were doing the last business with the Pegasus, and you realised you were going to be delayed and thought about sending Samuel home ahead? If you recall, George was in a temper that day and left early saying he felt ill. But, he had in fact seen his chance to kidnap Samuel, and he sent a quick note to the Rat and Barrel Inn telling his gang that an opportunity had unexpectedly presented itself. They had been told by George to meet him in an alley near your home. Apparently, four mercenaries and a fifth man, from the Rat and Barrel who wanted to earn quick money, turned up. This meant George had to be the sixth man. It did not go to plan. George's mask dropped, and Samuel recognised his uncle. It was then I believe Samuel was struck on the head and the plan changed from kidnap to murder. It seems when Ned and Eliza saw them, this had already happened, and the men were arguing over payment. Murder is more expensive than kidnap. The problem for George was the younger man would have no part in the murder." Jonathan stopped and looked at both William and Grace. "Are you both all right for me to continue?"

They had nothing to say as they tried to take in everything they had been told.

"George and the four mercenaries bullied the younger man with threats and somewhat reluctantly, he agreed. They had with them a larger jacket to disguise Samuel as they now intended to murder him and throw his body in the river."

Grace gasped.

"They hid somewhere until it was dark and then made their way to the dockside. It was late. At some point, they unrolled the rug and swapped Samuel's jacket for a larger one, hoping it would disguise him and make it more difficult to identify him. However, as they neared the dockside ready to roll Samuel out of the rug and into the river, the younger man refused to go any further and during the argument, the lookout on the Pegasus was alerted. In the confusion, Samuel was tipped out of the carpet and onto the Pegasus. They also got rid of his original jacket and telescope. It seems this rumpus is what young Billy Thomas must have heard. Either way, George made the comment Samuel wouldn't survive anyway so it wouldn't matter."

"What happens now, Jonathan?" added William.

"This is why I asked for this meeting."

"Do I understand the younger man will not give his name or any information in writing?" asked Grace.

Jonathan nodded.

"And it is improbable he would speak to a Magistrate or Constable?" concluded William.

"Exactly," said Jonathan. "As for the mercenaries, they will not come forward and admit to the abduction and attempted murder of a ten-year-old boy. Even if he survived, they would hang. As for George, he will deny everything and who would believe such a story? However," Jonathan paused, "somehow in the confusion the younger man ended up with the ransom note, and here it is."

Jonathan went to a drawer in his desk and pulled out an envelope addressed to 'Castles' Merchant Traders' in which was a piece of paper. He handed it to William and Grace.

"This was to be delivered to you the following morning along with Samuel's telescope as proof."

Jonathan opened the letter and handed it to William and Grace.

We have yor boy Samuel. Here is his teliscop with his name on it so no lies. If you want to see yor lad, then we will need fifteen thousand pounds. You have seven days. I will tell you where and when. Don't try anything stupid or yor boy will be returned to you in a coffin.

"The handwriting is not from an educated man," concluded William. "Unless someone has disguised it deliberately."

"There is only one thing to do," said Grace. "We need to confront George. He has expressed resentment and bitterness that William inherited the family business instead of him. He is resentful of Samuel inheriting the business. Now he is trying to find a way to become a partner in the family business. George is so angry, even unhinged. I dread to think what he is planning next."

Jonathan nodded. "There is evidence showing his resentment, but that is not a crime. Nor is being with a group of men arguing. They are simply normal family fallouts. We really need something that positions George as the instigator of this plot. We need a witness to point a finger at him and somebody with credibility. Now we either convince this young man to speak up and frankly, it is more than his life is worth to do that, or get George to admit being involved."

Jonathan grimaced. "This will be difficult, for George is well known in Bristol and a man of some prestige, if not a man of means, and most people will know that. The Bristol Merchant Venturers of which he is a member would ridicule the suggestion that he has kidnapped, or worse attempted to murder, his own nephew. We need firm evidence. I suggest we wait until the Pegasus arrives. Samuel is the key witness and young William Thomas may tell us more. Then, we may have sufficient to at least confront George and maybe go to the authorities."

"If the ship arrives in one piece, that is," said Grace. "I have just remembered. Whilst I was with Mrs Thomas, she made a comment about something Noah had said. It was to do with delivering our letter to George at the club when you were there, Jonathan. About how angry George was. It may be worth a chat with the boy. Will you be happy for me to do that?"

Jonathan nodded.

Noah had returned home. Grace sat in the kitchen with Noah and his mother. She explained as gently as she could to him she and his mother were really worried about his brother, William, and her son, Samuel whom he had met a few times. Noah, wide-eyed, nodded solemnly.

"William will look after your Samuel, Mrs Castle, he's good at looking after me and Florey," replied Noah.

"Noah, your mother and I know that. What puzzles us is we think they are both on the Pegasus and we wonder how they got there." Grace glanced at Edith who nodded. "I know you take messages for Mr Jonathan, and Mr William Castle. I know you take messages for Mr George Castle because you brought a message from him to us. Was Mr George angry at any time?"

Noah looked down sheepishly and then glanced at his mother.

"It's all right, Noah."

Florence, his sister, piped up. "Tell them about Mr George like you told me, Noah, shouting and, and."

Noah took a deep breath. "I took a message from Mr William to Mr George, who was in a good mood paying me extra to be quick. I ran to Mr George at his club. Mr Jonathan was there as well. When Mr George opened the letter and read it, he went mad. Something about Samuel will not inh... something. Mr George muttered to himself about getting rid of him. He then told me to get lost. He gave me sixpence, but he had promised me a shilling."

"Noah, well done. Can you remember anything else?" prompted Grace.

Noah paused. "He mentioned something on another day about a note."

His mother nodded. "Go on, son. Any little thing might help."

"A word I have never heard before. Ansom. A meeting about an ansom note."

Grace glanced up to Edith. "That sounds interesting, Noah. Tell us more."

Noah continued, "Grown-ups forget I am there and talk about things. Things sometimes I don't understand, like ansom notes."

"Noah," said Grace, "could that word be 'ransom' note?"

Noah beamed and nodded furiously. "That's it, a ransom note."

"Did you see the ransom note, Noah?" asked his mother.

Noah shook his head. "It had to go to an inn near the dockyard where Billy said I hadn't to go. So, I played stupid and somebody else went. It was the Rat and Barrel."

Grace smiled. "Well done. Well done indeed. If you remember anything else, tell your mother or Mr Jonathan." Grace went into her purse. "The six pence Mr George owes you. And here's another." Grace smiled at Edith Thomas. "Thank you so much."

Another step nearer, she thought. They now knew in which inn George and his mercenaries conspired. The Rat and Barrel. How appropriate, she thought, and how fortunate. It was close to the Ship Inn.

CHAPTER TWELVE

2nd September

It was daybreak and a normal day as far as days could be when stranded on a small rowing boat in the Atlantic Ocean. The three boys were asleep under the canvas cover. Billy on the left, Ottabah in the middle, and Sam on the right. As usual, Billy slept with his head slightly tilted, his jacket placed under his head so he could see the sunrise. In his opinion, a most wonderful and miraculous sight, a miracle he could not get enough of—a miracle he had learnt from Captain Fothergill.

His thoughts drifted back to the Captain and his lonely morning vigils watching the sunrise. Billy understood his captain's love and fear of the sea.

As the sun rose in great splendour, the three boys lingered a while whilst it replaced the dark and cold with warmth and light. After a meagre breakfast of yet more fish which was going rancid, the boys took to their posts. Billy, telescope in hand, scanned the horizon, for what he was unsure. Land or a ship maybe. Either way, he wondered where they were. He knew the Pegasus had been well on its way home before the storm. He also knew from talking to Gus the captain always kept his distance from the French coast because of pirates and of course the storm had thrown them off their planned route before finally exacting revenge by sinking the Pegasus. Was it possible they could be close to the South Coast of England? He shook his head in dismay before blinking hard and placing the telescope to his eye once again.

Ottabah was the best fisherman of the three and most of his time was spent leaning over the side of their raft with a piece of string or twine. Sam, the only one who could read, spent his time reading Doctor James's diary.

It was Billy who first noticed. It was the sheer stench, a lingering gut-wrenching stench. Nothing was to be seen through his telescope, so the nauseating smell intensified and there was a stillness that was difficult to explain.

Billy peered through his telescope with greater concentration. Nothing! The sea was calm, the sky dark and the clouds sagged lifelessly, and even the seagulls had stopped diving for fish or squabbling and shrieking. It was as if the world had come to a stop. Utter silence.

Another storm, surely not. Billy shook his head as if a bee buzzed in his brain. In the haze some way off and toward the rising sun was a large, dull, shapeless, mass. He frowned and then heard a loud sob. Turning, he saw Ottobah's eyes wide open, with sheer terror etched on every line of his face. He wept silently for he had recognised the smell; how could he forget it? The large shapeless mass was the hull of the slaver, the Black Swan, lumbering slowly in their direction.

Sam sidled towards his friend. Puzzled, he stared into Ottabah's eyes and saw the sheer terror and dismay on his face. He understood unbridled terror when he saw it, for that was how he felt when the three of them had stood on the deck waiting to make that leap of faith into the ocean.

"What is it?"

The young boy shook his head, gave a sigh of desperation, and then he pointed toward a hazy shadow.

Billy now understood. "Sam, it's that slaver we saw in Lisbon. You know when we first saw Ottobah. Remember! Can't you smell it? It smells of sewage. But it's off course. Seaman Johnson said when it left Lisbon it was to head west towards the Sugar Isles."

"Maybe the storm blew it off course? Or maybe it found shelter?" observed Sam.

They knew the Black Swan meant life to them if they were to be rescued. But a miserable existence for their new friend. Even death! Should they sacrifice him to save themselves? Catching the eye of Billy and holding his gaze, Sam shook his head. Billy nodded and smiled. They sat together to make their plans whilst head in hands, Ottabah wondered about his fate. Life was cruel. So many questions had been answered and demons lifted by these two white boys, his new friends, and now this. Could he hide on this tiny craft, for what? A return to slavery? Or should he end it all and jump into the sea and drown?

The Black Swan was getting closer. Billy and Sam sat on either side of Ottobah and gently each put an arm around him. They patted his head playfully and as he lifted his head, they grinned at him. Sam scuttled off under the canvass cover, muttering to himself, tugging a barrel here and pulling a piece of rope there.

"Ottobah, over here."

He pointed to a corner of the raft. Billy nodded to

Ottobah and with a flourish, gesticulated towards Sam who, like a magician, lifted a piece of canvas to reveal a small hiding place.

They both turned to Ottabah, pointed at him, put their fingers to their lips, and said "Shhhhhh!"

Ottabah nodded. He understood.

Despite the distance, the smell permeated every pore of Ottobah's body. He tried not to breathe in case it poisoned him. Billy closed his eyes, gritted his teeth, took a deep breath, and then whispered to Sam.

"When the Black Swan gets closer, we will go over the side, keep quiet, and let it pass us by."

The Black Swan

The Captain of the Black Swan cursed. Jack Mac Taggert had his feet spread out and his hands were placed on the table. He pursed his lips and concentrated hard on the map on the table before him. A piece of cord connected the West Coast of Africa, across the Atlantic Ocean to one of the Sugar Isles with a second piece of cord from the same point on the West Coast of Africa to the same island, but by way of the Port of Lisbon in Portugal. But for the detour, the Black Swan would not have been caught on the edge of a terrible storm that had damaged the mast and the hull, fortunately above the waterline. They had been most fortunate for the damage to the mast, sails and hull had been repairable. They had to find shelter close to the coast so they could drop anchor to undertake the repairs.

When it had been suggested to him by the owners of

the Black Swan the slave ship should sail from West Africa across the Atlantic to the Sugar Isles by way of Lisbon, where they would collect more slaves, he had protested as vehemently as he was able. He had felt there was more to this change in route than he was being told. This proved to be correct as a Portuguese Government Official had handed a parcel to him at the Lisbon docks.

Jack Mac Taggert thought whilst slaves were yet another cargo, a piece of property insured to be shifted about at will by their owners, they were a permanent source of trial and tribulation to him. Slaves were unlike any other property in his experience. Yes, slave trading was lucrative, but slaves needed feeding and watering and what went down their throats came out at the other end. He cringed. Slaves caught diseases too.

Captain Mac Taggert had been a sailor and a captain for a decade and more. He was a hard-nosed, no-nonsense Scotsman. Slaves were simply cargo to him and his crew. They were not well paid either, so every opportunity that came along to make money, he grabbed it. Selling off the weaker slaves made sense to Jack for they were going to die, anyway; weak slaves were open to disease and may infect the rest of the cargo. Better to get shut before.

It was simple enough, as long as he did not get too greedy. He had to take heed of his crew for in his experience, slaves brought the worst out of men, and a slave with the pox was damaged goods. Damaged goods cost money. However, the sheer power of his crew over men, women, and children was too great a temptation for some.

He left Lisbon sailing slowly north before preparing to tack to the west. They built the Black Swan as a slave ship to carry maximum slaves, not for speed or manoeuvrability. The captain was on deck when the horizon to the west appeared to be pitch black, a storm was brewing and heading their way. Lightning flashed and cracked, and thunder rolled. The storm heading towards them was of great magnitude.

And yet, above the Black Swan there was blue sky, clouds scudding idly across with a gentle breeze. It was like nothing he had ever experienced before. It was as if he was looking through a mirror, into another world, and it seemed to last an eternity. Eventually, waves came their way and eased the ship at first northwards, and off the ship's-chartered route. This continued for some time, and despite every effort by the captain and the crew, the ship proved helpless and hapless.

Finally, an enormous wave had simply plucked the Black Swan from the ocean, tossing it into the air before dumping it back into the sea, the ship shuddering and groaning like a dying old man. The waves disappeared as quickly as they came. They had been fortunate.

The captain's responsibility was the safety of the ship, its crew, and its cargo. He navigated the Black Swan closer to the coast where they could find a safer anchorage whilst they made their repairs. He would jettison some slaves overboard if necessary. Slaves were property and catered for in Maritime Insurance.

The report back from Able Seaman Price was the sail canvas and rigging had not been badly damaged, and his crew was already busy making the repairs.

Lost At Sea

Captain Mac Taggert was glad of this bit of good fortune. There was, however, a 'but' in the captain's mind. Autumn was approaching fast, and they needed to make haste to cross the Atlantic. The question was, how far had the Black Swan been blown off course?

Billy watched the ship. Its massive hulk was temporarily blocking the sunlight. It was not peaceful, Billy thought, more a stillness like death. It was as if the Black Swan had sucked the very life out of the sea and sky.

Billy put the telescope to his eye once more and scanned the ship from hull to deck and over the masts. It was still some distance away. They had little food, and he had not the slightest idea where they were. As for their small boat, Billy surveyed their little craft and grimaced. What chance had they of survival? None, if Billy was truthful.

What Billy did not know was none of the Black Swan's crew had seen their small boat and if they had, they would have ignored it. If it were in the Black Swan's pathway, they would simply run it down.

Ottabah sat beneath the meagre threadbare canvas cover. Knees bent, hands clasped round them, looking blankly at the sea. Life was a mystery. The elders of his village warned everyone about the dangers of the evil white men who had been raiding coastal villages for slaves but were now moving further inland. Their chieftain had moved the village to a more secluded place, hidden at the base of a gorge. They had also placed lookouts around the village.

Yet, the white men still came.

Ottabah had been practising with his bow and arrow,

aiming at a piece of cloth tied on a tree branch. The white men had pale eyes and white palms. He squatted on the ground so he would not be discovered but could not take his eyes of them. Being mesmerised was his downfall. Two black men were with the group. They were pointing at the village. One took a stick and made marks on the ground. The white men were divided into two groups, one running to the left of the village and one to the right. Ottabah realised they would surround the village. The two black men disappeared in the opposite direction. It had puzzled him, for these black men were betraying their own kind.

He sat enraptured like a startled goat. He then heard shouting close by, strange voices speaking an unfamiliar language. Two powerful hands grabbed him from behind and bundled him into a makeshift pen along with people from the village. Divided into men, women, and children. Nowhere to be seen were his parents, younger brother, or sister. In fact, he did not know whether they were alive or dead.

Ottabah had been fortunate or unfortunate depending on how you looked at it. He had been captured from his home village, manacled on the deck of the Black Swan, and then taken off to be sold in Lisbon. Then, he was bought by the captain of the Pegasus which sank in a storm. He had been fortunate in his two friends, but now he may be rescued by the slaver or drowned at sea!

Yet, his two white friends had saved his life. They had rescued him from below deck as the Pegasus was sinking but could have left him. The slaver could rescue them and he would be a slave once again, but he knew his new friends would not do that. Because the colour of your skin was not important; it was what was in your heart.

Sam and Billy planned to go over the side of their boat furthest away from the Black Swan. Neither boy was a good swimmer so as a precaution, they made two rope handles from which they could hang on should the slaver linger too long or come too close. If it did, the boys would have to go under the boat as they could not risk being discovered. They pointed to the hiding place. Sam grinned put his finger to Ottabah's mouth.

He said, "Shhhhh."

Ottobah disappeared into his hiding place whilst Sam and Billy slid quietly over the side of the boat and then put their hands through the rope handles.

The Black Swan was heading toward the small boat. Billy believed the crew of the Black Swan must have seen their small craft. He presumed they would have a lookout like the Pegasus for Seaman Johnson and Seaman Thomas would not have missed them. In Billy's mind, it had to appear no one was on the small rowing boat.

The waves from the large hulk buffeted the small boat and threw it away unceremoniously. Sam and Billy were dangling under the water and tossed about, hanging on to the small handles for dear life. It had not occurred to either of them that their small craft would have been battered about so much by the wake of the Black Swan. Ottabah held his breath and stayed motionless. He refused to breathe in the poison from the slaver whatever happened.

The Black Swan continued west, oblivious to the

small rowing boat with two young boys precariously hanging on and another hiding under canvas. After what seemed an eternity, Ottabah peered out from his hiding place. The stench had disappeared, and he was still alive. He knew he needed to help his friends to clamber back on board their boat. He laughed to himself about the foolishness of his thoughts: what if the men of the slaver were hiding? The Black Swan was out of sight and so he leaned over the edge of the boat to help his friends back on board. Billy was hanging onto his friend, who was now barely conscious, trying to keep his head above water with one arm whilst hanging onto the boat with the other. Billy was exhausted and freezing.

"Sam first."

Billy pointed to him in the water. Ottabah nodded and leaned over and dragged him onto the boat, trying to lay Sam upright the best he could. It shocked him how cold his friend was. He placed his ear against Sam's mouth and heard a slight breath, like a dying bird. He then went to help Billy clamber aboard. Billy, totally exhausted, did not have the strength to pull himself up. He was bigger and heavier than Sam. For Ottabah, it was like lifting a large sack of maize from the floor to his shoulder in one go.

Billy rested his head on the boat.

Breathlessly, he said, "I can't manage. I don't have the strength," and shook his head.

He did not need to understand what his friend had said; he instinctively knew Billy was in desperate trouble. He tapped Billy's arm, shook his head, and wagged a finger in anger. Ottabah grabbed Billy with both hands and heaved with all his might, dragging him halfway.

He took a deep gulp of air and shouted, "Billy, Billy," in his deep melodic tone.

He placed a single finger in the air. Billy understood and nodded. Once more, a big heave. Ottabah grabbed him under his armpits. Billy, with every ounce of strength he had left, wriggled, knees and legs scraping on the boat, and landed like a floundering fish on top of him. They lay still, momentarily winded. Ottabah cheered.

His friend was cold, so cold. Somehow, he had to keep both his friends warm. Slowly, he pulled Sam under the canvas shelter. It seemed to take forever. Ottabah then grabbed Billy and shuffled the best he could to drag him under the shelter too. His friends were desperate. He checked their mouths and then stuck a finger down their throats. Nothing there. His father had taught him how to clear the throat of someone near to death. He had never forgotten.

He checked the barrels for any food. All they had left was salted beef in the bottom of one barrel, but the beef seemed to have a life of its own. He knew the signs of rancid food—he had eaten enough of it, but the movements at the bottom of the barrel were in fact maggots. How they got into the barrels was beyond him. He checked the remaining. One held brandy which was untouched. They were going to drown, starve, or fall overboard drunk.

Ottabah then separated his friends, slid between them, and pulled the canvas over the three of them. He was quite warm, and he knew his body heat would help his friends. That was something his mother taught him. She had shown him how to keep newly born chicks alive by making a simple tent using warm stones from the fire.

Ottabah put an arm around each friend and pulled them close to him. He thanked his mother and father who were looking down on him and keeping them all safe, before drifting off to sleep. He dreamt of his homeland, the river, his friends, and the games they played together, and he laughed out loud. Hearing noises and soft voices, he smiled.

***

The Rose had done well. Its captain, Robert Benedict, was delighted with the success of their voyage. Captain Benedict worked for the Admiralty whose job it was to gather information about the activities of the Spanish. The Rose had sailed around the Mediterranean under the guise of a trader.

The Spanish, it seemed, had their eye firmly fixed on regaining the Island of Minorca. Minorca was a strategic jewel in the Mediterranean Sea and Port Mahon, which was a deep natural harbour, perfect for warships and frigates. With the expansion of the dockyard by the British, the port was also the Royal Navy's Mediterranean Squadron principal base. It was also close enough to defend the recent acquisition of Gibraltar.

Upon its return to England, the Rose would dock at a trading port, usually Bristol. The information he possessed would then be relayed to the Admiralty by

Lost At Sea

Captain Benedict, in person, where necessary. This was such an occasion, for he had maps and letters of significance.

It was the lookout, as sharp-eyed as a sea eagle, who spotted a small craft northeast. The captain ordered the vessel to be checked. Experience taught him never to ignore the smallest vessel as it was those who came back and bit. The lookout confirmed there were bodies on board but no movement. As the Rose closed on the small boat, Captain Benedict ordered the lowering of a rowing boat with four men on board to go alongside and check it. The crew knew the captain was a stickler for detail; he missed nothing. It had saved the Rose on many an occasion.

The men saw three lifeless boys under a canvas, but they could not board the small craft without it sinking and so they attached a rope and towed it to the Rose where it could be secured. The Rose's second in command and ship's medic, Seaman Dai Carter, clambered onto the craft and examined the three boys. They were in a bad way.

Seaman Carter shouted, "Captain, there are three boys—alive, but only just."

He organised the lifting of the boys onto the deck of the Rose and then sent a sailor back for any possessions.

Captain Benedict said, "What's the verdict?"

Seaman Carter shook his head. "Three boys on a rowing boat in the ocean is odd. There are two younger boys, maybe nine or ten years old. One is a black boy, with manacle sores on his neck, ankles, and wrists. The other is a white boy with an old nasty injury to the head, and a recent injury as well. He will be lucky to survive. The third boy is older maybe in his teens, thirteen or fourteen. The odd thing is, they were wrapped in canvas, with the black boy in the middle—his arms around them, their arms around him, as if they were trying to keep warm. I do not know what they have been living on, either."

Captain Benedict nodded. "Anything else in the boat?"

"Empty barrels which have had food in, also a battered telescope. They are exhausted and half-starved, Captain. And I found this."

Dai Carter handed a small book to the captain.

Robert Benedict took the small book and read it.

"It's from Doctor James on the Pegasus. A diary of some sort. Do your best for these boys. They have done well to survive."

Dai Carter smiled. "I need to find somewhere to keep them warm."

Captain Benedict went below deck to his cabin to read the small book. He quickly realised the two white boys were from Bristol, presumed to be stowaways. The ministrations of Doctor James had already saved the injured boy, who was least likely to survive. He expressed concern this boy had been beaten and thrown onto the Pegasus the night before the ship set sail. The other boy ended up on the Pegasus separately.

The doctor made an entry about a disturbance that had taken place the night before the Pegasus set sail from Bristol, and the suspicions he held.

Captain Benedict stopped. They had docked the Rose in Bristol around this time. One of his crew discovered a telescope and a jacket on the dockside and handed it to the Harbour Master. He needed to talk to Seaman Carter.

He continued reading. Doctor James believed the boy's injury to his head was quite deliberate. Certainly not accidental. The doctor also considered whether the intention had been to dispose of the boy's body in the river and that his ending up on the Pegasus was a mistake, if a lucky one.

The young black boy was indeed a slave, rescued by Doctor James and Captain Fothergill whilst docked in Lisbon. Reports of a dreadful storm had reached the crew of the Rose and they'd had sufficient time to make a detour. It was possible, of course, the Pegasus had been in the storm's eye, had capsized, and these three boys were the only survivors.

Seaman Carter was a canny Welshman. He had decided it was in the three boys' interest to be above deck away from hard-bitten sailors and anyway, fresh air was better than the fetid stench below deck. He knew of a cupboard on deck, which was behind the ship's wheel. It was sheltered and large enough to accommodate three boys if he cleared ropes, canvas, and other paraphernalia out. That was quickly achieved. The crew brought the three boys to him, examining them one by one for injuries or illness. He had also considered whether the boys had a fever and if so, he would need to isolate them. He believed they did not. Starvation, cold, and exhaustion certainly. He placed a canvas across the doorway for shelter and privacy and then left to go to the galley for food and ale.

The crew was most fortunate for Captain Benedict insisted if they were to undertake dangerous work for the Admiralty, then they should be well fed. So they were. Seaman Carter, along with a young sailor, reappeared carrying a pot full of broth, dried biscuits, plates, mugs, a ladle, and a pot of ale. Both sailors sat down at the doorway. The young slave boy, Ottabah, was sitting up and looking around at his surroundings and appeared quite puzzled. Dai nodded and smiled, and pointed to the food held by the other sailor who was not much older than Billy Thomas.

Dai gestured at the other two boys, Sam and Billy. Sam was still flat out, but Billy opened his eyes and stared in horror.

"Where are we? Dead or…"

The younger sailor shook his head. "No, you are on the Rose bound for Bristol. Quite safe. Your friend looks worse for wear though."

"Sam keeps getting hit on the head. Don't know how he manages it. This is Ottabah and I am Billy." Billy grinned at his friend and continued. "The Pegasus sank in a storm."

"Your friend, Sam," continued Seaman Carter, "has he been like this long?"

Billy composed himself. "Not really. A few hours. A slaver called the Black Swan was sailing towards us. We would not give up Ottabah. So, he hid on the boat, and we went into the water. I think Sam banged his head when we were getting out of the boat. We were in the water a long time and got cold."

Dai Carter nodded. "I see." He turned to the young sailor. "Jack, we need to feed them, and then we will have a good look at young Sam here. We must keep him warm. He will feel better with something warm inside him."

Young Seaman Nelson nodded, took two plates, and then ladled broth which the captain insisted must always be at hand for the crew, plus biscuits and two spoons. He gave one plate to Ottabah and the other to Billy. They were then given a small mug of ale. After their meal, Billy and Ottabah moved to one side along with Sailor Nelson who talked to them as instructed by Seaman Carter. Information was the bread and butter of Captain Benedict and his crew and so even the most junior and inexperienced sailor had to be adept at obtaining information. Jack had a gift, or so it seemed.

Dai Carter eased Sam into the light where he could see him better and where he could check his head wound. He had brought his medicine bag with him, and he carefully cleaned the fresh wound with neat brandy. Not the expensive stuff. The cheapest would suffice. He considered whoever had repaired the older wound was a man of exceptional skill and he thought he must ask the boys about Doctor Stephen James.

Ottabah and Billy sidled towards Seaman Carter and peered at their friend.

"How is he? We cannot lose Sam now. Not after all we have been through together." Billy's voice trailed away.

Seaman Carter said to Jack Nelson. "I need to talk to the captain and tell him how things are going. You must try to get Sam here to eat a little and sip the ale. These two must rest and keep warm. Understand?"

Dai Carter stared at the young sailor, who nodded.

He then pointed at Billy and Ottabah. "If you two want to help your friend, you must rest and regain your strength. More food later."

The boys nodded.

He then asked as an afterthought. "Tell me, what have you been living on?"

Billy grimaced. "After the Pegasus sank, there was lots of debris floating on the sea. Including barrels which we dragged on board our boat and opened them. There was salted fish, biscuits, some sherry, and brandy. Then a large fish landed on our boat. Biggest I've ever seen. We had a proper battle with it because it was slimy and strong and threw us all over the place. Ottabah ended up overboard hanging on for dear life. We also discovered he was good at gutting fish."

Billy laughed and cuffed his friend's head gently.

"That explains the stink then," laughed Seaman Nelson.

"It does. In the barrel with them," said Seaman Carter.

Upon joining the crew of the Rose, Seaman Carter organised the rigging up of a water barrel and overhead shower of seawater. As a chapel-going Welshman, he continued to remind the crew that cleanliness is next to godliness.

They took the two boys to the barrel. Seaman Nelson then showed them the ingenious system which had been devised by Seaman Carter, who was standing close by. It pumped water from the sea up and overhead and into the barrel manually. Billy clambered in and Seaman Nelson showed Ottabah how to work the handle before leaving them to it.

Lost At Sea

Seaman Carter nodded his approval and then went below deck to speak to the captain. He knocked on the door and entered. Captain Benedict asked him if there was anything to report. He told the captain what information they had got and how useful Sailor Nelson had been with the young boys. Captain Benedict confided in his second in command for Dai Carter had been with him many years and he knew he could trust him.

Pointing to Doctor James's notebook, the captain explained there was something odd surrounding the circumstances of the boy, Samuel who at the time was thought to be a stowaway on the Pegasus. At least that was what Doctor Stephen James believed. Dr James believed the boy, who he thought to be about 10 years old, may have been kidnapped and left for dead and it was fortunate he had ended up on the Pegasus rather than in the water. He was in a bad way apparently, and he had not fully recovered his memory, which may have changed since then.

The captain continued. Billy, after a somewhat loutish start, had matured and become a reliable sailor. They had rescued the slave boy it seems from a gang belonging to the Black Swan whilst in Lisbon.

Seaman Carter smiled and nodded. "They have only survived because of a strong bond between them and sheer doggedness. Their languages may differ but by God, they understood each other. I've seen nothing quite like it before."

"If I remember correctly, the Rose was docked in Bristol about this time and they found a telescope and jacket in the dock wall."

"It was Seaman Nelson who spotted something. When he had a closer look, he found a jacket and a telescope. The telescope had a name engraved on it. As we were ready for sailing, the lad took the jacket and the telescope to the Harbour Master."

"The Rose should be in Bristol in a few days, dependent on the weather," added the Captain, "so we must hope all three boys are alive and well when we dock. They have been fortunate to have survived at all."

In a change of plan, Captain Benedict decided to dock the Rose on the south coast of England; this would then enable him to go directly to the Admiralty in London. The letters and information he possessed were critical to the security of Great Britain and time was of the essence. They also had to be discreet about when and where the Rose docked, as they had to maintain their cover as a trading ship. There were spies everywhere.

Robert Benedict discussed with his second in command his decision, which meant Seaman Carter would therefore be the captain of the Rose and would take the ship to Bristol and wait for him there for fresh orders.

"Remember. The three boys are your responsibility."

The following morning just before daybreak, Captain Robert Benedict and Seaman Simon Leaworthy, a canny Yorkshireman, rowed ashore.

CHAPTER THIRTEEN

6th September

The Rose continued its journey along the south coast of England, docking briefly at Plymouth, a regular stopping point, before continuing its journey to Bristol. Samuel, Billy and Ottabah had recovered well enough. Rest, warmth and nourishment had done the trick and Billy was proving useful on board, helping where he was able.

Samuel progressed best of all. His memory was gradually improving, although he struggled with the events surrounding his abduction which Doctor James put down to the injury to his head. He could remember waking up on deck of the Pegasus, standing up and announcing his presence, then everything going black. Samuel's recollection of Dr James was still vague though. With fresh air and proper nourishment, he was getting stronger every day, for like his friends he had been badly dehydrated.

Samuel could remember his parents, his birthday gift of a telescope and the small present from Alice of a carved ship, as well as Mrs Harper's homemade fruit pies. To the amusement of his two friends, Samuel would sit with the small carved ship in his hand and talk to it. He found doing so prompted recollections. As for his Uncle George, his memory was patchy, although there was something quite distinctive about his voice. There were certain words he seemed to emphasise. The words 'boy', 'nephew' and 'you', sprang to his mind.

It was during these moments of recollection Samuel mentioned to Seaman Kennedy his telescope, a birthday gift from his father and which was engraved with his name and date of birth. Seaman Kennedy frowned. He had heard this before.

"Did you have a jacket on the day they kidnapped you, Samuel? Can you remember?"

Samuel frowned and closed his eyes in deep concentration. "The telescope folded up and fit inside an inside pocket."

Seaman Kennedy laughed then shook his head. "I need to speak to Mr Carter. A telescope was found on the dockside when the Rose was being loaded. It was engraved and in a jacket pocket."

Billy whispered. "If they found your telescope, Sam, with your name on, then someone could be looking for you—your parents, I mean."

Samuel was confused. So much to take in.

The Rose continued its journey along the coast passing Penzance and St Ives before heading on the last part of its journey towards the Bristol Channel. The three boys were on deck, staring at the coastline as the ship sailed gently onwards without haste. Each boy wondered what their fate was to be.

Billy wondered whether George Castle would still accuse him of theft and whether his efforts on the sinking ship would go in his favour. After all, the ship was partly owned by George Castle. He hoped his mother, brother and sister were living safely with Mr Jonathan and they did not believe he was a thief. That would break his heart and make him furious because he was no thief. Billy had learnt one thing on the Pegasus... the love of the sea. Perhaps, he wondered, he could stay with the Rose.

Ottabah was terrified he would be enslaved yet again. It was so confusing. His two friends who were white had saved him when the Pegasus sank. They did not have to do that. They also refused to give him up to the slave hulk, the Black Swan. They did not have to do that either. He hoped above anything he could live with his two friends in this place called Bristol, wherever that was. Surely, they would not abandon him, not after what they had been through together? He stifled a sob.

Samuel was apprehensive. Whilst recovering on the Pegasus he heard conversations between Doctor James and Captain Fothergill about the possibility of his being badly injured during a kidnap. Whilst on the Rose, he also overheard Seaman Carter and Captain Benedict when they must have thought he was asleep, talking about, 'Young Samuel apparently being left for dead.' It was all so confusing. After all, he was only just ten years old and why would anyone want to kill him? What had he done? If they were still after him, would they kidnap him again to make sure they killed him the second time?

The Rose continued into the Bristol Channel and then onto the tidal River Severn, and then the River Avon.

The crew of the Rose worked at full pelt, checking the sails, clearing the decks and checking the cargo below deck. Seaman Jack Nelson was ordered below deck to see the Acting Captain, Seaman Carter.

Seaman Carter wanted to speak to the three boys privately. Having returned with them promptly, Seaman Nelson was despatched back on deck to do his normal duties.

Ottabah, Billy and Samuel, stood shoulder to shoulder in front of Seaman Carter.

"You boys have done well, and as for you, Sam, I am glad to see your head wound has healed well. Until next time that is. Seaman Kennedy has told me about a telescope and a jacket. If I remember rightly, we found them hidden in the dockside. Seaman Nelson could spot a flea on a dog at a hundred paces. Could they be yours, Samuel?"

Samuel nodded shyly. "Yes, sir. But I don't know how they ended up in the dock wall."

Seaman Carter nodded. "You're full of mysteries, Samuel. Now, Billy, I know you had extra responsibility when the Pegasus sank. You did well too."

Billy beamed.

"Ottabah, they could not have survived without you. Now the question is, what will happen to you three when we dock at Bristol?"

Ottabah recognised his name and froze. Seaman Carter smiled, recognising the fear.

"Mr Carter, sir, please," said Samuel, "Ottabah saved our lives; without him, we would have starved."

Billy took a deep breath. He was not the most literate. *Here goes,* he thought.

"Mr Carter, Captain, please. Sam and I would not be here without Ottabah and Ottabah would not be here without us. Do not aba… leave him." His voice trailed off. He then continued, "Please. We could not bear for our friend to be sent on a slaver to the Sugar isles or wherever. Surely, he…"

Ottabah knew his friends were fighting for him. He stepped forward and sank to knees, hands clasped together, pleading. Even though he could not speak their language, Sam and Billy knew exactly what he was doing. They too got on their knees on either side of Ottabah and begged. They would have grovelled. Anything to save their friend.

"Boys, you do not have to convince me or Captain Benedict. We are on your side and can only imagine what you have been through."

Seaman Carter nodded at Billy and Sam. "You two can help. When we arrive in Bristol, talk to your families about what you have all been through together. That you would not have survived without each other, nor without Ottabah."

Bristol

It was three o'clock that same afternoon at 32 Queen Street. Grace and William were at Jonathan's home to discuss the progress they had made in the search for the two boys. After deciding to pool their efforts, the relationship between Jonathan, Grace and William had blossomed into friendship, whilst George's initial interest had faded somewhat. As events had transpired, this lack of interest by George proved to be a blessing in disguise as it had become clear George may well have been involved in the abduction of his nephew.

The initial discovery of Samuel's telescope and

jacket gave William and Grace a reason to hope they would find their son fit and well. Then there was the discovery a second boy, William Thomas, was missing, which added some confusion. Despite their efforts, in particular Grace's distribution of leaflets and posters, there was little new information until she visited the Ship Inn. It proved to be the luck they needed. The innkeeper, Harry Wetherell, and his wife, Gem felt sorry for the somewhat wet and bedraggled woman who had arrived with posters and was desperate to find her lost son. With the help of their friends and customers, information gradually flowed back to them, the most significant of which being Ned Champion and his wife Elizabeth whose information increasingly pointed a finger toward George Castle. Even the possibility George had instigated the kidnapping of Samuel and the subsequent ransom for an amount of money that may well financially ruin the Castles.

They had found a member of the group, a certain Jed Stone. Jed Stone had been unhappy at the kidnap and, when the plan went awry with the apparent murder of the boy, he wanted out. He also provided information and the ransom note but refused to give evidence to the Constable. Jed Stone knew if he did so, he would fear for his life. With his refusal to testify, Jonathan, Grace, and William had agreed they could not proceed down the legal route. However, they invited George to a meeting to discuss the missing boys and to see whether they could provoke him to make a mistake. They agreed Jonathan would lead.

Mrs Thomas had also been asked to attend, but she had declined.

"Begging your pardon, sir, I think you will make better progress without me, and you all know my feelings about Mr George. I'll just lose my rag."

Grace understood Mrs Thomas's loathing of him, as she too detested the man.

George Castle sauntered up the steps to 32 Queen Street and rapped on the door with his walking cane. Mrs Thomas answered and politely led him to Jonathan's study. As he entered, Jonathan and William got to their feet. Grace remained seated.

"You have news about the two boys?" said George. "I am sorry I could not help more. Really, I am."

George took a seat around the table next to Jonathan. George was determined to appear concerned about the two boys, in particular his nephew, Samuel. He had given considerable thought to the meeting. He would show pleasure at any good news and disappointment with any bad news. Of course, George must not give any sign he already knew Sam would not be found, and as for Billy, he could not care less.

"Good news, George," continued Jonathan, "it seems William Thomas, Billy as we know him, and Sam have been found."

George nodded, keeping his emotions in check about this unexpected news. Billy would know nothing about Samuel's abduction, so he was irrelevant. Samuel was a different kettle of fish though. George, however, because he believed the boy had been knocked unconscious, he would remember nothing anyway and therefore George would be quite safe. William and Grace smiled.

"That is excellent news," said George. "Are they

here? Have they said what happened to them?"

"No. Ironically, they were both found on our ship, the Pegasus. At first, despite there being the coincidence of two boys on the same ship, they were thought to be stowaways. Your nephew had a severe head injury and has been most fortunate to have survived. It was our very own Doctor James who came to the rescue and saved the boy's life."

"Ah. That was most fortunate!" George beamed.

Jonathan nodded. "In Lisbon, the Pegasus docked alongside the Swift which is owned by William and Grace here. Clive Fothergill was concerned that parents of both boys would have been worried about them and so he prepared a letter to be delivered by Captain Joseph Featherstone to the Bristol Authorities." He continued, "On his return to Bristol as owners of the Swift, he naturally told William and Grace of the two stowaways, not knowing of course the injured boy was most likely to be their Samuel."

George frowned. "I knew nothing of this. Why was I not told?"

Jonathan said, "It was all rather confusing, George, and no one knew their true identities. William Thomas had given the name Billy Wragg and the other boy, who has turned out to be your nephew, Samuel, had collapsed and was in a bad way. He had been struck on the head and it seems he had a nasty life-threatening wound. It appears he has lost his memory. He did not know who he was, or how he had ended up on the Pegasus."

George, whilst showing concern, inwardly gave a sigh of a relief.

Jonathan continued, "With good ministrations from Doctor James the boy has recovered. Now, here is the thing. Doctor James is of the opinion the injury could not be accidental. He believes the boy was assaulted and presumably left for dead."

George sucked his cheeks. "How can he possibly know that?"

"Well, firstly, the nature of the wound suggested a blunt instrument had been used, and secondly the position of the wound was on top of his head. Now unless someone dropped him on his head that would have been impossible."

George stared at his brother. "Doctor James is a criminologist and a doctor now, is he? That is ridiculous." He was angry.

"If anyone should be angry, George, it is Grace and I. Samuel is our son and it seems they left him for dead," said William.

George had been too anxious in his recriminations. His first mistake and he knew it, so he changed tack.

"I must apologise, William. You are quite right. Why would anyone wish to attack a 10-year-old boy? Did the boy improve as the journey progressed?"

"Yes. His memory has returned, if slowly. Oddly, Samuel was wearing his own trousers but not his own jacket. It was much too big for him," said William.

Jonathan shook his head. "Makes little sense to me. Why would anyone want to do that?"

George was alert and kept his thoughts to himself. He realised he needed to be asking questions, not answering them.

"And the other boy, Billy Wragg. What happened to

him?" asked George.

"That is not his correct name," continued Jonathan. "You remember young Billy Thomas? He was the boy that delivered my message to you we were needed on the Pegasus. It was the day you accused him of stealing. Apparently, after the fracas, the boy ran to the dockyard and hid in the cargo on the dockside by the Pegasus. The ship's watch was monitoring the cargo and when nightfall came, voices awoke young Billy Thomas. There was an argument of some sort. The lad thought one voice was familiar to him, and they were carrying what he thought was a roll of carpet." Jonathan deliberately paused at this point. "Then the boy fell asleep amongst the cargo and awoke the following morning on the Pegasus, heading across the sea to Lisbon."

"I see."

George paused for a moment. He needed to think. William, Billy Thomas that is, knew him and may have recognised his voice.

"Surely the local constables must have some idea who these men could be. Have we no idea at all? They need to be found before they do anything like this again," George added indignantly.

"Any suggestions, George?" asked Grace.

William and Jonathan turned and looked at Grace.

"Someone must know, surely? These things get around. I'll check at the Rat and Barrel, "he said.

"Maybe you will find yourself a rat?" said Grace.

Jonathan grimaced. It seemed Grace had had enough.

"Believe me, we have been searching everywhere.

Grace has been busy delivering posters to all the inns at the dockside. Samuel's telescope and jacket have also been handed in to the Harbour Master."

"Yes. In the dockside wall. They were well hidden, though." George cringed. He had slipped up again. "Apparently," George added as if an afterthought.

William frowned. Nothing had been said about how or where the items had been found. Was this the mistake they had been waiting for?

"We are unaware of this. Which well-hidden hole in the dockside were you talking about?"

Somewhat flustered, George tried to gather his thoughts. He had known the items were in the wall. After all, he was there when one man quickly removed the stones and pushed the telescope and jacket inside. The last thing he wanted was to leave any identification should Samuel's body be found.

"I have heard this from someone. Let me think."

William was furious. "When was this? Why didn't you tell us?"

"A while ago. William why, are you so angry? Calm down, man."

William seethed with anger. "George, did it never occur to you the only people who knew Samuel's jacket and telescope were in the dockside were those very people who had abducted him and left him for dead? This person who has told you may well have been one of them."

Grace smiled to herself. She was the one who was expected to lose her temper, not William. It was so unlike him.

"George, this is important!" said Jonathan. "Who

was this man? We need to go to the Constable with this information."

George had to give himself time to think, at least he had not blurted out the name Jed Stone. He had to be careful.

"I am sorry, William. You are quite right. I should have told you straight away. At the time I simply did not understand the significance and I apologise. I recall it was soon after Samuel's disappearance and..." George had to think quickly, "and it was someone in the Rat and Barrel who was drunk. I did not take it seriously. I will talk to the innkeeper this evening."

William shook his head in dismay. "George, your nephew was abducted on the 22nd of July, and you give us this information which could be vital on the 6th of September?"

George looking glum, shook his head.

He is convincing, thought Grace. *I will give him that.*

"Is this man a regular at the Rat and Barrel?" asked Grace.

"No. Just now and then and I do not think I have seen him since."

"That's unfortunate," added Jonathan trying to be conciliatory. "We will now have to wait for the return of the Pegasus. Hopefully, Samuel's memory will have returned, and we know young William Thomas had recognised one voice that night at the dockside. George, would you try to find the name of the man at the Rat and Barrel who knew about the hole in the dockside wall where Samuel's telescope and jacket were hidden? It may still prove useful."

George nodded. He still felt secure enough, for neither he nor the men dared admit to their part in the kidnap and attempted murder of a young boy. They would all hang for this.

In his rooms above the Bristol Gentlemen's club, George was deep in thought. He was in a bit of a mess if truth be told. All his best-laid plans seemed to disintegrate around him.

George reflected. He had been making plans to kidnap Samuel and demand a ransom from his brother and his wife for some time. George had known if he was to succeed, he would need information about the daily routine of the Castle family and their finances. He needed to rekindle his friendship with William and through him, get access to his family and his finances. He had partly achieved his goal when he wrote to William, offering him friendship and an investment opportunity. Then after gaining their confidence, he needed to get their daily routines and establish any weakness, financial or otherwise, in Castles' Merchant Trading. In fact, George himself had to be beyond suspicion.

However, gaining the confidence of William and his wife proved to be more difficult than he had expected. It was not helped when Jonathan questioned George's hostile attitude to his brother and his nephew.

George established what the largest amount of money Castles' Merchant Traders could raise was. Namely £15,000. If he abducted Samuel or had him abducted more like, a ransom of such a large sum of money would nearly bankrupt the company. With the

£15,000, George could step in and take over the business.

He cursed to himself for he had nearly given the game away to Jonathan. First, when he showed a fit of temper when a note from William was delivered to George by the boy, Noah, in which William had said he was now preparing Samuel to join the business. Second, earlier that day at the meeting in Queen Street when he challenged Doctor James on the opinion =Samuel had been attacked intentionally. Finally, when he mentioned the hiding place on the dockside. He thought William was going to have a fit.

That the abduction plans had gone awry did not help his temper, either. He thought it was a bit of good luck when an unexpected opportunity to grab the boy appeared whilst William and his son were on the dockside, and William had decided after some deliberation to send Samuel home to say he was going to be delayed. George left smartly as he realised the boy would be on his own. So, feigning illness, he made his excuses and left, heading smartly to the Rat and Barrel.

Then all his plans went up in smoke. He could not get all the hired hands he needed and so they ended up two men short. This meant not only did George have to step in, which was the last thing he wanted to do, but also, they had to get another man from the Rat and Barrel, with an offer of easy money. That man was Jed Stone. George rolled his eyes and shook his head. A mistake.

He should have waited, but he was too eager not to lose such a golden opportunity. Not so golden, as it turned out.

The six men waited near Samuel's home. The boy was dawdling and distracted as he was constantly looking through his telescope. It was easy enough to catch him unawares, snatch him and drag him down an alley. It was during the scuffle that George's mask slipped, and Samuel recognised him. In sheer panic, George whacked the lad over the head with the end of his cane. Stunned by the blow, he dropped like a stone, blood oozing from his head.

One mercenary said, "You've done him in, George."

George hissed. "Not my name, you fool."

He realised he had to get rid of the body for he truly believed his nephew was dead. The idiot from the inn had cold feet, but they all threatened him. They could all hang for this. They decided the body would have to be disguised, weighed down, and thrown into the river. Even that went wrong. They went to the dockside at dusk, but the lad, Jed Stone kept arguing which not only delayed them, but they were making enough noise to alert the dead, let alone the guard on the Pegasus. His own ship! So, they tossed his body, which was wrapped up in a large coat, into the river, or so they thought. Then they hid the boy's telescope and his own coat in the dockside wall. At least Jed Stone had his uses. It was his idea. Of course, he had intended to return and retrieve the telescope and coat. Or more likely, get someone else to do it. George could not be seen to be involved.

Because of the chaos surrounding the kidnap of his nephew, George decided if he was to achieve his heart's desire of owning Castles' Merchant Traders, he needed to have an alternative plan. George had approached his solicitor, Jeremiah Sykes and sought his opinion on family law. Did he have any right of ownership of Castles' Merchant Traders should his sister-in-law, Grace Castle inherit the business? Jeremiah Sykes was of the opinion whilst women could inherit, it was uncommon. George would need to prove she was unsuitable. Women were strange, unreliable, and flighty creatures and George was not only a male relative but also a successful businessman. Jeremiah Sykes did not ask about the deaths of William and Samuel. After all, this was an unlikely event but something that may have to be considered in the future.

Finally, his investments with the South Sea Company had not produced what he had hoped. He knew he had got a little too greedy. After all, Jonathan warned him to sell, and, as usual, he was right. He had got out in time with some funds, but had been lucky not to go bankrupt. George really needed a good return from the Pegasus.

The fly in the ointment now was the younger man who he had grabbed at the Rat and Barrel to give a helping hand. Jed Stone had got quite squeamish at the end and George realised he had to get rid of him, so he headed for the inn to speak to the leader of his hired mercenaries—a man known to him as Bart. Jed Stone was a risk to them all, including George.

"Consider it done."

The only other issue for George was he could not find their ransom note for love nor money. George needed a bit of luck.

Lost At Sea

7th September

It was mid-morning by the time the Rose entered the Avon. The ship docked on the northern bank of the Avon briefly to collect Captain Benedict. He had conducted his business quickly with the Admiralty in London and they had provided him with new orders to return speedily to the Mediterranean Sea. However, he was determined the three boys in his care would be safeguarded.

As the Rose was approaching the docks, heading their way was a small tugboat to act as a pilot and guide the Rose to the berth allocated by the Harbour Master. The Rose docked on a typical autumnal day in Bristol. Jeremy Bryant walked briskly along to meet the ship.

In all his experience as Harbour Master, Jeremy Bryant never imagined a ship docking would have two boys on board that had disappeared from Bristol. Boys who had then been discovered on the Pegasus on its journey to Lisbon, and had arrived back in Bristol on a totally different ship, the Rose, and with a third boy—a slave at that! Quite astonishing. These were indeed strange times.

The Harbour Master was delighted with the return of Billy Thomas and young Samuel Castle but unsure what to do with the slave boy, who it seemed was called Ottabah. So many questions! God only knows who his owner was and where he is now. He was totally flummoxed and for once glad the slave boy would be the responsibility of someone else. It was a matter for the Constable.

By the time they had dealt with the formalities of the Rose, it was late afternoon. The Harbour Master then despatched a message to the Bristol Constabulary Office advising them the two missing boys had turned up on board the Rose. However, there were other issues that needed to be resolved. First, the kidnap of Samuel Castle, and second the allegation of theft by George Castle against Billy Thomas. Also, the ownership of a slave boy. Could Constable Norris who was dealing with these matters be available at eight o'clock at the Harbour Master's office the following morning?

He sent messages to William and Grace Castle and Jonathan Jerome for the information of Billy's mother, informing them of Samuel's and Billy's arrival on the Rose and requesting they be at the Harbour Master's Office at nine o'clock tomorrow.

Jeremy Bryant understood such a request may well puzzle the families and wonder why the boys could not simply go home. He added because of the disappearance of the boys and their befriending of a slave boy who was also on board the Rose, he felt obliged to ask Constable Norris to attend to resolve legal matters.

The messenger had barely left the Castles at their home when there was a knock on the door. William opened the door. Standing there was Joseph Sykes, their solicitor.

"Joseph, this is an unexpected pleasure."

"Unexpected perhaps, Mr Castle. A pleasure I am not so sure. I am not the bearer of good news, I am afraid. May I come in?"

Confused, William took the solicitor into the study,

where a happy Grace Castle welcomed him with a broad smile.

"I have a legal matter to discuss with you both, urgently."

"We have just received wonderful news, Joseph, have we not, William?" Grace continued. "Samuel and Billy Thomas have arrived in Bristol on the Rose. We will see them tomorrow."

"Ah. Wonderful news indeed! There is a but..."

If William and Grace had any doubts about the loyalty and dependability of Joseph Sykes, they were going to be dissuaded quickly.

"Information has come to me quite by accident. If truth be told by an incompetent clerk—fortunately, my father's and not mine. I have information your brother, George has in fact sought legal advice from his solicitor, my father of course. Fortunately, that advice was mistakenly placed into my personal box at my father's office. Having read the advice given to your brother, I had to consider my ethical position, for it related to you, Grace, my client. My loyalty is to you."

Grace frowned. "I don't understand."

"Let me explain. The legal advice sought by George Castle relates to the possibility of a woman inheriting a family business, namely Castles' Merchant Traders in the event of the death of her husband and son. Women taking over the running of a business from a husband or son is not unknown, but a man who is the natural heir as far as the bloodline is concerned can challenge it. George that is. If he could prove you were also unfit to run the family business, then Castles' Merchant Traders would pass to George. My father is of the opinion this is indeed a legal possibility."

Grace and William knew George was seeking legal advice but were stunned and outraged at what George was actually planning. Even worse, that George could be so duplicitous, and that the appalling action to disinherit Grace may well be legal.

Joseph continued. "We are fortunate my father is fully occupied with providing legal advice to the Bristol Merchant Venturers and is blasé about any other work including his advice to your brother, George Castle, as well as having an incompetent clerk!"

"I am at a loss here, Joseph," said William. "Grace has been part of Castles' Merchant Traders long before my father passed away. Father deliberately left the business to me partly because of Grace and partly because he did not approve of George's attitude towards the business. A fact that was mentioned in his will. He gave George a sum as his inheritance."

Grace had gone quiet. "I remember vividly your father's will was quite detailed. There was a first will. He had hoped to leave the business to both his sons but had realised this would be a mistake. If I remember correctly, it was because George was lazy and because of his attitude to business. George wanted to trade in slaves which their father found abhorrent. So the will was changed in William's favour." Grace paused. "I wonder if Samuel's disappearance was part of his plan. After all, for George to inherit the business then both Samuel and William would have to die. Oh, my God."

"I have not seen your father's will, William. I need to get my hands on it. Do you have a copy?"

Grace and William shook their heads.

"It was lodged with your father," said William. "Surely it cannot have disappeared. There are enough witnesses. Grace, George, your father and I."

CHAPTER FOURTEEN

8th September

It was the following morning and Captain Benedict hoped the issues surrounding the three boys would be speedily resolved. This would allow him to concentrate on his orders from the Admiralty, as well as re-victualling the Rose. Whilst seven days to prepare for the departure of a ship may seem ample time, experience taught him there was never enough.

Seaman Carter poked his head around the captain's cabin door.

"It is nearly eight o'clock, Captain, and you are due at the Harbour Master's office. Seaman Nelson is waiting at the dockside with the boys."

"Look after things here."

Seaman Carter nodded. "Aye, sir."

The captain had considered allowing Seaman Carter to attend the Harbour Master's office, but Robert Benedict had vowed to do his best for the three boys, particularly the slave boy, Ottabah. Not only did the boy need his help, but he deserved it.

Jeremy Bryant was well prepared for what was an important meeting. Better in his office than on board the Rose where space was limited, or indeed in the Constable's Office which he believed would have been too formal. The Harbour Master was a shrewd man, and he believed common sense. Tact was needed.

The kidnap of Samuel Castle was a serious offence and the culprit or culprits needed to be apprehended.

However, the allegation of theft by a very drunken George Castle against young Billy Thomas was, in the Harbour Master's opinion, frankly ridiculous. He knew the likes of Jonathan Jerome would not employ nor indeed tolerate a thief. The slave boy was a different kettle of fish, for as slaves were simply property, they had to have a legal owner. Jeremy Bryant recognised there may well be a special bond between the three boys. After all, they had been through a lot together.

The Harbour Master's office was indeed a grand representation of Bristol's importance as a port and therefore its Harbour Master. Jeremy Bryant was a person of esteem and influence. The office comprised not only the living quarters of the Harbour Master, but also a spacious office and meeting room, complete with a large table. He also had his own housekeeper—grumpy she may have been, but efficient she certainly was.

Captain Benedict, accompanied by Seaman Nelson, Samuel, Billy, and Ottabah, arrived punctually. Constable Bernard Norris was already there. They placed the three boys in the parlour in the housekeeper's care, who it seemed for once was in a good mood. The captain insisted Seaman Nelson should be present and assured the Constable the seaman had the highest level of integrity. After the introductions, for Robert Benedict had never met Constable Bernard Norris before, the Harbour Master began the meeting.

"To business, gentlemen. Captain Benedict, I am unsure how much of the details of the disappearance of the two boys you are aware of. May I suggest we start with Constable Norris here? It may be of help," said Jeremy Bryant.

Robert Benedict nodded and listened to the background outlined by the constable of the disappearance of Samuel Castle.

"Captain Benedict, perhaps you will tell us where you found these boys?" said the Constable.

Robert Benedict nodded. "It was the second of September, late afternoon. We were just south of the English coast when our lookout spotted a small boat. Three boys were discovered, two in a bad way, both cold and wet. I am told the slave boy who is called Ottabah was in the middle of the boys, apparently trying to keep his two friends warm. They owe him their lives, so my second in command tells me."

Constable Norris interrupted, "I hope, Captain you are not telling me the slave boy should be dealt with the same as the other two boys? He is a slave, and that is the end of the matter."

Robert Benedict showed not a flicker of the contempt he felt for the Constable.

"It is clear you do not have the slightest idea what the three boys have been through. Yes. Three boys, Constable. The captain bought and paid for the slave boy, as you call him. He was taken on board the Pegasus by Doctor James to save him from penury and to tend the wounds caused by the chains that bound him. It is also worth mentioning Ottabah was placed by Doctor James into the care of Billy and Samuel. We were told the Pegasus was caught in a violent storm and sank. These three boys are the only survivors. One of the last memories they had was being surrounded by hundreds of rats leaving a sinking ship. Now think on that."

Captain Benedict knew the future of these boys was in his hands and so he had to impress on the Constable what the three boys had gone through, and each of these boys had been brave and indeed heroic!

"Despite the Pegasus being in a dangerous state, Billy and Samuel risked their lives to search for Ottabah. They found him below deck. They have told us they stood on the edge of the sinking ship, staring into a stormy, treacherous sea, and simply jumped for their lives. It was Billy Thomas here who dragged the other two boys onto a boat which saved them from drowning. Since then, they have been at sea for a month or more surviving together, finding food and making shelter the best they could. Now I believe to get an understanding of what these three boys have been through, you need to talk to each of them. In my mind, they should be congratulated for their sheer courage and determination. They survived because they battled together. They survived because they shared everything. There was no slave on board. By the time we found them, they were in a bad way: cold, wet, starving. I placed these three boys under the personal care of Seaman Nelson here. Seaman Nelson, what state were these young boys in?"

"Not good, Captain. Not good."

Seaman Nelson, with blue eyes, looked even younger than his sixteen years. He pursed his lips and shook his head, blonde curls moving about.

"The three boys were huddled together, sir under a canvas cover. Ottabah was in the middle and Billy and

Samuel were clinging to him. They told me they hid from the slaver, the Black Swan. Billy and Samuel agreed they would rather drown than give Ottabah up. Ottabah could not swim and so he hid in the boat whilst the other boys went over the side and stayed there until the slaver was out of sight. They were in the water for some time, Captain. Ottabah had to drag both boys into the boat and, realising they were so cold, he laid in the middle to give them heat."

Jack Nelson grinned. "Clever. Really clever. Billy and Samuel saved Ottabah's life, and he had saved theirs, I am of no doubt. These three boys knew they would only survive by sticking together. They have a friendship that…" Seaman Nelson sighed, "I've never seen before."

The Constable was not as savvy as Jeremy Bryant who kept his own counsel and was not fooled by the lad's angelic face, a face that did not have any facial hair. The Harbour Master knew Captain Robert Benedict well enough, and he would not have a fool, young or otherwise, as a member of his crew. Constable Norris sniggered.

Jeremy Bryant stepped in before Bernard Norris had time to spit.

"If I may ask Seaman Nelson a question, Captain?"

Robert Benedict wondered where this question from the Harbour Master was going, but it would have been churlish to refuse. He nodded, and the Constable grinned as he believed the backslapping by the Captain and Seaman would now end.

"What do you think should happen to the three boys? You know them better than anyone else, I believe."

"There's more to these three boys than the sinking of the Pegasus and their survival. God only knows how. Each boy had gone through so much before. Samuel was kidnapped and beaten and left for dead. Billy Thomas at thirteen helped to care for his family by delivering messages and was then accused of theft when he asked for the payment owed to him. His employer, George Castle threatened and bullied him. Lastly… Ottabah."

Jack Nelson shook his head, sighed, and then paused for effect.

"Slavers kidnapped him from his family; sold and treated no better than an animal, so cruel men could profit. He cannot speak their language and they cannot speak his, yet Samuel and Billy searched for him, despite the risk they might go down with the ship. Then these three boys took a leap of faith together." Seaman Nelson smiled. "What they had to do and eat explains the stink, Captain."

Constable Norris was furious. "Have you lost your wits, lad? You cannot compare the kidnapping of Samuel Castle with slavery. Captain, deal with this boy."

"That is enough, Seaman Nelson. But Constable, the lad is quite right."

It was Robert Benedict who interceded. "I believe Seaman Nelson is simply saying that the kidnap of young Samuel Castle from his family is no different to Ottabah being taken by force from his. After all, we are not savages."

Seaman Nelson nodded.

"Fetch the boys. All three if you would."

"Aye aye, sir."

Seaman Nelson made a hasty retreat. He knew he had stirred a hornets' nest. A short while later, Seaman Nelson appeared with the three boys. Ottabah stood in the middle. Jeremy Bryant smiled at Samuel and Billy but was unsure what to do or to say to Ottabah.

"Samuel and Billy have something to say to the Constable if they may, Captain?"

Captain Benedict nodded. Billy and Samuel put one arm each around their newfound friend. Samuel was the spokesperson of the group.

"Constable, sir. Billy and I wish to beg for the freedom of our friend." Samuel nodded towards Ottabah. "Captain Fothergill who released him into the care of Doctor James, told us to look after him. He bought him in Lisbon. The Pegasus sunk in an almighty storm. Billy here took charge, and we all jumped off the ship together. Billy saved us from drowning. So, we owe our life to Billy. Ottabah fished for food and kept us warm when we were wet and frozen. So, we owe our lives to Ottabah. Without them," Samuel struggled to control his emotions, "I would have died."

Billy smiled and shook his head. "Samuel will not say what he has done. He has gone through so much. When the Pegasus was sinking, Sam helped me save Ottabah. On the boat, it was Sam that was always so calm, and it was Sam who said to hide Ottabah when the slaver was approaching. So, we owe our lives to him. Constable, please! Do not send Ottabah back to slavery. It is evil," said Billy.

Lost At Sea

Constable Norris was speechless.

Robert Benedict continued. "These three boys have been with us for seven days since we plucked them out of the sea. In that time, Billy, Samuel, and Ottabah have conducted themselves with great credit. I for one would have Billy as a Seaman on the Rose tomorrow. He is hard-working and honest. Samuel has survived abduction and a life-threatening injury to his head. He is made of stern stuff. He is a clever lad and a leader. My admiration is the greatest for Ottabah. Despite his different background and being unable to speak the same language, he put his faith in two young boys, and they put their faith in him. Ottabah has been through enough. He wants and deserves his freedom. For that is the greatest gift of all."

Bernard Norris remained silent. There was a kidnap, a thief, and a slave.

Jeremy Bryant said, "Now, Constable, where do we go from here?"

"I need to report to the Justices of the Peace, and I would be grateful if the three boys could stay together for the moment. I need to speak to them again tomorrow. Also, the ownership of the boy...."

As he nodded towards Ottabah. Constable Norris had moderated his tone.

A knock on the door provided a slight impasse. Jeremy Bryant's housekeeper poked her head around the corner.

"Sir, it is nine o'clock and Mr and Mrs Castle have arrived along with Mr Jerome."

"Give them some refreshments, Mrs Blunt. We will be with them shortly."

Bessie Blunt smiled through her teeth and cursed the day Grace Castle had visited the Harbour Master. He had gone soft in his head since that day. The housekeeper directed the visitors to a room where they could wait in comfort.

"I see Mrs Thomas is not with you, Jonathan," said William.

Jonathan nodded. "She felt she may be a hindrance. Mrs Thomas believes, as I do, that Billy is no thief, and he would only take from George what he believed he was owed. George Castle is my business partner, and she feels my speaking on his behalf would in her words 'carry more clout' than hers."

William and Grace Castle sat talking to Jonathan Jerome, whilst the housekeeper huffed and puffed around them. There was a loud knock on the door and the housekeeper, temper frayed at the edges by now, growled and walked to the door. Upon opening it there stood George Castle. Grace frowned at the familiar voice and in he strutted.

"I called to see you, William but you were not there, were you? You were here." He laughed at his own joke. "Your housekeeper told me where you were. I thought we were all friends together now, searching for the missing boys. Apparently not."

"We did not need you at this meeting, that is why," snapped William.

"And Jonathan is?"

Jonathan shrugged his shoulders. "I am simply here on behalf of Mrs Thomas. To make sure her son is not accused of something he has not done. Ironically accused by you, George. I am here to ensure fair play."

Lost At Sea

George visited the Castles' residence hoping to speak to William and Grace as well as try to discover the latest information. He was worried Samuel's memory had returned, and they had deliberately kept him in the dark. Samuel or Billy hadn't heard or seen him, or had they? Was he simply getting paranoid? He had taken a chance to attend the meeting, feign ignorance, and use bluster. Whatever it took, he had to be there and be able to defend himself if he needed to.

"Mrs Blunt, you can send everyone in. I did not expect you, Mr Castle, George that is," said Jeremy Bryant.

"Well. I am here now. I am here to see my nephew."

There was a gasp from inside. "That is the voice, Billy," said Samuel as he collapsed on the floor.

George was the closest to the door leading to the Harbour Master's office and had heard what Samuel said. He panicked for he knew it was his voice Samuel had recognised. The others present would not know, or so he hoped. He had to hasten. He pushed his way into the Harbour Master's office and saw Samuel on the floor with his two friends kneeling at his side. Samuel's eyes were shut, and he was still. Not so much as a flicker. Billy knew his friend was unconscious.

"Get back, get back. My nephew needs fresh air," shouted George, whereupon he scooped the boy into his arms and headed for the door and outside onto the dockside.

George had not the slightest idea what he was going to do. Think. Think.

He could make a dash for it with the boy, but that would surely seal his guilt. He had to silence the boy or rescue him. Madness. Madness. George walked slowly and calmly to the dockside making soothing noises.

"The boy is awake. Thank goodness," he shouted towards the bewildered group.

A plan was forming in his head.

George exclaimed, "You are safe, Samuel. Quite safe with me. Who? What are you frightened of?"

George bent his head towards a still unconscious boy, but what did they know? He shook his head in disbelief.

"Surely not. Surely not."

William stood. Could it really be someone else had kidnapped Samuel, and George was innocent? Grace gasped and put a hand to her mouth.

"Have we been looking for the wrong person, William? All this time."

George, whilst supposedly soothing Samuel and nodding and whispering to him, sidled slowly to the dockside. He had cleverly, or so he had believed, put seeds of doubt about the identity of the kidnappers in their minds whilst also appearing to come to the aid of his nephew. He smiled to himself, missed by everyone but Ottabah and Billy, for they had followed George outside.

Billy had smelt a rat from the beginning. He knew George Castle of old. He was nothing but a cheat and a liar. Billy had seen Samuel unconscious on the Pegasus and so he knew he would not come around sometime soon. What was going on? Ottabah also instinctively sensed danger. Something was wrong.

The two boys moved closer to George so they could get a look at their friend. Samuel's eyes were shut. His body was limp. But then Samuel coughed, spluttered, and blinked. He stared long and hard at his uncle who was so close he could feel his breath upon his face. There was a dawning like the sun rising in the east, of recognition and absolute terror.

Samuel gazed at Uncle George and tried to scream. But before he could say a word, George placed his hand firmly over the boy's mouth. In absolute panic, George looked around him. In a daze, he staggered with the boy in his arms toward the edge of the dock. Samuel froze.

"What on earth is going on, George? Are you trying to strangle the boy?" shouted Jonathan Jerome.

Jeremy Bryant, Jonathan Jerome, William Castle, and Grace Castle stood still in silence. They dare not breathe never mind move. Constable Norris watched George Castle intently. He stood perfectly still.

George's plan, if he had one, disappeared into thin air. He then decided. One last-ditch effort. He was going to jump, fall, or trip whatever it took to end up in the water. Samuel had to die. What had he to lose? Nothing. After all, it had been total chaos. A lot of shouting. Who had heard what? Could be nothing. Simply a misunderstanding.

George's heart pounded, and his breath quickened. Samuel was going in the water all right. At least a twenty-foot drop.

"Keep still, stop moving about. I might drop you," shouted George Castle.

The boy in George's arms, still rigid with fear, stared in terror. Samuel did not dare take as much as a single breath. Not even blink. The look on his uncle's face was pure hatred.

George dropped the boy into the water.

He delayed his reaction deliberately and then shouted, "I'll get him."

George jumped into the water, arms and legs flailing, coughing, and spluttering as if he was drowning, hoping he was showing concern whilst causing chaos. In the confusion and with a bit of luck, the boy would drown.

However, Samuel had barely hit the water when Billy jumped in and landed at his side. Ottabah did not know what to do. He could not swim, and he did not want to distract from the rescue of Samuel. So, he remained quiet but ready to help his friends if need be.

Quickly by Ottabah's side was Captain Benedict and Seaman Nelson.

Captain Benedict said to Seaman Nelson, "In you go, lad, they need help."

Seaman Nelson grinned at his captain and jumped. The drop from the dockside to the water below held no fear for an excellent swimmer like Jack Nelson. Samuel had disappeared under the surface. Billy and Jack Nelson both dived under the water. They grabbed the boy's jacket and between them they hauled him to the surface. Fortunately, the shock of cold water made Sam gasp, and he started coughing.

George Castle was in shock. Floundering and gasping, he had drunk too much water and was struggling to get his breath.

The Harbour Master quickly joined Robert Benedict, complete with a piece of light wood for exactly such a situation. Jeremy Bryant threw the piece of wood

Lost At Sea

expertly to the boys. Jack Nelson grabbed hold of it and placed his hands under Samuel's armpits, then held onto the piece of wood.

"Well done, lad," shouted the Harbour Master. "Hang on, it will keep you afloat."

Young Jack Nelson knew exactly what he was doing, kicking his legs to keep afloat.

"We need a rope," shouted Captain Benedict. "We have to get the boy to the dockside wall, and we have to tie a rope around him so we can pull him up safely."

The Harbour Master nodded and disappeared momentarily, returning with a rope. Captain Benedict quickly took hold of the rope, securing a loop on one end. He called Jack Nelson.

"You know what you have to do?"

Jack nodded and grinned.

"Billy, we have to put this loop under Sam's arms and one of us will have to go up with him so he does not hurt himself on the wall. You are taller than me and have longer legs. Do you think you can go up with Sam, arms around him, feet on the wall to stop him from hitting it?"

Billy frowned and then understood what he had to do. Jack quickly placed the rope around Sam.

"Arms under and hold the rope for dear life, Billy. Understand?"

Billy nodded.

"Billy will come up with him, Captain." Jack then turned to Billy. "Feet on the wall. Keep your legs straight."

Billy followed his instructions and Jack signalled to his captain for Sam to be hauled slowly up the wall side. Jeremy Bryant was quite adept at this, and he gently pulled the rope, hauling the two boys slowly to the top, watched by a growing group of spectators, including the crew of the Rose.

Meanwhile, the floundering George gave up after an irate William Castle bawled at him.

"What are you doing you, fool? You can swim."

Jack, a most competent swimmer, rested on the piece of wood and shouted encouragement to Billy, and, when both boys had reached the dockside, they were met by a tearful Ottabah and cheering from the crew of the Rose.

Robert Benedict and Jeremy Bryant lifted both boys over the edge of the dock and onto the dockside where William and Grace Castle were waiting. William stooped down and picked up his son who was exhausted and wet through and carried him to the Harbour Master's house. He needed to get Samuel warm and dry. Unceremoniously, William walked into the parlour and asked Mrs Blunt for a blanket.

Jack swam to the steps to a wet and miserable George Castle. On the dockside stood Constable Norris who had been closely watching the proceedings.

"Are you all right, lad?" said the Constable. "Well done. Well done indeed."

"It's young Billy you should thank, Constable not me. What I don't understand is how he," he nodded towards George Castle, "can speak to someone who is unconscious. Must be a miracle."

"Indeed. As you say, lad it must be a miracle," said Bernard Norris.

The Constable glared at George Castle.

Robert Benedict shouted, "Well done, Jack. To the Rose with you. Get Seaman Carter to come and have a look at Sam and get yourself dried off."

Samuel Castle was the key witness. The Constable needed the lad to have a clear recollection of the kidnap otherwise George Castle could dig his way out of yet another hole. Perhaps it went some way to explain his clumsy attempt to drown the boy whilst pretending to save him. Constable Norris had to get Samuel away from the influence of the abhorrent George Castle and he needed to draw in a few favours and seek advice.

What the Constable had learned these last few weeks was George Castle had lived a charmed life, and he was unpopular in many quarters. He may be a well-heeled rogue, however, but he was still a man of influence.

Constable Norris spoke to Jonathan Jerome for he knew George Castle well. It was odd, or so the Constable thought, how Jonathan Jerome had distanced himself from George Castle since the disappearance of Samuel and Billy. He also recognised with the sinking of the Pegasus, which was jointly owned by both men, that even if they were properly insured, money would be tight. He decided he would speak to the boys the following day. But first, he needed to speak to his senior constable.

Grace Castle stood on the dockside along with Jeremy Bryant, Robert Benedict, Jonathan Jerome, Billy, and Ottabah. She thanked Robert Benedict for the care of the three boys, and Jeremy Bryant for his help in the rescue of her son. She then turned to Billy and shook his hand, then to Ottabah and shook his, and thanked them both.

"Would you boys kindly check on Samuel for me, please?"

Billy nodded. With an arm around Ottabah's shoulders, he guided him towards the Harbour Master's office.

As the two friends departed, Robert Benedict nodded in their direction.

"Mrs Castle, Mr Jerome, if I may have a word? Samuel and Billy pleaded with the Constable this morning to give Ottabah his freedom. Should we return Ottabah to slavery, then I believe they will forgive none of us. Use your best endeavours to secure his freedom. He has earned it."

Grace looked towards Jonathan, and they agreed.

Constable Norris had watched in amazement at the events that had unravelled before his very eyes. The most astonishing part of the dockside events was the sudden appearance of George Castle. Not only had he not been invited to the original meeting but also, he seemed somewhat agitated. Bernard Norris pursed his lips. Most odd. Samuel had muttered something about 'the voice' then from nowhere George Castle appeared, or so it seemed. He picked the lad up, left, and ended up by the dockside. He watched the reaction of the two boys. Curious, the Constable followed them to the dockside. It quite intrigued him. He could see Samuel was unconscious, and yet George Castle seemed to have a conversation with him.

When George Castle, with the boy in his arms, ended up in the water, Bernard Norris thought there were people better equipped than he to help and so he stood to one side, observing the unfolding events. Captain Benedict had taken charge along with Jeremy Bryant. Constable Norris's opinion of some of those present had changed. Billy, with no thought for his own safety, had jumped into the water, swiftly followed by Seaman Nelson. Ottabah, in absolute despair, was leaning over the dockside watching the rescue.

Constable Norris, if he was going to be honest, now better understood what Captain Benedict and Seaman Nelson had said about the strong bond between the three boys. Could it be right or fair that Samuel and Billy should be praised for their actions after the sinking of the Pegasus, whilst Ottabah was simply returned to slavery?

He was also a little embarrassed by the tone of Captain Benedict and Jeremy Bryant towards him that morning. There must be a way this matter could be resolved. He turned to look for George Castle, but he had disappeared. How unfortunate.

They agreed that all three boys should go to the home of William and Grace Castle and they would visit the Senior Constable's office the following morning. Bernard Norris believed the unravelling of the mystery behind the abduction of Samuel would depend on the boy's memory.

The Constable also realised much of the evidence had been down to the persistence of Grace Castle distributing posters and visiting inns and taverns, as well as talking to people from the Harbour Master to the Customs and Excise Officers. It was surprising how local people had rallied to her cause and had given her their support. She was very popular and well-liked, particularly by the men.

Then there was Captain Fothergill's letter, which had been delivered by Captain Featherstone of the Swift to the Bristol Authorities and which had really set the hare running. For it was that letter that made the Castles realise the two boys on the Pegasus were in fact, Samuel and Billy.

Harry Wetherell and his wife, Gem, not forgetting Ned Champion and his wife, Elizabeth, had also come up trumps. Bernard Norris believed they had unwittingly witnessed the abduction and that George Castle had been present.

The Constable was not without his own contacts. He had received news which he needed to pass on to the Castles and Jonathan Jerome, that the man, Jed Stone who had given information and handed over a battered ransom note, had been found with his throat slit in an outhouse at the back of the Rat and Barrel. There was enough information to arrest George Castle, but he was a well-known trader and investor and would have his supporters. The Constable needed to proceed with care. Many prominent Bristol citizens were slave traders or at least profited from slave trading and they would not take kindly to a slave boy, even though he may have earned his freedom, undermining them or their trading.

Constable Norris needed advice.

George Castle was standing on the dockside, soaked to the skin. He was angry and frustrated, but he was not demoralised. Far from it. Such was his self-belief at the righteousness of his claim to his inheritance of Castles' Merchant Traders, nothing would dissuade him from righting that wrong. Nothing.

In his mind, he had been patient. Tolerant, even. He dismissed the mistakes he had made, not least the bodged kidnapping, everything else had worked well. He needed time to think about what he should do next.

George watched as his brother, William, his wife, Grace, along with Jonathan and the three boys, followed by Constable Norris and Jeremy Bryant, walked back into the Harbour Master's house. They were oblivious to him and his sodden state. None of them had shown any concern about his safety despite his apparent effort to rescue the boy. George took a deep breath, turning abruptly and walking along the dockside before turning down Wapping Road and stopping near its junction with Guinea Street, where he could discretely observe the Castles' house and adjacent warehouse.

It was much later when George saw an approaching carriage. As the carriage drew nearer, he could see William, Grace, and the three boys. Now that puzzled him. Why the slave boy and why young Billy Thomas? After all, had not young Billy Thomas stolen from him? The slave boy should have been back in chains where he belonged.

Life was unfair. A plan was fermenting in his mind. Whilst at the dockside, George overheard the boys would be seen the following day at noon in the Senior Constable's Office, which was within the Petty Sessions Court Building. The frustration for George was he did not know what his nephew could remember, nor whether he had confided in Billy Thomas.

He pondered a while and considered what Billy

Thomas may or may not have heard or seen the night of the kidnapping. George now knew when he and his fellow kidnappers were carrying the carpet with Samuel inside and approaching the dockside, Billy Thomas had been in hiding close by.

He, George, may well be in the clear, but he simply did not know. The fracas earlier could be explained away as an overprotective uncle who had simply tripped and dropped the boy in the water. Unfortunate, but a crime surely not.

George returned to his room. He felt much better now and clearer. He had a plan, but he needed help. Help from Bart—Bartholomew Holroyd to give him his full name. George quickly had something to eat, but no alcohol as he needed his wits about him. He left his room just before ten o'clock. It was dusk, and he knew Bart would be at the Rat and Barrel in the back room where crimes were planned, proceeds divided up, and back handers paid.

As expected, George found Bart in the back room talking to Colin Bickerstaff the innkeeper. Although the events at the dockside stoked the boiler of his anger and the hatred of his brother and his family, he was determined to keep his anger and frustration under control.

George found an empty table and nodded at Bart who wandered over, placed both hands on the table, and leant towards him. Bart nodded but said nothing.

"Bart, I have a proposition for you."

There was an edge in George's voice which made the hair raise at the back of his neck. Bart was alert.

Keeping a calm tone Bart said, "Sounds something

important, Mr Castle."

George snarled. "I have a job. A proper job, not for cocking up. Sit down and shut up."

Bart sat down, pursed his lips, tempted for a moment to pick George Castle up by the throat and chuck him headfirst through the nearest window. Alarm bells were ringing.

"Must be dangerous. How much?"

"One hundred guineas."

Bart blinked. A small fortune to the likes of him.

"What do I have to do?"

George smiled a wolfish smirk. "The Castles. Wipe them out. Kill them all. Lock, stock and barrel." He laughed out loud.

Men huddled together on separate tables and talking in hushed tones stopped and turned their attention to George and Bart. George had let his anger show. He bit his lips, cursing inwardly, then he glanced downwards at his shaking hands. He needed to compose himself. Despite George's efforts, Bart could see he was also a deeply troubled man. Insane even. This was not the place for loose tongues and careless words.

The kidnapping of the lad had raised its head again, for Bart had contacts and he knew the Castle boy was back. What could the lad remember? He had to tread carefully; he already had to dispose of a loose-lipped Jed Stone. Could Bart trust George Castle to be discreet and hold his temper?

Bart sucked his teeth, something that irritated George.

"Good god, man. Keep your voice down. This is dangerous talk. Serious stuff. When are we doing it?"

said Bart quietly.

"Tomorrow morning."

Bart was shocked. "So soon?"

Bart had done many things in his life, including being a mercenary. He had been paid well mind. You name it and he had done it. It was a dangerous game that could send a man to the gallows. Having a good leader who not only had a calm head but who also was good at planning was why he was still alive. George was neither a leader nor indeed temperate. Bart could smell danger at a hundred paces, and he felt swamped in it.

He glanced at George. "It needs thought."

"I didn't take you for a coward," snapped George.

Bart glared at him and hissed. "I am no coward, you lily-livered man, and I am no fool. Whilst you have been messing about as a trader, strutting about Bristol with your airs and graces I have been scrapping and killing. You, with your fancy clothes and your money and rich friends. What do you know about anything? Nothing."

George's eyes nearly popped out of his head at the implied insult.

"I'll tell you what I know. My nephew, Samuel who you helped to kidnap and who we thought to be dead is in fact very much alive. He has returned home and earlier today I am sure he recognised me. If he identifies me, then they will be onto you. Now at noon tomorrow, Grace and William Castle and Jonathan Jerome, Samuel, Billy Thomas, and a slave boy will visit the Bristol Constable's' office and be spoken to by the Senior Constable. A Justice of the Peace will then make a judgment on what happens next. So, it is in your interest and mine to stop this from happening."

Bart sat back on his stool, and leaned against the wall, deep in thought.

"The thing is, George, your nephew never clocked me, did he? In fact, they have got nothing against me at all. I will deny everything. I'll get someone to swear I was blind drunk and somewhere else. Like here at the Rat and Barrel."

George shook his head. "Trust me. If I hang, you will be next to me taking the drop. Do you really believe any judge will believe you before me?"

Bart took a deep breath. George was right. He needed to change tack.

"I see. We need to finish this, then. You have a plan?"

"We could murder them in their beds. Or perhaps set fire to the warehouse, which will spread to their house. I thought of hijacking the carriage on the way to the Constable's Office, but that will be difficult as it would have to take place in public and would be too risky."

Bart considered. "So, you have no plan at all, then. If we set fire to the warehouse, the flames will simply spread and kill many more folk."

"So what?" George shrugged.

"There is another way," glowered Bart.

George Castle glared with arrogance and spite. "Yes? Go on."

"Do nothing."

"Nothing?" snapped George.

Bart nodded. He leaned forward.

"It was something you said to me earlier. Who are

they going to believe? You or your nephew? The boy with a battered head? No."

"I am an upstanding gentleman, trader and… there's a thought."

Bart held his breath, waiting. He had his own plans.

"No. It needs to be done in the early hours tomorrow when it is pitch black. We will set fire to the warehouse close to their living quarters. I will deny my involvement and as you say, I am an upstanding gentleman and member of the Bristol Merchant Venturers, and I will have an alibi."

Bart kept silent. Clearly, George had given no thought to Bart or his alibi. George was an arrogant, selfish man. This stiffened his resolve. Bart was neither upstanding nor a gentleman. He knew he needed his wits about him.

CHAPTER FIFTEEN

They would meet an hour before daybreak in the alley near the Castles' residence on Anchor Road, the very alley in which they had hidden to kidnap the boy. Bart was to bring grease or some other sort of accelerant and rags for the fire. The rags would be placed as directed by George as he was familiar with the layout of the warehouse.

Bart kept a straight face. He had watched experienced arsonists plan a fire. They took a great deal of time and care and certainly did not set fire to anything simply thought up the night before. The place, the weather, the material that a building was made of, even the wind direction, had to be considered. Not forgetting what was being used to set the place on fire. Grease would take some setting alight. George was looking at a quick fix and Bart had a bad feeling about it all.

" Be better with rum, not grease," said Bart, "and, I want 50 guineas up front and 50 when it is done."

Angrily, George snarled, "Don't take me for a fool, Bart."

"Please yourself!" Bart stood up, shrugged his shoulders, and turned to leave.

"I do not carry that amount with me. I will have it ready for you in the alley."

Bart shook his head. He placed both hands on the table and leaned towards George.

Looking him in the eye, he whispered. "I don't trust you. I want half now or you're on your own."

Bart stood up and glared at him. George had half the money with him. He was simply trying it on.

"Outside. I'm not giving you money in here."

Bart and George got up and left the Rat and Barrel by the back door, known only to the crooks and murderers and thieves. The back alley was in fact where Bart had slit the throat of the unfortunate Jed Stone, who he had quite liked if it was possible for Bart to like anyone. Bart was tempted to slit the throat of George Castle there and then. However, George was a bigger fish than poor Jed, and anyway, fifty guineas was up for grabs, whatever happened.

One hour before dawn, Bart waited for George Castle as arranged.

He carried a bag over his shoulder and wore a jacket with a high collar and a face covering. He had not set fire to property before but had been with men who had. Bart had been with soldiers who used black powder to blow up bridges, but he had no intentions of using the black stuff. Too deadly for a start.

Bart had his own plan and his own method. He was prepared and waited for George in the alley's shadow, and as he did so, he saw him walking down the road. George attempted a disguise, but it was unconvincing. Bart would know him anywhere. It was the strutting arrogance of the man, which gave him away.

George approached the alley where Bart was waiting. Bart made himself known to George quietly. He opened his sack, showing him its contents: strips of rags.

"I have a keg of rum and wooden staves hidden by the warehouse."

George nodded and grinned. "The warehouse is wooden and there is plenty around the back. It has not rained for a while so should be dry enough."

"Show me the rest of the money."

"Don't you trust me?"

Bart did not say a word.

George held his nerve and tapped his jacket pocket. "The rest is here and yours when they are all dead."

Bart stared at him. "Follow me."

He turned and walked down the alley towards the rear of Castles' Warehouse.

Grace and William got little sleep that night. They spent some time trying to understand what happened to Samuel on the day of the kidnapping and talking to the three boys, hopefully gaining the confidence of Billy and especially Ottabah. Grace and William also agreed they would ask the Senior Constable if Ottabah could remain with them. Whether it was possible, even, to become part of Castles' Merchant traders in some capacity. Billy had matured and Grace did not believe for one moment he would have stolen money from George. It made little sense.

As for Samuel, it seemed his memory was returning, if slowly, and certain events and possessions prompted his memory, in particular Alice's gift of the carved ship.

Grace was unsure, but she thought Samuel recognised George at the Harbour Master's House, and seeing him had provoked both a memory and a reaction. She had not been close enough to hear what he said when George picked her son up. But it appeared to her to have been very contrived and

George seemed anxious.

It was daybreak when William and Grace were awoken by a loud banging on their front door. Puzzled, and a little confused, William got out of bed. He quickly put on a pair of trousers before picking up a small lit candle.

"I will see what the racket is all about, Grace, you stay here."

She nodded but instinctively got out of bed and got dressed. Something was wrong.

William went downstairs where he was met by Mrs Harper.

"What on earth is all that racket, Mr Castle? Enough to waken the dead, never mind me and you."

William opened the front door and there stood Constable Norris.

"Sorry to trouble you at this unearthly hour, Mr Castle but you need to come with me."

William wrinkled his nose. "Do I smell smoke, Constable?"

"You do. Quickly now."

Before William could say another word, Constable Norris set off running, turning down the street that ran down the side of the house and warehouse.

"You are worrying me now, Bernard."

The Constable ran down the side of the warehouse. The stench of acrid smoke stung William's eyes, which made it even more difficult to see in the darkness. As they approached the backend of the warehouse, William could just make out two figures. One kneeling on the ground holding a lantern over another, who was moaning and gasping for breath.

Lost At Sea

At one side was a sack and a barrel, which were surrounded by burnt rags, wooden staves, and a distinct smell of liquor. It was rum. How odd! Two young lads were standing by the burnt rags which had been extinguished. William frowned.

As they approached, William recognised Brian Whitehouse who owned the horse and carriage business on the street directly behind William's warehouse, and where William was a regular customer. Brian was holding the lantern.

"Brian, what on earth is going on?"

"It's your brother, George. He is in a bad way. "

Brian held the lantern over the slumped figure on the floor. It was George Castle right enough. He was bleeding profusely. George was pale, sweating, and had lost a considerable amount of blood. Not that William could see, but he knew his brother was in a bad way.

"I have done the best I can to stem the bleeding, William but…" Brian shook his head in dismay.

"None of this makes any sense," said William. "Why is he here and what are all these burnt rags?"

Brian took a deep breath. "I heard angry shouting from behind the stable yard, which of course is at the back of your warehouse. It got louder, and I thought the racket would frighten my horses. I called two of my stable lads." He nodded towards them. "We went to look. We could smell smoke which worried me even more. Nothing worse for frightening horses than flames and smoke. As we got round the back there were two men. One was on the ground and the other a big chap, was standing over him rifling through his pockets. I shouted at him, and he ran off cursing. There were rags still burning and scattered about. One wooden stave was still aflame which the lads put out. I went to look at the man on the ground. I recognised him straight away. It was George. He is in a bad way, William."

"The man who got away. Any idea who he was?" said William.

Bernard shook his head.

William knelt at his brother's side. He lifted the edge of George's jacket and as he did so, blood oozed from a gaping wound in his stomach. William grimaced. His brother was dying.

"George! My God! What happened?"

"I'm done for, William. If you only knew what I had planned for you." George gasped and grinned. "You would not feel any pity for me then, Brother. Come closer, William. I have nothing to lose now."

William leaned towards his brother.

"Closer," whispered George.

William placed his ear as close as he could to his brother's mouth.

"What is it, George? What has happened to you?"

George managed a laugh and a cough. Blood oozed from his mouth and splattered William's face. William was oblivious.

"You have no idea, have you, William? No idea how much I hate you!" George coughed and gasped for breath. "I hate you. I hate your wife. I hate your son. It was me who kidnapped your boy." He spat the last word with venom. "I was going to set fire to your warehouse and kill you all."

George gasped. "I should have inherited. Not you, not your wife, and certainly not that, that, boy of yours." George closed his eyes and he grimaced in pain. "I made a vow I would get Castles' Merchant Traders back. I did not care how. By fair means or foul."

George gasped for the last time and died.

Silence shattered the calm.

William looked at his dead brother, the burnt rags, and the keg of rum, and shook his head.

"I had no idea he hated me so much. I do not understand."

Brian Whitehouse approached William and said, "Harsh as this might sound, William, you are all safer now your brother is dead."

Constable Norris nodded. There had been a fallout between George Castle and his accomplice, whoever he was. His accomplice had stabbed him and was robbing him when he was disturbed. The Constable would keep his opinion to himself for the time being, at least.

With the Constable's approval, Brian Whitehouse removed George Castle's body. He placed it in a secure outhouse in his stable yard and covered it with a horse blanket whilst arrangements could be made to take the body to the Bristol Mortuary. George Castle was a well-known Bristol citizen and formalities needed to be followed.

Constable Norris walked with William back to his home.

"Things need formalising, William. I will see you at noon as arranged."

William nodded. Grace stood by the opened door and knew from William's face he was in deep shock.

Bart sat behind a wall not that far from the side of the Castles' Warehouse, his chest heaving to get back his breath. He had got away just in time and without being recognised, or so he believed. He shuffled his feet to get more comfortable and moved closer to the wall. His senses were alert to the slightest movement. He held his breath momentarily as he heard a slight sound, then sighed with relief as two small eyes peered at him. A fox. He would remain where he was until he felt the coast was clear but before the hue and cry.

He regretted many things he had done in his life. In fact, if truth be told he was sad to have had to slit the throat of the young lad, Jed Stone. The kidnapping of Samuel Castle was an utter shambles, and it was down to the rushed planning of George Castle. He was the murderer, not Bart. Bart had learnt his lesson that day. He knew he would have to kill George as he would not hesitate to kill him or have him killed. Unless, of course, Bart ended up dead because of one of George's shambolic schemes, which was more likely.

He grimaced. Bart would trust a snake more than George, and he had met a few snakes in his time. Bart was quite right not to trust him. Whilst they were wrapping rags around wooden staves ready to be dipped in the casket of rum, Bart again asked to see the second pouch containing the fifty guineas owed.

George tapped his jacket and said, "We need to get a move on."

They continued to wrap the rags around the wooden staves and dip them in the keg of rum. Bart had already had a plan in his mind to finish George off, but he was biding his time. He needed to catch him unawares. A dozen or more staves were ready to be lit and placed around the warehouse.

"Come on, George this is the dangerous bit. I want to see my money."

George ignored him and lit the stave he held in his hand. Frustrated, Bart made a grab for George by his coat collar, swiftly turning him around, pulling him close so he could look into his eyes and feel his breath.

He snarled. "No messing. The purse, George, or I swear I'll break your neck this very second with my bare hands."

George gasped. "My inside pocket. The pouch is there. You have seen it."

Bart shoved his hand into George's coat and grabbed the leather pouch which was secured by a leather strip at the top. He shook it and glared at George.

It was then they both realised the stave which George had dropped on the ground was now ablaze. Not only that, but it had also set fire to other staves and torn rags.

"Bart, quickly!" George picked up his lit stave. "We need to place these. Before it's too late."

Now Bart never intended to involve himself with the latter part of George's scheme. He shook the purse. It did not sound right. Bart pursed his lips, opened the pouch, and poured a variety of pebbles into his hand. George watched in horror as the pebbles dropped out. The time seemed to George to be a lifetime, but it was barely to the count of five. He was done for. He knew it.

Bart put a hand into his belt, drew out his knife, and as quick as you like, he stuck it in George's gut.

Bart hissed, "You are a lying…" He twisted the knife. "Cheating…" He twisted it again. "Man…"

Before more vitriol could pour from Bart's mouth, the shout of 'fire!' stopped him in his tracks. He could hear but not see anyone in the darkness and so ran off down his pre-planned escape route at the back of the warehouse. Bart knew he had to prepare for the plan going drastically wrong.

He hid behind a wall for a little while. He pulled his knees to his chest and shuffled as close as he was able in the cloak of darkness provided by the wall. After what he considered sufficient time, he stood up and silently slipped away. At least he still had his fifty guineas from last night. It was a goodly sum and should provide him with some security for his future.

Bart felt sure no one would have known about his and George's night time activities. The death of someone of George Castle's standing would be investigated. That he murdered George before they could have completed their plan would have to remain his secret until his death.

The problem for Bart was he had been seen regularly in the company of George Castle and had a reputation for violence, known to the authorities. He knew he needed to lie low, perhaps leave Bristol, and even travel.

There were many ships sailing for France.

EPILOGUE

At eleven o'clock the following morning, a carriage driven by Brian Whitehouse arrived to collect William and Grace Castle along with Samuel, Billy, and Ottabah. Despite the death of George Castle, Constable Norris still wanted the meeting to go ahead, and, importantly in the presence of Senior Constable Elton. The three boys were nervous about the meeting. Brian could see William looked exhausted and Grace's face was etched with concern for her husband.

"Come and sit up here with me, William. The fresh air will serve you well."

Making sure everyone was safely on board the carriage, William joined Brian at the front. The carriage slowly set off.

"How are things, William?"

William shook his head. "What can I say? When my brother was dying, he told me he hated me and my family. Not only had that he also planned to murder us all. What possesses a man to do such a wicked thing?"

"George was unhinged," commented Brian. "If your warehouse had caught fire, it would have spread quickly. How many more people would have died? It was madness."

"George must have had some help though, an accomplice even. Otherwise, how would he know what to do and where to go?" added William.

Brian nodded. "The stable lads got there before me and they both said there was another man with him, and they were having a real argument. The other man, a big man, had George by the throat."

"Would they recognise him, do you think?"

"Not so sure. They seemed to be nervous of him, frightened even. I wondered if they knew him."

The carriage arrived in good time. Awaiting their arrival outside the Petty Sessions Court Building was Jonathan Jerome who helped Grace Castle and the three boys down from the carriage. He lingered a while to speak to William Castle quietly.

"Constable Norris has told me about the death, or should I say the murder, of George and the attempted arson of your warehouse. I cannot imagine what you and Grace are feeling right now or what possessed George."

William was in no mood for any small talk and so he kept his own counsel. They entered the office of Senior Constable Elton. Constable Norris was already seated.

William and Grace Castle, Jonathan Jerome and Samuel, Billy, and Ottabah answered the questions posed to them. Occasionally, Constable Norris would provide additional information or clarify some details. The experience of the three boys was unknown to the Senior Constable, and they needed time to go through the events and allegations appertaining to each boy.

First, the kidnap of Samuel and what he could or could not recollect. Second, the allegation of theft by the now deceased George Castle against William Thomas. Third, the purchase of Ottabah in Lisbon by Captain Fothergill. Not forgetting the sinking of the Pegasus in the storm and the miraculous survival of the three boys.

Finally, what was to be done with Ottabah? Ottabah

was a slave. A slave was property. Property had to have an owner. Simple enough. The ownership of Ottabah was a legal matter, a judicial matter, and one for the Courts. A conundrum.

Shortly before two o'clock and before the Petty Sessions Court was due to start, Senior Constable Elton and Constable Norris left and joined Walter Fairfax, Justice of the Peace, in his private rooms.

The Bristol Justices of the Peace had from the outset been told of the kidnap of Samuel Castle, the allegation of theft against Billy Thomas by George Castle, and the docking of the Pegasus in Lisbon. Also, they were aware of the meeting between Captain Clive Fothergill of the Pegasus and Captain Elliott Featherstone of the Swift.

More recently, indeed only the day before, the Justice of the Peace office had received Captain Robert Benedict's report. This was the first time the slave boy and question of ownership had come to the notice of the Bristol Authorities. A thorny issue.

Added to this, Walter Fairfax had been told of the events of the early hours of that very morning. The murder of George Castle, the attempted arson of the warehouse, as well as the confession by George Castle of the kidnap of his nephew.

George Castle's sheer hatred and jealousy of William Castle and his family had been frightening. Then finally, there was his attempt to exact revenge for the perceived cheating him of his birth right, the inheritance of Castles' Merchant Traders. Setting the warehouse on fire was the action of a madman. Walter Fairfax's questions were answered, but there were still so many lingering.

They also believed George Castle had an accomplice who they were presently seeking. It was a relief to the Constable they had caught George Castle red-handed. Constable Norris knew if George Castle had survived, he could challenge whatever memory Samuel had of his abduction, which was vague. He could also continue his accusation of theft against Billy, although George's drunken demeanour and very odd behaviour made his explanation of events questionable.

Walter Fairfax needed to speak to the three boys himself and asked Constable Norris to bring them to his private quarters along with William and Grace Castle and Jonathan Jerome. The Petty Sessions would have to wait.

Jonathan Jerome vouched for the moral character of Billy Thomas. Grace, William, and Jonathan begged for the freedom of Ottabah. Walter Fairfax recognised the bravery of all three boys and believed Samuel and Billy should be rewarded. What to do with a slave was much more difficult. As a trader himself, Walter Fairfax knew should he release Ottabah, there would be an outcry from traders. Where would this end? If the slave boy committed suicide, any insurance in existence would be invalid as suicides were not insured —simply classified as a dead loss.

Throughout the meeting, William, Grace, and Jonathan were speaking to the Justice of the Peace and representing the interests of the three boys the best they could. Billy, Samuel, and Ottabah had not said one word, and so William Fairfax decided he wanted to hear from the boys themselves. He needed to get a sense of what these three boys were like. There was something about their bond, but he needed to better understand what they had been through together.

He spoke to Samuel and Billy and as he did so, he watched the boy, Ottabah intently. Walter Fairfax listened to the two boys and was quite enraptured, if truth be told, about how they had survived. A violent storm, the sinking of the Pegasus, the rats, the starvation.

It was, however, when Billy and Samuel had gone over the side of the small boat to protect Ottabah as the Black Swan approached that convinced the Justice of the Peace of the strong bond between the three boys. Ottabah had to drag his two friends back on board the boat and keep them warm if he was to prevent them from dying of cold.

The difficulty for the Justice of the Peace was the legality of the ownership of Ottabah. The law was the law, and a slave was property. No more, no less. That was the truth of it. If Ottabah was to have his freedom, he had either to earn it, pay for it, or be given it by his owner.

"Who actually owns the boy?" asked William Fairfax. "Did the men from the Black Swan own him?"

Samuel and Billy shrugged their shoulders.

"Did Captain Fothergill own him?"

They shrugged their shoulders.

Billy told the Justice of the Peace it was Doctor James who asked the boy to be given his freedom, and it was Captain Fothergill who threw coins on the pavement to pay for him.

"Any legal documents to prove ownership?"

Billy said not. The men on the dockside simply wanted rid of him.

"Who looked after the boy?"

Samuel stated Doctor James was given responsibility for Ottabah by the captain and they, Billy and Samuel, helped.

Walter Fairfax was an experienced Justice of the Peace, but he was well and truly stumped. In his opinion Ottabah's freedom would have to be given to him by his owner, but the man who had purchased him sank with the Pegasus. Even if the boy became a free man, he would still need some sort of proof, written proof at that. Otherwise, he may be enslaved again.

Samuel whispered to Billy, who then nodded in agreement.

"Sir," said Samuel, "without Ottabah, we would have died. Without Billy and me, Ottabah would have died. If he is not free, then neither are we. He belongs to us, and we belong to him."

William Castle stepped forward. "Sir it is our wish that Ottabah should be a member of our family and in time have employment with Castles' Merchant Traders. My wife and I would willingly act as guardians if that would be of use to you finding a resolution to this matter."

Jonathan B Jerome stepped forward. "An amicable suggestion. I would support William and Grace in any way I can."

Walter Fairfax stared long and hard at Samuel, Billy and Ottabah, and nodded.

"By the authority invested in me, I hereby give Ottabah as property to you, Samuel Castle, and to you,

Billy Thomas. That is my order."

Justice of the Peace Walter Fairfax banged his gavel. Samuel and William stood confounded and confused. Ottabah burst into tears at the bang of the gavel.

The Justice of the Peace waved the three boys forward.

"Come closer. Ottabah belongs to you. He is your property now, legally. That means you can do as you wish with him. Might I suggest you give your friend his freedom?"

Samuel frowned, shook his head sadly, and then suddenly he realised what the Justice of Peace had actually said. He laughed out loud.

"Billy, this means we can give Ottabah his greatest wish!"

That very day, William Fairfax signed three orders. The first order simply gave the ownership of Ottabah to Samuel and Billy. The second order, with the approval of the new owners, Billy and Samuel, simply rescinded the order of ownership of Ottabah and gave him his freedom. Thirdly, William and Grace Castle were appointed as guardians of Ottabah.

Ottabah, Billy, and Samuel had therefore been given their wish. The complicated legality of the ownership of Ottabah had been dealt with at the stroke of a pen.

Ottabah was free.

Free at last.

Bronwyn Harrison

AUTHOR'S NOTE

Trade

The beginning of the 18th Century saw major conflict in Europe. **The War of the Spanish Succession (1701-1714)** between Spain and France was intended to decide whether the possessions of the Spanish Empire should pass to one claimant or be divided between the two. This impasse was a benefit to other European trading nations, including Britain. The war concluded with **the Peace Treaty of Utrecht 1713.**

Also important after decades of mistrust and suspicion between England and Scotland, was the **Act of Union in 1707** which united both countries and helped reduce obstacles to trade. Both countries could look outwards to trade rather than looking over their shoulders.

This expansion of trade in Britain also encouraged investment and speculation. One of the beneficiaries being the **South Sea Company.**

The South Sea Company was established in 1711 as a British Joint Stock Company. Subsequently, the company was granted exclusive trading rights to the Spanish South American Colonies (South Seas) as part of the treaty of the War of the Spanish Succession. In return, however, the company assumed the National Debt. Naturally, the Government wanted to reduce the interest on its debts and it did this by placing a tariff on South American goods. In reality, this meant the main activity of the South Sea Company was funding the National Debt. It seemed to be a win-win for the Government whilst the South Sea Company had to find increasingly imaginative ways of selling their stocks and shares. This included lending money to customers to buy its own shares and it appears the company was eventually able to dictate its own share value.

Of course, as the Government was involved with the company and other eminent figures were investors it was thought the company was a good and safe investment. In 1720, the share price of the South Sea Company rose from £128 in January, £550 in March, £890 in June, and later that year to £1,000.

Due to the success of investments in general and the South Sea Company in particular other companies were 'floated' on the stock market, some with extravagant claims (including to manufacture square cannon balls) some downright fraudulent. In June 1720 an Act of Parliament was introduced to control 'The Bubbles' known as 'The Bubble Act'.

Price of goods.

I found that estimates of the value of goods and services varied considerably, and therefore I chose the Bank of England's currency estimate. The main currency was pound sterling.

In 1710, £100 would have an estimated value £13,643 in 2023. Whilst in 1720, £100 would have an estimated value of over £16,540 in 2023.

Bristol, where our story is set, was the biggest port in

England second only to London. It was a vibrant trading port particularly in the slave trade. The Triangular Trade of slaves was thriving. Merchant Trading Ships left British ports loaded with goods for sale in West Africa which were exchanged for slaves. The slaves were then sent across the Atlantic and were sold at great profit for labour in plantations. The ships re-loaded with export crops and commodities, the products of slave labour (cotton, sugar, rum, etc.) and returned to Britain.

Whilst it was legal to purchase slaves in the colonies, slavery was neither legal nor illegal at this time in England. Also, there was a growing opposition to slavery but Merchant Traders were a powerful lobby. Walter Fairfax, the Justice of the Peace, had a real conundrum. How could Samuel and Billy be rewarded and Ottabah enslaved?

Milton Keynes UK
Ingram Content Group UK Ltd.
UKHW040634131123
432470UK00001B/47